Ripples

Alicia Charron

Published by:
Alicia Charron
Independently Published

Cover created using public domain and personal properties arranged and designed with Adobe Creative Cloud.

No AI used.

ISBN: 9798386105099

Ripples

Alicia Charron

Dedicated to

middle children, the silent sufferers, and the ones
who had to self-actualize early to survive

Disclosure

Before you begin, please be advised that this book depicts scenes of domestic violence and grapples with themes of mental illness. The first-person narration provides an example of what it can be like inside the mind of a teenager struggling with mental illness and abuse. Therefore, the language in this book can be harmful or triggering to those who have dealt or are dealing with depression, anxiety, hallucinations, suicidal ideation, PTSD, and/or C-PTSD.

Elle Groeman came from the mind of a depressed and anxiety-ridden teenager (me) and is by no means meant to be an example of how to handle living in these conditions, but instead be a fictional vessel through which I hope others find that they are not alone and that they too can find the brighter side amongst the darkness.

Content

I. It Isn't Real 13

II. All Eyes 22

III. Safehouse 30

IV. Patchwork 43

V. It Has a Name 55

VI. Misguidance 67

VII. Strange and Unusual 83

VIII. Someone Gets a Papercut 99

IX. Blaming the Victim 113

X. First Dance Ready 125

XI. Disappearing Act 137

XII. It Isn't Real? 145

XIII. At Least Once 159

XIV. An Audience 177

XV. In Deep 191

XVI. Truth in Memory 206

XVII. Happy Things 221

XVIII. King of Shadow 232

XIX. Rally 242

XX. Home 255

XXI. Aftermath 272

XXII. Loss 279

XXIII. All There Is is This 292

XXIV. Not Out of the Woods 300

XXV. Obstacles 314

XXVI. Fear 328

XXVII. One of Us 340

XXVIII. What Is Real 350

Epilogue. 359

Acknowledgement 363

CHAPTER ONE

It Isn't Real

I'm surrounded by demons every morning, so it should be no surprise that when I open my eyes I am met with the slow cyclone of shivering shadows. My arms and legs are stuck to the sheets and I can't close my eyes again. I have to watch them watching me.

A small wispy movement offsets the darkness as my other senses awaken. Something glides over dead leaves, the rustling like a hollow, rattling breath. Then there's the smell of a cold breeze across damp logs and mud. Whispers begin to fill the silence and I try to rise from the bed again but can't seem to find my own body in the darkness.

Bright flashes of light blind me as the shadows start to sway. In the light, they are decaying figures, hollow molds of humans turned grey with crumbling skin and deep set eyes glazed over grey.

They crowd around me as a singular mass, sucking in with their dry mouths trying to take something away from me that I cannot give. The air grows colder and acceptance turns into desperation to end the torment, the tease.

It's not real, and this thought brings me back to my body. Except, I don't believe myself because they're here, they're all I can see, their darkness is all I can feel. They're dangling death in front of me, toying with the idea, and I can't have it.

Each time the light appears, I reach towards it, fingers spread desperately towards its warmth. Every time I think I am close, the darkness grabs a hold of my wrist, thrusting it back to my frozen body, the bony touch lingering as a stinging coldness on my skin.

Shivers run up and down my spine, along every appendage, and goosebumps flood my skin, tightening against my bones as if their resumed inhale is taking something away from inside of me. Then, they let go.

And they scream.

They scream like children in danger.

They scream until it turns into a singular high pitched ringing that ebbs into the stagnant buzz of a fluorescent light that appears on the ceiling above me. Slowly, I turn my head to see scratches in the wall that weren't there when I went to bed, that won't be there after I look away.

My bedroom door creaks open with the sharp cry of scraping metal. My door is made of wood, so I know it isn't my door that is actually opening. I am still seeing things, still hearing things, still feeling things that aren't there.

One of the pitch black figures from before slowly covers the light, engulfing me in the shadows once more. The man has eyes that glow yellow and his lips are curled into a smirk of triumph. I open my mouth to scream, but no sound is made. I can't hear anything beyond the buzz of the light I can no longer see.

I shut my eyes to stop seeing the man's face, but it sticks in my vision like staring at the sun. Only when the buzzing stops, abruptly and totally emptying the room, do I open my eyes again and breathe. Sweat beads down my forehead as I sit up abruptly, finally back in control.

Something about the cold dark dimensions tries to pound itself into my skull leaving a message at the front of my thoughts. I have to physically shake my head to keep my brain from drilling the hallucination into my memory. All I succeed in doing is replacing the thoughts with a nauseating headache.

I've learned the difference between reality and my mind playing tricks on me. It only took a couple of beatings to learn that there are no such things as whispering shadows and men with glowing yellow eyes. Lately, though, it's been happening a lot more frequently and I've been a lot more sore coming out of it, a lot less certain of reality than I'd like to be.

That's why when I reach over to turn off my alarm, another goes off immediately after, and another after that. It's to make sure that at least one time I hear my phone ringing, I believe it's actually ringing and know that I am awake and back to reality.

A stiffness remains in my limbs, but I force myself up anyway. Tiny black blotches start to blur my vision, but they slowly fade away as I topple over losing my balance and falling on top of my bed. The covers beckon me back to their vise grip, but I ignore the call and shove my phone in my patchwork backpack before getting back up off the mattress. Something to wear is better than nothing, so I'm wearing my black hoodie and jeans for the who-cares day in a row.

There's a floorboard that creaks between the doorway to the kitchen and the other end of the hallway where my parents' bedroom is. Again, no one is here. No one can hear, but it's become a habit to sneak around when it comes to breaking into the master bathroom where my mother keeps the extra strength pain relief.

I throw a few more than I should into my mouth without washing it down with water. Their weight sits alone in my stomach, and although my brain knows that I haven't eaten in a while, my body doesn't seem to mind as there are no grumbles of hunger erupting from my bowels.

The multitude of alarms ringing remind me of the things I need to do. The lights take turns going on and off as I shift from room to room, ignoring the shadows creeping up the walls. In the bathroom, my breath turns minty fresh, the feeling and scent making me feel enclosed in a neat, clean package. In the living room, the rickety brown couch gently creaks as I let my whole body relax and sink into its worn out cushions.

The screech of tires braking at the end of my driveway wakes me from my half-asleep state. There's drool on my cheek and I hope this is one of the times my mind's tricking me, but one look out the window says the bus is definitely at the end of the driveway; so I snatch up my book bag and run out to the bus with neither of my shoes tied. My own laces trip me on my way up the bus steps.

Sitting myself in the first available seat in order to avoid people, putting my book bag on the floor and leaning my head against the window, I close my eyes and listen to music. I don't want to think. The rumbling of the bus as its frame shakes with every turn of the tires keeps me from falling asleep and aids in the persistence of my headache, but the throbbing drum of my brain colliding with my skull has already numbed to familiarity.

I don't bother looking around me at the other students slowly trudging onto the bus and into their seats, there's nothing new to see about it. Every day is exactly the same boring routine of seeing the slightest glimpse of the truth only in the morning—grey eyes and quiet—until the unhappy and exhausted teens meet up with their friends inside the building and the facade takes over.

Everyone's ready to move when the bus finally turns into the parking lot of the only high school in the city, Norwood

High: Home of the "ever-so-brave" Mavericks. The school likes to prepare for pep rallies early, meaning whichever unlucky soul who decided to get out of gym by volunteering to parade around as Marvin the Maverick this season has to be on the grounds before everyone else and welcome students into the building.

The cartoon eyes stare blankly above everyone's heads, but I still actively try to avoid them. The only thing I succeed in doing is throwing myself right into the student in front of me's shoulder. He whips around, knocking other students' bags with his own as it hangs lazy off a single shoulder.

The irritation pulling on his eyebrows lifts when he recognizes me. "Groeman."

"Alex," I say from behind my teeth, still trying to forge ahead, but he matches me step for step.

"What's the rush? Gates aren't even open yet."

I hate that he has a point. There are still about five minutes before we're allowed down the halls to the classrooms, the lockers, everything other than the cafeteria and gymnasium. I usually cut to the auditorium, hide until the first bell, but I'm not about to lead him there.

"Rough morning, not in the talking mood, I got you. Catch you later." Alex turns smoothly back around on his heels, cutting through the torrent of students like a knife through butter, slipping through the cracks or parting the seas, whichever means the world bends in his favor.

Returning to an invisible state, I silently groan and push my way forward. The cafeteria is always crowded, so I lean against the wall right beside the accordion metal grate blocking the hallways. The pale blue paint peels away as if aware of its own uselessness.

DING- DING- DING

The annoying scheduled chime of the warning bell tells all students to act like they're in a school, say goodbye to their friends, and go to class. There's nothing more fun than being pushed around by people who don't give themselves enough time to get to their first period while all I do is try to get ten feet down the hall on my own. Bookbags collide, my heel is stepped on, and I shove a freshman three feet over to get through the door.

Mr. Feldon looks at me as I rush in, finding my place in front of his desk. He doesn't pick on the kids who get up close and pay attention, or at least those who are really good at pretending they are.

"Good morning, Miss Groeman," Feldon says as he drops today's worksheet in front of me. "How are you?"

"Just fine." My voice is all gravelly and raw.

That's as far as pleasantries go before the rest of the twenty students walk in as the late bell rings. Lanni takes his seat beside me, waving to a girl in the corner before turning to me. "Good morning, sunshine."

"Oh, fuck you." I throw my foot out to kick his shin.

"Shh, class is starting," he says while rubbing his shin and grinning.

I steal glances at Lanni every now and then to make sure he is there, really there. He always is right where he is supposed to be. Honestly, he is the one decent consistency in my life. His brown hair, blue jeans, and schoolboy smile is everything a normal person would want, and everything an abnormal person needs.

Sure there are times when I imagine what he looks like under his skin tight t-shirts, but there isn't a single person out there who doesn't imagine what their best friend looks like topless. The only person I'd actually consider trying to get a peek at is Spencer, though I really shouldn't be thinking about that.

When I catch Lanni's glance again, he's smiling and I can't stop the blood from rushing to my cheeks. He *has* to know what I was thinking and, oh god, can this class go by any slower?

DING-DING-DING

I practically jump out of my seat, not bothering to put anything away, just scooping it into my arms. Everyone else is rummaging around, packing up their stuff, and ignoring every word Mr. Feldon says about the night's homework assignment. They walk out in their groups of four or five, laughing at some picture they pulled up on their phones, not actually communicating with one another except to say "look at this" or "haha, that's a good one."

I jump when Lanni speaks, "See you at lunch."

Before I can respond or play things off, he's already running out of the classroom as part of the crowd. A familiar self-pitying thought crosses my mind wondering whether or not he wants to be involved with more normal people instead of being around me.

To break that train of thought, I leave the classroom as well. In the white-washed halls, it doesn't take long for everything to feel the exact same as yesterday, rolling through the hours like sheep on a farm. Every period is forty minutes of begging to leave because acting like a good student and a likable person is anything but satisfactory, yet I do it anyway.

The more I think about the simplicity of fooling people into thinking I'm normal, the sadder the world seems which isn't something I thought was possible. I try to imagine myself as the type of person who could just live in the moment and be who I need to be whenever I feel the need to. I would walk out of this building right now if I wanted to and no one would stop me, but all I need to know that I am not like everybody else appears in front of me as if on cue.

Flawless and dressed in the most innocent of whites like a child prepared for a baptism, the girl with jet-black hair who isn't real stands at the end of the hallway. *She isn't real,* I repeat to myself, and watch her flicker but never leave.

DING-DING-DING

She's gone, and I'm late for class.

CHAPTER TWO

All Eyes

Dismissal comes at a slow rate, but once it does, I practically run onto the bus, repulsed by how accustomed I am to this yellow mobile smokeroom. There's no more comfort in the crammed green seats than usual, but it's the one place where, when I'm alone, I actually feel alone. There are no shadows watching me, no voices whispering, just nothing. I can press my back against the window and put my feet up to block the space. There is quiet, for once.

The moment is short-lived. Someone walks on with a vape in their mouth and head dripping sweat for some unknown reason. Teenage boys are always sweating. I shut off, plugging my ears with the sound of music, and resume the waiting.

The neighborhoods are endless rows of neat houses that are all identical to one another save for the lawn ornaments. Hordes get off at different street corners until I'm rattling against the window with the rumbling of the bus as the brakes struggle down the hill to get to the end of my driveway. When it finally comes to a halt, inertia lurching the cabin forward before settling in place, I can't manage to utter a single word but I wave farewell to the bus driver as I step off.

The exhausting length of my cracked, gravel driveway makes me feel even more sluggish than I was before. But I remind myself of the sweet relief of dropping my bag and falling onto the rickety old sofa, of the hour or so of time that I get when it's just me. The shadows aren't as scary in the daylight.

Instead, the eyes that watch me are the ones in the picture frames. It would be easier to say the pictures were a lie, but I can see the truth clear as day. My mom never found the right concealer, and my father doesn't smile. It's not just because he's a man, it's because he doesn't know how. And me? Four-years-old and dress coated in a thin layer of pink chalk dust, I'm matching his expression.

Under our watchful eyes, the ones that know our secrets and mock any attempt to act normal, I unpack my bookbag to start on homework. I'm forever grateful that I don't have siblings. This house doesn't need any more eyes.

An hour has passed by and I have only just finished my math homework. The day I never have to prove why a triangle is a triangle again can't come soon enough. When I get up to stretch my legs, the floors squeak. The sound sometimes scares me. I forget that it's me and become convinced there's someone behind me, waiting for the perfect moment to cover my face with chloroform and kidnap me.

I do another turn around just to double check that I am alone. My mind plays tricks on me. I know my mind plays tricks on me, and it especially acts up when it can fill a void. Blank spaces are occupied by whispering shadows or the little girl.

So I avoid looking at the empty spaces, but then I catch the eyes in the photograph. A different photograph. The same three people are in it. Mother, father, daughter. The same three faces. Forced smile, stone-faced, and mini stone-faced. Taking family photos is some Martha Stewart home-making hack we desperately cling to.

But I remember having to put effort into looking disinterested this time. I remember who was behind the camera and I love the miniscule face of the dog trying to shove his face through the porch banister in the background.

We'd spent a lot of time at my grandparents house before they passed. It was further from the city, somewhere between the suburbs and the endless cornfields which meant they had a lot of land. That fall, maybe eight years ago now, my grandmother kept us all busy setting up a corn maze for the county's Halloween festival. If I try hard enough, I can still smell the straw.

"What's that?" My grandfather startled me as we set up another yard of fake cobwebs. I followed his pointed finger to a dark spot sticking out above the wall of corn husks. At first, I was just glad that he saw it, too.

Then it started coming towards us.

And it growled.

And it jumped out from the corn, flailing wildly, writhing in awkward, bent positions on the ground.

I screamed.

My father laughed. Everyone laughed as they came out of the corners of the maze.

"Sorry, sweetie. Are you okay?" Every bit of panic the thrown scarecrow had given me disappeared in that moment. My father patted my head, couldn't stop laughing, was checking on me, and was smiling.

"I'm okay," I squeaked out before catching the laughing bug and we were all cackling.

We took the photo when we gathered all back together at the house where there was a camera. Staring at it now, I want to do nothing more than press it to my chest and go right to sleep, right into a dream of that memory.

I rub my thumb over a smudge, but it doesn't wipe off. Looking closer, I see it. I see the shadow. Why would there be a shadow in this photo?

The shadow's here.

I feel its cold touch coax my chin to look out the window where the little girl is crouched in the garden, plucking weeds.

The sound of tires wheeling up the driveway steals my attention, but doesn't resolve the growing dread in the pit of my stomach. It's only four o'clock, so it can't be them. It's probably just someone using our driveway to turn around. Still, I rush around the living room, packing my school things away and rushing them to my room.

The door unlocks and footsteps stumble heavily in the entryway as shoes are kicked off and discarded.

My father is home early. Very early.

There's nothing but shouting as my parents come inside, so I take my place behind the wall before the living room. I look around the corner of the wall and watch what is happening. It is like walking in during the middle of a movie scene, so I have to piece together the missing pieces of information, but that doesn't stop it from being a scene.

My father has his hands wrapped tightly around my mom's wrists and she's shouting demands for him to let go. Of course, he doesn't listen. The sound of his hand smacking her cheek makes me jump, but I continue watching. I can't stop. I can't move. Like when I woke up, there's a grip on my limbs keeping me from moving.

My mother's face turns red with the sting of the slap and her eyes water. He doesn't have to say anything for me to understand what is going on because I know this part of the movie very well. He's blaming her for getting them sent home early.

All I can hear is the hopeless screaming between the two of my parents as they dispute over who is to blame for whatever happened this time.

"You always have something to say, don't you?" My father spits. "What do you have to say now? Huh?"

In my mind, I'm begging her to keep her mouth shut. But he got to her, she's bothered, and she can't help herself. She shakes her head to flick the hair out of her face, breathing heavily but not letting her exhaustion show. She never lets it show. Am I supposed to think that's strength? She speaks evenly, "No point. You'll have the final word. You always do."

Then her hand escapes his grip and despite the odds, she lands a humiliating blow with the palm of her hand on my father's face.

The air is still.

Even the shadows are silent in their spectating.

No pain registers on his face, but his eyes fill with a different sort of rage, a blind fury. He shoves my mother into the wall and pins her arms against it.

The brute force makes picture frames rattle. A young version of my father and grandfather fall to the floor and they frown as they shatter. My father's aggression is a thunderous storm that shakes through the house making room for the shadows to grow.

I attempt to stifle a cry, but the sound escapes before I can cover my mouth. In hopes of being neglected as some random sound, I crouch behind the wall and keep my hand over my mouth to silence my breathing. I'm paralyzed, I can't move. The shadows are keeping me in place. They're whispering again, more of their incoherent echoes.

The sound of my mother pleading, "No, please, no," is the only indication to the fact that my father is on his way towards me.

I could close my eyes but it would make no difference.

His footsteps come first, and then a single hand reaches through the darkness and takes a hold of my hair. The shadows follow me, helping my father carry me to the living room, to the stage, front and center.

My dad pushes me to the ground and my mom tries to hold him back by grabbing his arm, but he shoves her away. She disappears into the darkness and my father grabs my hair again. I'm forced to look up at him so that I am staring into his half-interested face.

It is all I can do to refrain from resisting, because if I resist, I won't be able to control myself and something worse could happen. I can't speak. I can't move.

"Snooping, good for nothing—" He grits his teeth and spits insults at me under his breath. "Messed up, little—"

Without warning, though I know it's coming, he slaps his hand across my face just as he did to my mother.

But it doesn't stop.

One motion after another after another, and I cannot get up in between. I won't because I will only be struck down again. My face gets hot, I reach for it, but I am hit again. I move my hand away from my face and my fingertips are sticky and red from the wound on my now hot cheek. I stop trying to move, stop trying to do anything.

There's only darkness, growing deeper with every strike.

He pulls off his belt, but after the first hit, it stops.

Just one word escapes his lips, "Leave."

CHAPTER THREE

Safehouse

And I do.

Taking my mother's keys from the counter, I walk right out the door. I get into my mother's car, still stiff. I have to readjust to having control of my own movements again, and thankfully, it doesn't take long.

I know the shadows are watching, they're creeping up the sides of the house like vines, but I don't look back. The brisk autumn atmosphere burns the cut on my cheek, and I swipe at it with my sleeve as if I can make it go away, but it only makes a mess and burns the abrasion. I'm more frustrated than hurt, the pain no longer makes me cry as it did when I was younger.

I can only ever think of one place to go and I hate myself every time that I do this. But I always leave afterwards. Especially when I'm told to.

The drive there is easy, practically around the corner which isn't far enough but I can't keep my hands on the wheel any longer. Not only am I trembling, but I don't want to drive safe. I want to veer. I want to crash. I don't want to appear at Spencer's all broken again, but he's the only one who can fix me.

Spencer is, well, my friend in the simplest terms. He found me the first time that I was mugged. I was lying against a dumpster in an alleyway on a street downtown. It was just after I had bought a gift for my mom. It had been her birthday and she had lost the baby. She was pregnant with what would have been my little brother.

The man who mugged me didn't take my present, but he took my only purse which had a twenty dollar bill in it. Unfortunately, that twenty also happened to be my bus money. I sat there slightly tattered like a rag doll left on the shelf over many years and disappointed with the lack of aesthetics about the scene. There wasn't rain, it wasn't dark, and the alleyway was tidy.

Spencer happened to be riding down the street, parked on the side, and came into the same alley way with spray cans and stencils. He wore black jeans below his waist with chains on them, a blue T-shirt that read "Suck It" in large black letters, and headphones over his head probably listening to something atypical like classical music. It took the small voice in my head that wanted help to make me try to get his attention.

He didn't notice me until I grabbed a stick and banged it against the garbage can. He jumped, his pants falling lower and his headphones falling off. I would've stood up, but my ankle had been twisted when the mugger shoved me down. He turned on his heels and saw me. He quickly rushed to my side, told me his name and that he was going to take me to his apartment. Before doing so, he tagged his name on the wall, well, his street artist name.

I know his address by heart because his place is the only place I go after I've been beaten. I don't want to go to a doctor, that would mean contacting my father about it and possibly worse injuries. I would only ever go with my grandfather, but ever since he passed, I refuse to walk through those glass doors. Our lack of insurance renders going for care useless anyways.

To get myself out of my head like I often do, I press my foot harder on the accelerator. Relief hits me immediately as I pull into the parking lot of Shady Palms Apartment Homes. The building is twelve stories tall and made of various dark-colored stones. A waterfall with two palm trees bending over it serves as the street sign.

The smoothed parking lot has little to no parking spaces at times as everyone in the building tends to stay inside. The occupants consist mainly of older folk who are on the less wealthier side of retirement, but none of them are bitter enough to repel visitors such as myself.

I yank the keys out of the ignition and grab a napkin for my face. At the door, I hold it up like I am blowing my nose so that the person watching the feed from a camera that is pointing directly at me doesn't see a girl with a bloody face trying to get into their building. As I have so many times before, I type his room number in the keypad and the door unlocks. Quickly, I get up the stairs to the third floor and go straight into his room.

"You want to try moving a couple flights lower?" I say jokingly, walking inside and sitting myself on the bar stool he keeps in the corner where he has already tied off a dish towel containing ice for me to hold to my face.

"Hey to you too. What's up this time?" He already got out his medical kit, he knows the routine.

Without saying a word, I pull the napkin away to show him the damage. "Ouch, what happened?"

"Same old, same old." I take a long pause to stop myself from possibly getting too emotional about it. "My parents were fighting and he noticed me eavesdropping."

"I don't get it." He stops talking after that and pours rubbing alcohol over the tear in my cheek. It burns deep under my skin and I try to keep from wincing.

It's funny how he tries to understand because there is no possible way he can. The only person that might have an idea about why this happens is my father, but that reason is hidden under many layers and can be so complex that my father is too dense to put together himself.

All there seems to be is silence. Spencer is usually left speechless when I come by, but this time it's so quiet that it scares me. It makes me think that he knows something about my situation that I don't.

I close my eyes and feel the heat force the area around the wound to puff up around the break in my skin. As if I wasn't already ignored at school, now rumors will arise and I will hear the tiny whispers of what will sound like my name and possible snickers from an incorrect assumption.

I've been in this position enough times, I shouldn't even care, but I start to cry, and the salt from my tears makes the wound burn even more.

"I know, I know," Spencer consoles me and all it does is make me cry harder. Shadows creep up the walls and their whispers try to drown him out, but I hold onto his words. "You're okay."

A small bandage goes over the cut on my cheek. Spencer is careful not to press too hard into the bruised skin, his fingers like the softest feather-duster. I melt into his touch.

"Not here," Spencer says and then his hand grabs a hold of mine. I follow him to the sofa where paisley patterned seat covers welcome us.

Spencer holds me to him when we lay down on his couch. The cushions are softer than the ones at my house, worn from decades of use, and the warmth of another person being with me is a comfort I can never get anywhere else.

"Are we going to talk about it?" He asks, drawing circles on my arm with his thumb.

I consider it, but only for a moment. He doesn't know about the shadows, the eyes and their whispering. If I've told him about one beating, I've told him about them all. There isn't anything else to say, so I just close my eyes. "Not today."

Thankfully, unlike Lanni, he accepts my answer and just holds me.

Spencer is exactly the kind of person that I would have wanted Toby to be. Toby was my name for my unborn sibling. No matter what they called him, I would call him Toby. We would care about each other, and always be there for one another. Perfect siblings. I would be there for him when our father goes off. Like how Spencer is for me.

Okay, maybe not *exactly* how Spencer is for me.

His hand slips from my arm to wrap around my stomach and hold me to him and I think this is it. The shadows retreat, bored in the quiet and I wish they would go away forever. I wish they would choose someone else to watch because there has got to be something worse for them to consume. My life is nothing.

They're not real, stop thinking like they're real.

As if he knows that I need to get out of my head, he whispers softly in my ear, "Go to your home."

I say in my head, *this is my home*, because he knows that, and that's why I come here. Those four words are the ones that got me to come back here after the first time we met. He felt more like home than my own and I let that convince me to glue myself to him. Like a stray puppy dog attaching itself to the first person who gives them food, I went home with Spencer and now I always come back.

The night sky takes over, creating a natural dark, *real* shadows, and it's too easy to fall asleep.

○◎○

When I wake up, Spencer is gone but it's because he actually isn't here. I can move, I can see the walls. I am here. As I look around, I spot a note on his refrigerator door. Quickly, but carefully, I walk around the couch to get to the kitchen. The note was hastily written, but neat, on a piece of yellow legal pad paper. It reads:

> *Eat. Pancakes, eggs, syrup and milk in the fridge.*
> *If throbbing hasn't gone down, I shouldn't be long*
> *If it has, you should go home.*
> *I know you don't want to, but you*
> *will have to eventually.*
> *~ S*

Can I pretend I didn't find the note? Maybe if I go back to the couch and lay down, I can fall back asleep or at least pretend to still be sleeping when he gets back. Only, I don't want to go back to sleep and risk being surrounded when I wake up again. It's nice to have a shadow-less morning.

Fortunately, there is still throbbing, enough in my opinion to mean I can stay. Sure enough, there are three pancakes and a few scrambled eggs shoved into a small plastic container. I'm still not completely sure why he helps me, but I'm glad he does.

After getting the food out and ready, I eventually find a fork and sit down, disregarding the few miscellaneous items he keeps in some of his drawers. The chair scoots, the chair leg cracks, and I miss it by half of my body. The floor shakes as I crash onto it, without a doubt disturbing the kind, elderly couple downstairs.

Dust fills my nostrils as it is swept up off the ground by my fall. The amount of dust is so thick that it is almost as powerful as breathing in smoke and as I stand up, I realize that Spencer doesn't clean. So, after gobbling up the last bits of fluffy batter and yellow eggs, I do the dishes. It's strange how much easier it is to do someone else's chores. I quietly turn the hot water on and sweep while I wait for it to get warm.

Dark piles form as I take the broom to every corner and crevice, sticking to the bristles so that I have to use my hands to pull the clumps out. The water running from the faucet doesn't feel any warmer when I rinse the dirt off of my hands, so I take a moment to lean, realizing a moment too late that there is a thin-legged spider sitting innocently against the manilla wallpaper in direct line with my shoulder.

At least I know the water is now warm when I wet a rag to wash the wall. A few plates and forks later and the task is all done, so I lounge around and consider attempting a sneak peek at what he might keep under the couch. I think better of it and, instead, go back to looking at the walls which have dents in some places and a lot of pictures hanging on it, pictures that do not suit Spencer, like pastel bouquets instead of cityscapes.

Don't, I start to think, but a shadow whispers into my ear, *snoop.* I ignore it.

Every now and then I try to imagine what it was like when his grandfather lived here. I've only ever seen pictures of him, facial expressions matching Spencer's nearly exactly. He lived here alone because he and Spencer's grandmother got a divorce when Spencer's dad was a teenager.

The type of business Spencer is mixed up in has nothing to do with his grandfather, though he didn't try to stop him. Instead, he supported Spencer's free will and let him keep all of his equipment in this apartment to keep it hidden from his parents. I've always imagined him as a humorous man. It's too bad I never got to meet him.

Snoop.

The nostalgia of it all lures me to find a photo album, so I find my usually timid hands searching through his cabinets. They're wooden curio cabinets with silver handles. Nothing out of the ordinary is found, much to my disappointment. So I proceed to look beneath the couch as I contemplated earlier. I kneel on the scratchy blue carpet, but something pushes down on my shoulders.

A clamor makes me jump, getting rid of the pressure holding me down. But I hit my head on the couch and bump into the coffee table with the back of my legs. A slight little squeal comes out of me and I am glad no one is here to ask me what just happened.

When I look to see what had shattered, I can't find anything amiss. I didn't think anything but the shadows followed me here, but I guess anything in your head travels with you wherever you go.

Rubbing my head where I had just hit it, I stand up straight and observe what I need to fix. The couch hadn't moved from the collision, but the coffee table seems to have had its top knocked off center. When I reach out to put it back into position, it's surprisingly easy to move.

There's a darkness in the gap that had been created by the shift, like the tabletop is a lid. Where the wooden top is supposed to be covering air, there is a space, like some secret compartment hidden under the tabletop.

My eyes shift towards the door, watching and listening for signs of Spencer's return.

Snoop.

After enough seconds, I decide to look. Pushing aside the top of the table, the light makes its way in to reveal a purple lined interior. As I trace my fingers across the soft, velvety material, I find a break from the fabric where it turns into something hard and cold like metal.

I push the table further back and see a gun placed into its outline beside six perfectly placed bullets. My heart stops for just a moment before it starts beating way too fast, and my eyes grow wide as the shock takes one wave over me. Once it fades away, I put the normal, unassuming, wooden tabletop back in place.

My entire body jumps again when Spencer comes in and drops some bags on the counter without glancing my way.

Instantly, I check that my jump didn't knock the tabletop out of place again. It didn't.

"Everything okay?' Spencer says as he shuts the door behind him. He noticed me jump.

"I'm fine." I've had so much practice, you'd think I'd sound more convincing by now.

"I'm sorry it took longer than I thought. I had a run in with some… friends."

"The cops are your friends?" I say in a mocking tone, trying to shake the bit of shock that is still leftover. Talking in general makes my cheek hurt.

I can tell he sees the pain on my face when he says, "Come over here, Little Fawn."

I blush at his nickname for me. "I'm fine really."

"Did you move around a lot?"

"Not really, I'm fine." I try to sound as convincing as possible, but he sees right through me. No one who's fine says "I'm fine" more than once in a conversation.

"Oh, please, stop talking. You need more ice. Did you eat? It's a yes or no question, so just nod or shake," he says all of this as he gathers ice from his freezer.

Glad that he asked me to keep my mouth shut, I nod and walk back into the kitchen. I sit at the table when Spencer hands me a bundle of ice wrapped in a dish cloth. It's cold, too cold. My face is still cold from yesterday's dosage, and I feel as if my blood would freeze if I placed it on the healing wound. But I do it anyway, to please Spencer.

I stay still, getting as comfortable as possible on the wooden chair. My back aches and I point it out to Spencer. Quickly, as if giving attention to my pain was the most important thing to him, he comes over to me to observe.

He lifts my shirt and discovers a single pink colored stripe across the surface of my skin, and I remember the belt. I move the ice bag from my face to between my back, giving him a nervous smile as he takes a seat on the other stool, clearly refraining from asking questions.

My phone buzzes and we both jump. It's my father. Somehow, Spencer gets even quieter as I answer the call.

My father speaks before I can, and he's terse. He hates phone calls. "Where are you?"

"I crashed at a friend's place." *Don't ask.*

He takes a moment to respond and I hold my breath. He says, "Come home."

"Fine," I barely utter before the line is dead.

A million words are written on Spencer's face. *Is he mad? Will you be safe? Don't go.*

"I have to go."

He only nods. He doesn't want to say anything either.

Every single time this happens it is like we are both being sucked back into reality again by a force that neither of us can control. So, giving him a quick thanks that I'm not sure how well he interprets, I slowly make my way out of the apartment. If it's not quick, it doesn't happen, and I really have to go.

I steal a last look at him and his worried yet smiling face, like an old man watching his only visitor leave.

Thoughts plague my mind as I descend the metal stairwell, an indiscernible voice trying to make me comprehend its words. The feeling of it pounds against my skull and I'm dizzy. My walk turns into a hobble as I start making my way down and the black spots come back adding warped vision to my waddle.

It's leaving that gets me every time. I hate the goodbye. I don't think normal people understand the true meaning of a departure, no matter how much time passes between then and the next time they see that person. For me, my mind convinces itself that every time is the last time and each goodbye is permanent. It absolutely tears me apart when I have to leave Spencer.

The black spots in my vision grow larger, pulsating in a pattern so I can only see glimpses of my surroundings. I'm resisting too much, navigating myself too well, and I can feel it happen before it actually does. My knees buckle beneath me.

I fall.

I fall down the metal stairs and stop after my body hits the freshly painted wall near the exit. I sit there, the tear in my cheek splitting open, and I am bleeding again. I sit there and want to cry. I sit there and part of me hopes Spencer heard and is coming down, but the other part hopes he doesn't. I am too dizzy to think of much else.

My face is sticky again, but that's not what I care about.

The spots won't disappear, Spencer is not coming, and I can't move.

CHAPTER FOUR

Patchwork

My head's in my hands and I just sit here. *Move*, I try to will myself. I have to get home.

Seconds, maybe an hour, pass by before there are footsteps on the terrible metal stairs. "Elle?"

"Lanni?" I ask, waking up my voice as a whisper. But it isn't Lanni who comes around the turn of the flight.

It's Spencer.

Did he hear me? How long have I been sitting here?

"What happened?" He asks as I take his hand to help me off the floor. "You're bleeding again."

"I fell."

His face falls just shy of a laugh in a no-duh sort of way. "Come on."

"What?"

"A Band-Aid clearly isn't working."

He raises me off the floor, and I strengthen my voice to say, "I'm not going to a clinic."

"It's not that serious."

"Where then?"

"I know a guy." We slowly make our way down the rest of the stairs, Spencer's hands on me the entire time.

"Spencer," I say his name like a plea.

"Trust me, Little Fawn."

I don't really have a choice once I see myself in the reflection of a car window, all bloody-faced and in no state to return home in. I can hear my father's words already gearing up for another round because how dare I leave the house looking like I lost a boxing match. But Spencer opens the passenger door for me and shuts me in, sealing the decision to prolong the inevitable.

Like riding the bus, I drop my throbbing head on the window and shut my eyes from the streaks of color made from driving past tree lawns and storefronts.

○◎○

My eyes open and my head is pounding.

But I am not at the bottom of the stairs, and I cannot smell the paint. Instead, I smell rubbing alcohol.

I open my eyes to find myself in the passenger seat of Spencer's car with a brown bottle swirling in front of my face. If anything was going to be used to wake me up, the last thing I'd think of was a bottle of rubbing alcohol. Thankfully, Spencer's the one wafting the fumes my way.

He moves the bottle away the second I move my head to face him and says, "Come on."

"You've got to stop saying that," I jest to convince him that I'm fine without saying the words this time, because I am. I am fine.

He parked in the grass. It gives beneath my feet like a mattress as I follow Spencer to the rotting wooden porch of a mobile home. The whole thing shifts with our weight as we step inside past the sliding screen door. The air is stuffy, holding all the humidity without the A/C unit running to improve airflow. The box sits in the window without making a sound.

There's a cigarette burn on the sofa where Spencer tries to sit me down and it's like a switch has flipped inside me. "Where are we?"

His response is just a look and I wish the shadows would rise between us so that I can't see him looking at me like that, all red-eyed with his thumbs picking at each other.

"What's going on?"

"There's nothing to worry about." His voice is flat as he walks over two steps to the sink to wet a cloth and clean me up again. The rag irritates my skin but the water is cooling. "No one knows you're here."

"Where is here?" I gesture to the cramped space that Spencer can't even raise his arm in without hitting the ceiling.

"You needed a bit more than my dollar-store first-aid kit could provide."

Another sliding door that I can only assume leads to where a mattress is kept shuffles awkwardly over and back as someone comes through. He doesn't have to duck to get through the doorway, but he does turn to his side. His jeans are worn low, bunching at the ankles, and he's wearing a sports jersey overtop of a black sweater. Just looking at him makes my skin grow hot, and then I realize I'm nervous.

This is a stranger. I'm in a stranger's trailer, not even a house. Even if I wanted to, I wouldn't know which direction to go if I tried to leave.

All the stranger has to offer is a gesture pushing forward a blue plastic bag in one hand and a crumpled tube in the other. His voice is unconcerned, like this is any other day for him, "Found the glue."

"Spencer..." I have no words for him other than his name. I can't believe he's involving someone else.

"That's Andrew. He has glue," his voice is small as he offers his defense, his hands shoved deep in his pockets as he tries desperately not to make eye contact.

I would try to say something, to comfort him, to tell him that he didn't have to do this, that I'm fine; but I'm too confused about how I feel about it to say anything I mean to say. "Have you checked my phone?"

"I, umm…called—" He winces.

"Spencer!"

"I told him to," Andrew joins the conversation, physically stepping towards us from his resting place by the flimsy slab of wood I generously called a door. He makes a motion with the tube of glue and asks, "May I?"

My jaw tenses and shifts, but I nod slowly. That doesn't stop me from wincing when his hand reaches towards my face. He stops inches away and Spencer takes my hand, squeezing it reassuringly. I nod again and Andrew applies the glue, pinching my cheek until the glue does its job.

Spencer looks as sheepish as I've ever seen him and I can't be mad. I just can't. No matter how much I wish none of this had happened. "I shouldn't have come over, I should've handled it myself, I—"

"Stop it, Little Fawn." That name makes me smile for a second, and then so does he. "I'm glad you came to me."

"What did you tell him?" My eyes flit to Andrew who can hear me, but I don't care.

Spencer shrugs. "That you fell."

"The least convincing lie that immediately gives away what actually happened." I actually chuckle until we're all laughing, and I ease a bit. They seem close, like friends, and if Spencer trusts them, I can too. I can try, at least.

Seeing the pain that laughing brought, Spencer says, "It's looking better, though. It'll be easier on you when you get home."

The sad look reappears and he turns his head toward the window that is covered in layers of newspaper so that you can't actually see through it. "Spencer. I'll be fine, really. This has happened so many times and—"

He cuts me off, only he's mad, "No!"

Andrew takes the outburst as a cue to leave the room and I am grateful for it even though I know there is nowhere he can go in this trailer where he won't be able to hear.

"You should've seen yourself compared to the other times that you came to me for help. From the looks of it, you've been beaten all week, so God knows how many more times you've been hurt without coming to me or anyone else. You shouldn't have to live like this. You shouldn't have to go home." He stops yelling and a dark cloud looms over us.

I am scared for him. It only hurts me more to see him this way, how I changed his life.

Tears well up in my eyes, but I can't let him see. Deep breaths make me inhale the antiseptic scent of the medical supplies that were discarded on the counter, and I realize that this entire time I hadn't once thought about how seeing me made Spencer feel.

And it disgusts me. I am so selfish. I get so emotional, and since I'm so used to no one being there for me, I don't notice or take the time to think about the other person when they are.

A tear escapes my eye and it all goes downhill. At first, he sees me crying, but thinks nothing of it. Then, I hiccup and he looks worried. I try to stifle any more from escaping my throat, but I can't. I need to show him that I am strong, that I'm not a child incapable of handling my life.

But my own selfishness makes me angry and upset. The thought of him caring this much makes me sad. The thought of going home, seeing my father, being in a stranger's home, and everything that has happened in this one night starts to break through the surface. I am a burst dam.

"Elle." He continues to look worried and scared."I didn't mean to, I—"

My turn to cut him off, sniffing to clear myself up first. "No. You're right. I'm sorry for putting you through this, for making you put up with me.

"I'm sorry that I'm a child and didn't warn you." Apologies start flowing through me, moving me, so I stand or else I won't be able to get it out. "I'm sorry that I've been so selfish and never once thought about how badly I hurt you. You shouldn't have had to see that, you shouldn't have to clean up after me. I can stop coming, I can stop making you feel bad."

"That's not what I want." He pauses to calm himself and I do the same. He takes my hand and waits for me to turn my face towards his, for our eyes to meet again, and then goes on, "You remind me of who I used to be. I used to need help, but I never had anyone. I'm never more happy than I am when I find out that I can help you. Please, not another word about it, let's just get you home, okay, Little Fawn?"

"Okay." And he leaves to talk to Andrew.

Once alone, I finally stand. My entire body aches as I walk around the unfamiliar room hoping the other door leads to a bathroom and not a closet. I'm wrong. The closet door has a mirror lining the inside of it that reflects my strange body back to me and I stare at it.

Spencer was right. The bruising on my cheek has subsided and all that's there is a small scratch where glue is holding my skin together. They hadn't looked at anything else and I can't stop myself from pulling my sweatshirt over my head to see the rest of the damage.

Bruises and red spots riddle my skin, marking me up with no pattern or reason. I move my hands over everything, some spots protruding slightly and others sensitive to the gentlest of touches. It's hard to tell what's from the fall and what's from before. The doorknob wobbles and I pull my shirt back down, wiping away tears with my sleeve once I'm covered. I can only imagine what my mom looks like.

Desperately needing to worry about something else, I check to see that all of my things are still in my pockets: keys, phone, change, and chapstick. Holding the keys, I notice that the car might still be in the parking lot of the apartment building. If my dad saw the car on his way to work, he'll be even more mad, and Spencer will be even more worried, so I make a note not to mention it as I go to join them.

The wooden slab of a door jiggles as I wrap my knuckles against it to warn them of my approach.

"Meet us outside," Andrew calls through the plank.

I step out into the fresh air, the wheels of the screen door squeaking in protest to being opened.

"Don't worry about me," Andrew says, his voice thin from holding it in until he exhales and smoke drifts up into the air.

"I don't know anyone and I'm not interested in telling people others' business anyhow."

"Thank you," I say.

"Ready to go?" Spencer asks.

I force a smile and straighten my shoulders, "Have to be."

"Wish we met under better circumstances," Andrew says while opening an arm for some sort of half-hug. It's hard to tell when his other hand is in the front pocket of his jeans and tendrils of smoke drift from the cigarette between his fingers. Then he makes a bring-it-in gesture and I give in, stumbling into the awkward, armless hug.

Soon enough, I'm back in Spencer's car and watching Andrew's trailer disappear from view as we drive away with the radio off. The sound would make my head pound and I don't want to show any signs of pain. I need to stay strong, to show him I'm okay, to make him not worry.

Like there is nothing he can say without hurting one of us, he lets me out in the parking lot of Shady Palms.

"I, umm," Spencer tries to say goodbye.

"See you," I offer.

"Yeah, maybe we'll go roller skating next time." He grins, trying so hard to act like he doesn't know what saying goodbye means, like it's nothing.

I want to believe it, so I play along. "Roller skating?"

"Everybody should do it at least once."

"Okay," I smile, but I'm sure it's just as convincing as his own. Still, it's better than saying goodbye.

My fingers pull the keys from my pocket and I make a point not to look back at him as I get into the car. I hate to think about the repercussions of taking my mother's car out of their use and move even faster because of it.

Then I'm on the road, leaving Spencer and going back to my life. The drone of the car rolling on the pavement is the only sound filling the silence. The one-turn drive is not nearly long enough to let me breathe, to let me think. I can feel the tears threatening to come out of me thinking about what the hell just happened and just how much I never want it to happen again.

Obviously, there's something far worse going on with me. Surely, any other person would go to a doctor or psychiatrist about this. I know I have tried in the past and no part of me wants to try again. They just call parents even when they are the problem, so it only makes things worse. I'm so afraid all of the time.

When my grandma didn't respond one morning, my grandfather broke down in front of everyone. It was a sad sight to see, a man that was always so strong suddenly crying in that hospital lobby. I overheard some doctors suggesting therapy or counseling for him to help him get over the loss. All that made me think was that they were going to put him in a home and I'd never see him again.

Once my grandfather regained his state of emotion, he refused to go to a home. Of course I was happy to hear him say that, but I was also being selfish. Things might have gone differently for the both of us if he had gone to a home. I'm just not sure whether it would have been better or worse.

It wasn't long before he became ill and had a heart attack one night that killed him. I nearly lost my mind and would have if it had not been for the advice he gave me.

Teachers wouldn't stop stopping me in the hallways. Unfortunately, one of them caught me with bruises on my wrist and they thought I was hurting myself. I let them believe that because I didn't want to tell them the truth. Saying that only caused more injury for "not being   careful to cover up" as my dad said that night while beating me again.

I was sent down to the guidance office where I learned to avoid ever going there again. They can't know what it's like to be beaten and filled with all the demons that I hadn't realized I was making. To have no safe place to go during the weekends or long breaks off of school.

Being in that office just allowed all of the negative things in my life to appear in the front of my mind. My dad was getting more drunk and stronger. My grandfather left me, rendering me without an escape from home, and I know he didn't want to, but it still bothered me.

Everything was getting worse, but no part of me wanted to share it with anybody. The sad part is, the counselor believed me when all I told her was that the bruises were from myself because of my grandfather's death. I thought counselors were supposed to tell when someone's not telling the whole truth, but this one seemed to have no interest in "helping" me at all.

Then, so many years later, I met Spencer.

Opening up to Spencer was so easy because he caught me in a time of vulnerability and he didn't talk to me like I was some overdramatic experiment. Sometimes, the best people to talk to are the ones who have their own share of problems that they're going through. I could never bring any of this to Lanni. He wouldn't be able to handle it.

It's the middle of the day and I'm not at school, but my parents aren't home—thank God my parents aren't home—and I can walk back inside with the only eyes to watch me being the ones on the walls.

Without playing music and without changing into pajamas, I lay down. No covers, no anything, just me and the bed. For now, I just want a quiet and calm sleep, to stay in the moment, to live right here, right now, to know that I am alive somehow.

And that maybe next time, I'll let Andrew deal with the sight of me and keep the ugliness from Spencer. I'd like to keep my ugliness from Spencer.

CHAPTER FIVE

It Has a Name

The morning is cold, and it's not that I'm not used to the cold, it's that this particular cold is clammy and prickly with the looming shadows surrounding me like athletes in a huddle. They're making some sort of game plan and I'm the ball, or the field. I don't know sports well enough to finish the metaphor.

Slowly, in my elusive manner, I get dressed. Same look, different items. A different pair of jeans and an olive green sweatshirt, no hood or pockets. It's when I look at myself in the bathroom mirror that I actually consider my appearance.

Andrew's glue did its job, but it isn't pretty. I brush my hair to one side to hide the patchwork of my face as much as possible. Some cover-up helps it look less red, but it cakes up.

This morning is just another one in an empty house with eyes watching like people idly sitting on their couches as the opening theme of a show plays on, the same montage of the character going through the motions. Then, the episode begins.

Today feels different like that as the wind blows on my face, cooling my cheek. I stand here and count the cars passing by on their way to my right. And when I look to the left, I watch the cars traveling that way disappear past the hill.

Not as much time is taken for the bus to arrive today even though part of me prayed it would take longer, that I could keep standing here, keep counting and watching, standing still without a care in the world.

"Groeman," the driver grunts, and I climb on.

I look back as far as I can out the window, and watch as the hill itself disappears.

The jostling of the bus tests the tactfulness of my bruises, and all are functioning as bruises. I do my best not to move, but then I become restless. I've been immobile for what feels like forever. Standing still to listen to my parents fight, going numb when the palm turned to me, lying paralyzed by embarrassment or shadows that aren't real, and all of the sleeping. I'm never in motion.

Except for when I'm moved.

Turns out thinking about pointless subjects that I can't do anything about makes the time fly by faster. The bus stops, abruptly causing my body to lurch forward, and my bruised knee crashes into the scantily padded seat in front of me.

The struggle to gather myself leads to a long wait as the rest of the students shuffle off the bus without allowing me to shove myself into the middle of it. As if the bus driver has no patience, he practically shuts the doors as I walk through them in a hurry to start his next route.

Between the bruises beneath my clothes and horribly parted hair, I can't help but feel like people are looking at me and judging me as I walk by. How conceited? God, I need to turn off my brain.

Lanni sees me first today and, unfortunately, there is no way of avoiding him.

"Look, I already feel like everybody's looking at me—"

"Elle," he looks concerned, very concerned. "You're face… Elle?"

"You know I'm fine." I initiate a hug and do so tightly to let him know I am here and always will be.

"Would you please at least tell me what happened? So many br—"

"Shh, be quiet please. And most of it *is* from actually falling." He gives me a skeptical look and I return it with a serious one of my own.

DING- DING- DING

We silently agree on dropping it for now and head to first period, immediately opening our notes pretending we can pay any attention as Mr. Feldon finishes writing the lesson plan on the whiteboard.

The day never goes by fast when you need it to. Then again, at the end of the week, I find myself wondering where the time went. The seconds tick by on the clock. Even though I know it only makes things worse, I watch and listen as the long red needle rotates. But a watched pot never boils.

My fingers find the edge of the desk and scratch the ridges in the wood with warndown nails, somehow comforting my uneasy mind. The teacher drones on and on about the biblical allusions represented in John Steinbeck's *The Grapes of Wrath*. There couldn't be a more dry topic to discuss.

Mr. Feldon looks to me every now and then as he tries to move his eyes around the room and make eye contact with any student who is actually looking towards him. In those passing glances, there's a desperate plea for participation. It almost seems rude to make him think that I'm actually listening to what he's saying.

Mostly, my head hurts. Partially, my mind is numb. The day is passing by more hazily than normal. I don't even see Lanni at lunch, which is for the better because I don't think I would have been able to pay attention to what he said. The exhaustion consumes me, drowning out everything, even my thoughts, until the only thing I can actually focus on is the fact that I can't get focused.

The only comfort in the fog is that it isn't accompanied by too many more shadows or unreal people. Even my demons are too tired to play.

By the time I get home, I have no homework left and nothing on my mind. Lanni was the only one who seemed to notice anything wrong with me, as I should have suspected. The discoloration should clear up by tomorrow and I'll continue to keep my head down to hide the cut that is definitely going to scar.

The familiar eyes at the house watch calmly, satiated for now by yesterday's drama. I leave them behind for the shadows of my bedroom where I sit at my desk and find myself staring out the window. The picture nature paints for me today is serene.

Daffodil weeds grow, spotting the back yard with yellow and white, making it look almost exotic. It hardly feels like a choice when I reach to slide the window open to feel this oddly sunny day of autumn.

A breeze unlike any other that I have felt before enters my room swiftly. The soft, gentle touch of the wind lingers for a brief moment before escaping my grasp. If I close my eyes, I can picture myself at five years old in the meadow outside my grandfather's old home.

I miss the sweet smell of wheat and corn growing in his plantation in Pennsylvania. I miss seeing him and running after Rover, my grandparents' cocker spaniel. I move my hand through the air, pretending to pet his soft red fur.

Desperate to return, I lift the screen, brush aside cobwebs and bug carcasses, and jump out the window. My bare feet grip into the earth and then I run until I fall and I lay there.

I breathe.

The damp soil wets where my shoulderblades push into the ground and I let the earth make a mold of my body, hugging me. I stare at the baby blue sky above me and make images out of the clouds. A shark, a fairy, a turtle, a hat, and so many other things that remind me of the Fourth of July nights also spent with my grandparents.

Longing to see him, thoughts come to my mind. Thoughts I want to avoid thinking. If I think, I'll think about death and my demons that haunt me, but it's too late. The precious moment, a brief moment of bliss, of fireworks and the Fourth of July, of Pennsylvania and my Grandfather's farm, gone, gone, gone.

Instead, she appears, that girl from the garden. I'm in my backyard, and so is she. The same wind sweeps our hair to the side. Hers falls into her face. She is only a few feet from me, but I cannot see whatever haunting expression lays behind her flowing locks.

She could have a smirk, planning her tricks and schemes to get me to cower in fear. She could look sad and need help, but I am too blind to see it and too struck with horror to do anything about it. No matter what it is, I can't trust it. I don't even know her name.

I will move. I will not be still.

But I'm afraid to move. My knees are up, heels touching my thighs, and my elbows hold me up. The fresh grass that I had laid down upon is now squished from being under my body. Daffodils also flatten beneath me, and my back is now covered in dirt. I don't know what to do, what she wants me to do.

She's never been this close before, and it terrifies me. She watches me as my elbow slips and I fall back down, knees still up.

A giggle, a childish giggle, penetrates the silence that I hadn't realized was surrounding us. It leaves as quickly as it came, and when I sit up again, she has already disappeared. She's never appeared to me in such a haunting manner, and I definitely want to keep this one a one-time only sight. As if I have any control.

A name repeats itself over and over in my mind before I crawl back into my room through the window: *Lilith*.

The name repeats itself in the hushed voices of the shadows as I try to distract myself by cleaning.

My drawers are now organized.

Lilith.

And my bed is made.

Lilith.

The floor is vacuumed.

Lilith.

And the window is locked.

Lilith.

I start towards my bed to lay down and nap, but now that the shadows are saying something discernible, I can't rest. More so than usual.

There is no other demand in my body than to see Spencer, to run to him. Not to tell him, just to get out of here, to get out of my head, to break the cycle of only coming when I'm in real bad shape.

The eyes seem only slightly intrigued as they watch me leave. My parents drove to work together, so I can take my mom's car again. If I can keep up a habit of being gone all day, maybe I'll never get that lecture that was surely waiting for me when my father wanted me home yesterday.

On the counter next to the keys is a five dollar bill with a note on top. It's from my mother, of course. The note reads simply, "For food."

They must have dinner plans. In this moment, instead of trying to think what the hell I could possibly get for five dollars, I try to picture my mom at her best because maybe she meant well. I prefer to think that she meant well.

The image I conjure is a stranger. That small smile seen so infrequently lifts her face, and she's got colorful hair that I have only seen in old pictures. I hate to think about how quickly the greys set in, how I've only ever known my mother to be grey. To wonder about how she got stuck with my father goes in a million directions.

Sometimes I fill in the timeline with how they met innocently in high school. I imagine my mom wanting to break up the relationship for whatever reason. Maybe he turned out to be a bad kisser or he didn't pay on dates or he didn't leave her cute notes or something.

But by then, he must have gotten so obsessed with having her that he didn't care how and became aggressive about it. I've read about abusive relationships. There's no doubt that my mom just fears he might kill her if she tries to leave.

There's also another reason why she might not leave, that reason being me. Folding up the bill to let it burn a hole in my pocket, I know she can't afford to take care of me on her own, so she stays because she doesn't want to leave me alone with him. I'm an anchor, the leverage my father has over my mother. For that reason alone, I've wanted to remove myself from the equation, but cowardice is apparently hereditary.

Trying to forget my family's misfortune, I shift focus from my mind to my body. One foot in front of the other to the door, never forgetting to lock it, and then continue to the car where I pull on the handle and get into the driver's seat. Mirrors, brake, ignition, reverse, and swerve out onto the road.

This will be good, I tell myself as I spot Spencer's car in the parking lot and ring his apartment to get buzzed up.

There's a shadow on the steps where I had collapsed yesterday, but I run past it.

No shadows, no bodiless eyes, no darkness.

I knock on his door, he opens with remorse, but as soon as he sees me smiling a real smile, he smiles too. "Surprise."

"No kidding," he breathes a laugh. "Come in."

Once I'm in, not being rushed to a stool or otherwise fussed over, I realize I have no idea what I'm doing. We stand here, looking at each other like distanced family members at a reunion.

I begin to turn, to find a seat or something to fidget with, but he reaches up and stops me with his hands awkwardly positioned on my shoulders. I blush and turn my face away so that he cannot see me. My hair covers my face like a curtain, and Spencer pulls it away as if he's trying to let the sun in.

Only I am not the sun, and my smile can't possibly be that bright. I fear that my face may scare him away, that my sunken eyes and hastily patched cheek only remind him of bad things. That I only remind him of bad things.

My smile begins to settle and Spencer brings me closer. We hug. He whispers in my ear, "I'm glad you're here."

"Me too," I utter, and hold him even tighter, afraid that he might let go. Always afraid. But he holds me too and my head fits perfectly on his chest. And suddenly, mine is growing warm.

I can feel the color rushing to my cheeks as my heartbeat picks up and, oh my god, he can feel it. We're so close, there's no way he doesn't feel it. I know because I can feel his.

Right when I'm about to stutter for words or twitch and ruin everything, he lifts me off the ground and I scream a girly shriek that I try to stifle enough so that we don't bother the neighbors. He wrestles with my flailing limbs until I'm upside down. My hair flies towards the floor and gets in my mouth as I shout between laughs, "Stop! Put me down!"

He has my ankles at shoulder-height and I let my hands fall to the ground as I try to crawl up and out of his grip. But as soon as my hands touch the ground, he rolls me over into some sort of somersault.

I sit there on the ground, my chest aching from laughter and not breathing as he creeps up behind me to give me another big hug.

"Gotcha!"

"Got me how?"

"Made you laugh. A *real* laugh." He pokes a finger at my face, daring to touch a dimple or some other cutesy crap. It's so romcom, it makes me sick.

I swat a hand at his shoulder but can't get rid of my smile. "Jerk."

We laugh and his laugh is so perfect. I try to silence myself to hear him. We have never played before. I like it.

He helps lift me up off the floor and gestures to the couch. "Sit."

"What are we doing?" I ask while obeying.

He lifts the phone from its base and begins dialing as he explains, "*I'm* ordering pizza and you are picking something to watch."

He gestures passed me to the coffee table and I stretch my hand out to grab the remote before a chill spikes through me, stalling my reach. It's heavy knowing what's underneath the tabletop. Does Spencer know what's there? I can never ask, I just can't.

Instead, I swallow and shake the rest of the chill out of my body to take hold of the remote and lay down to start channel surfing.

When the order's placed, Spencer joins me by sitting on the floor near my head, and that's how we stay through countless reruns of Storage Wars. All the while, I dance with the thought of pulling him onto the couch with me, or simply tracing his arm.

He eats my discarded crusts after the pizza arrives and I wonder if this is how to get rid of the shadows.

CHAPTER SIX

Misguidance

While I'm half asleep, Spencer kisses my forehead and says, "Wake up, Little Fawn."

Calmly, even though I'm growing less calm as my senses catch up with me, I sit up. I couldn't have been here all night, could I have?

"You slept the whole night," he answers almost as if he read my mind. "It's time for school."

"School? You're waking me up for school?" I can't remember the last time somebody woke me up for school.

"Are you telling me you want to play hooky?" His smile is coy, but I'm fully awake now and not in the mood.

It's not like I have to get dressed or care that I don't have a change of clothes. This won't be my first time wearing the same outfit twice in a row, but having the car out all evening yesterday was pushing it and now I've had it and myself out *overnight?* "Why'd you let me sleep?"

"You didn't tell me not to," he responded, his smile dropping at the panic in my voice.

"But you *did* know how pissed my dad sounded on the phone yesterday when I was out for a couple of hours. How could you think a sleepover was okay?"

"As far as I'm concerned, you can stay here forever and never go back there."

"Well, as long as everything revolves around what you're concerned about, I guess it's okay."

"I'm sorry," he mutters, but not in the genuine way, more in a questioning way without wanting to actually ask why I'm so upset because he doesn't want to get yelled at anymore. And I shouldn't be yelling at him. This isn't his fault. I'm responsible for myself so I only have myself to blame for falling asleep and staying asleep *all night.*

"No, I'm sorry," I mutter and hope it sounds sincere. "I have to go."

As I try to get away, Spencer stops me. His eyes are silky, and his voice is as soft as his grip on my hand as he asks, "What do you think you're doing?"

"Umm, going to school."

"No, I'm taking you," he says with a bit of that coy smile returning to his lips, and he grabs his coat as we both walk out the door.

"I need to grab my book bag from the car, and get the car home" I say as a friendly reminder, but as I reach into my pocket, I can't find the keys.

"I took your car back to your house so that your mom could get to work, or to make it look like you were home, whichever works best."

I blush, embarrassed. He *had* been thinking. "Thanks, but what about my school books?"

"I moved them to my car. There is nothing to worry about." We stand here for a moment with me completely in awe and once again feeling the temptation to touch him.

He keeps his hand in mine as we make our way down the staircase and we play a sort of game of tag as we approach his car. He keeps his car clean. The scent is quiet, not sweet or fruity, but almost nature-like. The sheer perfection of it keeps my mind in this tranquil state, one I wish to wake up in every day, one I wonder if normal people are used to.

We roll down the windows allowing the chill autumn air to whip around what it pleases. My hair is blown in and out of my face, strands getting caught in my teeth as I laugh at something Spencer says. He presses harder on the accelerator for just a moment, picking up speed and intensifying the air pressure. I feel like shouting, screaming something dumb like teenagers do in the movies.

Normal. I feel normal.

I remember when my grandfather put me on the back of his motorcycle late at night so that Grandma wouldn't know. Oh, how she would've freaked out if she had any idea. There were a few rare occasions when the weather was so hot that I was allowed to get on without a jacket or with sunglasses on instead of the bulky helmet he usually made me wear.

It was the most amazing feeling when the wind went through my hair instead of just watching the bike move and holding onto my grandfather. He'd let me take my hands off of him and hold them out as if I were flying.

No one ever understood me as much as my grandfather, not then and especially not now. The thought of going back in the beige prison-like building makes me want to enjoy this moment even more. I lean my head in the frame of the window feeling everything directly on my face, cleansing everything before having to dirty it with irritated looks again.

We arrive at Norwood High and Spencer finds an open spot in the parking lot—*how?*—of dropping me off in the bus lane. "What are you doing?"

"Just saying hi to some people. It's been a while."

I squint at him and he shrugs in response, but I don't question him any further.

As soon as the thought crosses my mind that he intends to follow me throughout the whole day, he makes a turn into the main office. My smile immediately disappears and I hunch over to assume the invisibility I prefer to wield within these walls. Something about the building turns me into a hermit, but the smile tugs its way back onto my face.

Even though I'm walking in a mere minute away from being late to class, Lanni finds me outside of the classroom. With only one strap of his book bag over his shoulder, he perks up at the sight of me as if he has been waiting. "You look particularly chipper this morning."

"Chipper?" I make fun of him, smiling at the ground. "I got a ride."

"You know people other than me?" He makes an equally ridiculing joke and all I can do is start creating a mental venn-diagram.

Lanni on the left (classic boy-next-door, light hair, blue eyes, thin skin so you can see the veins underneath) and Spencer on the right (complete safety and transparency, spunky dark hair, melted chocolate eyes, tall and fit from running). The gorgeous cross-section is complete fiction, but it feels better than trying to decide which one of them I like more.

We walk to class without another word, not much room for conversation in the midst of everyone else's chatter. I stare at everything else as Lanni does his thing. The walls have been painted tan, covering murals that previous art students were probably proud of. The tile on the ground is a disgustingly textured swirl of beige, blue, and green colors, intermingling in a regurgitated fashion.

The bell rings just as we step into the classroom, everyone's heads turning towards us as if they didn't just walk in seconds ago like I know they did. Mr. Feldon barely glances at us, not caring all that much because we aren't exactly late and we aren't troublemakers. Then the lesson ensues and the routine commences.

The day carries on like normal until midday.

As everyone in the classroom is supposed to be working on a research paper about the medical implications of skin grafting, the classroom's phone rings. Everyone in the class either begs it to be something about them leaving or uses the fact that Mrs. Ingrim is distracted to start their own conversations.

After she sets the phone back in place, Mrs. Ingrim turns towards the class and asks my name like she doesn't know who I am, "Leighanna Groeman?"

I roll my eyes at the sound of my full name. "Yes?"

"They wish to see you in the guidance office," she says, staring back at her computer screen.

I grab my things and the desk squeaks with the movement, but nobody's watching. *Nobody's watching, no one cares, just get it over with.* I glue my eyes to the floor as I go down the halls again, this time keeping the shadows out of sight. *It's nothing, it's nothing, it's nothing.*

The guidance lobby is a gross blue color, a regurgitated blue, dilapidated steam-engine blue. Dark blue carpeting, pale blue walls and crinkled ceiling, and even blue cushioned chairs. The odd green plant in the corner seems fake in this blue environment, just like the smile on the secretary's face.

"May I help you?"

"I'm Elle."

"Do you have an appointment?"

I sigh and roll my eyes to the ceiling while clarifying, "*Leighanna*. You *just* called me down."

"Ah, yes. Ms. Rayas will see you in her office at the end of the hall." She points her long wrinkly finger towards Ms. Rayas' office. My stomach turns to knots.

"You wanted to see me?" I ask when I walk in, closing the door behind me.

"Hi, Leighanna—oh! Or do you prefer to be called Elle? I thought I overheard you at the desk." Ms. Rayas is one of those adults who try to connect with the youth by following their trends—years behind—and the fact that she has a scrunchie around her wrist in addition to the one keeping her up messily in a bun screams overkill.

I set my books underneath a chair and then climb into it. I look around the room, taking note of all of the toys and trinkets that she keeps available like we are all five-year-olds whose problems can be solved with a little playtime.

"It's whatever," I answer.

"Feel free to mess with the trinkets, that's what they're there for."

"Um," I pretend to consider while noticing the miniature sandbox and rake. A zen garden? Really? "No thanks."

"We got a notice from an anonymous student that stated you may need some help," she says and two things go through my mind as my body stiffens. One is that she said anonymous *student*. And second, what kind of help does she think she can give me?

"It must've been a mistake, I'm fine. I'm great actually," I say with the same forced smile that was manufactured into the secretary's face, but it doesn't convince this perky and inhumanely optimistic person before me.

The conversation picks up pace as she notes me being difficult. "Well, they came into my office and said that they've noticed you acting a bit unusual."

"Then they don't know me, I'm an unusual person compared to everyone else."

"This was one of your friends—"

"If it were one of my *friends*, they would talk to me, not send me in here." My voice raises, but I don't care. The shadows have crept up to the ceiling and I'll be damned if I let them cover the ceiling and swallow me in this child's playroom. I sweep up my things, knocking the small table, making the trinkets wobble.

"Leighanna!" Ms. Rayas calls to me, but I'm already out the door.

I speed-walk angrily to my locker because I don't know where to go, racing pointlessly against the shadows as if they were real and not attached to me. I'd begin to curl up on the floor next to it, but the bell rings and my need to avoid attention overcomes my need to break down. So, instead, I go into one of the bathroom stalls. Before I know it, I'm crying.

So many questions stir: Who called me in? Why? What did Spencer want when he went into the office? Why did I snap at the guidance counselor? What do all those students think about me being sent to guidance? Whatever it is, I will never know. The rumors will remain obscure to my ears, never reaching me.

Everyone knows me as the kid with a problem. Whether they heard that my parents were terrible or that I have some mental disease really doesn't matter. By the third grade, everyone knew that I was different. Everyone has something they deal with and I somehow became the scapegoat.

It never occurred to me before that someone might feel bad for me. It's a shame that they would rather tell a guidance counselor than talk to me directly. They probably think I'd ignore them or get snarky as I tend to do whenever a teacher tries to talk to me.

Perhaps whoever it was has listened to me talk to Lanni about bad things and didn't want me to run away or something. Speaking to Lanni is the only time anyone would ever have the chance of hearing me talk about... my condition.

I wipe my eyes with the toilet paper realizing that I had been sobbing loudly as I had these thoughts. No one really comes in here, it smells like an old woman and the mirrors fog up easily when you breathe too close to it. No girl would try doing their lipstick or fixing their mascara. Well, as long as they didn't hear loud crying.

Nervously stepping out of the stall, I see some girl with long brown curls and porcelain smooth skin adjusting her outfit. "Freak," she glares at me, inspecting my whole self like I'm an object at a store. I just keep walking.

Somehow convincing myself not to leave the building, I make it to the cafeteria for lunch. Lanni is already there waiting for me, and he looks way too happy for the mood I'm in.

"So, any crazy stupid rumors going through the popular crowd?" I tease him, spooning a mouthful of baked beans into my mouth.

"Nah, just that some girl got sent down to the guidance office. Apparently, she has issues and needs to go through therapy. They say that she might even have to go to an asylum," he says with an equally playful grin.

"Are you just teasing, or is that what they're really saying?" I say suddenly serious.

"No, I'm totally messing with you. You know I don't get into all the drama that goes around at this school. You shouldn't worry about it either," he says while taking a giant bite of his hamburger.

Finally away from all of the seriousness, I get up to throw out my trash, but when I come back to the table, Lanni's gone.

The only place he could go without me seeing is outside, so I go out the exit and start shouting his name, unable to make any logical reason as to how he got away so fast. The brisk autumn breeze makes my sweatshirt whip against my skin and my hair slaps my face.

All I see are trees, trees that are just now beginning to grow their leaves back. I don't see a teenage boy running over fallen tree trunks or dodging branches, there are only trees. I sit on the small patch of pavement that makes up this exit. I hear the faint ringing of the bells, but I don't move. I don't want to, how could I? My best friend just disappeared. He can't possibly be—

"What are you doing out here?" I don't know who says it until I turn around and he is right there by the door. "You are *so* late for class."

"Where'd you go?" I say, wiping my face with my hands to stop the phantom tears.

"The bathroom." He says it so matter-of-factly that I feel like an idiot. "C'mon. You don't want to miss all of history, do you?"

I smile, letting my confusion out in one big breath, and run in. He walks behind me, and every now and then I have to look back to ensure his presence.

Before I know it, the school day is over and I catch a glimpse of Lanni before he runs out the door. I sigh in relief that he didn't just disappear again and head out, but I also don't really know how to talk to him right now, so I don't make a point of breaking the flow of foot traffic to catch up to him.

Invisibility is key. Part of me is scared that as soon as I am off school grounds, someone is going to come after me with some comment about my trip to guidance or something, but that's just my mind. What I find instead is Spencer in his jeep waiting for me.

He rolls down the window and calls out to me, "How was school, Little Fawn?"

I turn my head, frantic, hoping no one heard his pet name for me. I don't want people thinking that he's my boyfriend or something. "It was awful, if I'm being honest."

"Well, wanna talk about it?"

"I guess." and I sigh, I don't want to throw my drama at him again, we finally started something apart from that.

"So, let's begin then," he says, starting the engine.

"First, I'd like to know what you did in the office." I throw that in his face before I start so that we can begin with what will hopefully be something to laugh at.

"Oh, it was nothing," he plays it off like that's how it really is, but I don't believe him.

"Okay, I was just wondering because in the middle of fourth period, I was called to guidance." I give him a look that says "I-know-it-was-you-so-stop-pretending."

"Oh, and what happened?" He ignores my look.

"She said an anonymous 'student' called in," I added air quotes around the word student, "saying that I was acting 'unusual.' And I said I am always unusual, and left."

"Just like that, with no complications?" He gives the same look that says "I-know-you-did-something-so-stop-pretending." Only, he means what his look says. I'm still unsure just who sent me to the office.

And so I tell him everything from yelling at the counselor to the girl in the bathroom to ignoring people, not mentioning the intensity of the shadows. I've never told him about the shadows, or the eyes, or the girl, Lilith.

Relieving myself of repeating the events over and over in my head by saying it out loud feels surprisingly good and I wish I felt comfortable enough to do it more often. We stay silent the rest of the time until we start towards his apartment, then I ask what he did all day.

"I just did stuff." He shrugged when he said stuff and part of me thinks it was bad stuff like illegal "stuff."

"Mm, okay." And I shrug too. Then, my mind gets to thinking about my thing. "Spencer?"

"Yeah?"

"Do you think they're going to try calling my parents?"

He hesitates to answer like the thought of it frightens him the way it cripples me. He says what we're both thinking, "They shouldn't."

The silent suspense as if we could find out any minute is eventually replaced with tranquility as Spencer takes us the long way out through the nature parks, the beautiful quiet sending away the bad thoughts. This time, the windows stay up and Spencer plays something on the radio. Some station he likes is playing soft music, instrumental.

The sounds are flowing and gentle and if I close my eyes, I can picture us in an open field in the middle of the night, enjoying the senses of nature as it surrounds us. The relaxation presented by the absence of manmade structures is incomparable to anything anyone may deem calming.

When we pull into the Shady Palms parking lot, the jostle of the car from the road to the driveway knocks my head back to an upright position and I wait patiently for the car to stop so that we can get out. It is nice to be driven here and walk in with someone rather than coming all alone uncertain whether or not he's home or if he even wants to see me.

As soon as we get in, we resume the positions we were in last night with me laying on the couch while he sits on the floor. My eyes glance at the coffee table, but I quickly push any questions I may consider asking out of my head. The entire day peels away, fading to a distant memory that may have been a dream. I just lay here, breathing in all I can of Spencer.

Then my heart starts beating fast again, only it's not with the excitement of intimacy, it's the sudden onset of panic. I rise quickly, scurrying around the furniture like a rat in a maze.

"What?" He starts to get worried too. "What is it?"

"I just, I—" *don't know what to say.* "I should go home."

"Why? I thought we were hanging out again." He looks sad at the thought of me leaving.

"My dad, he'll notice that I haven't been home eventually," I try to explain and I think he understands. "I should really get back."

"Are you sure?" His milk chocolate eyes are begging me not to go. He still doesn't understand. Right now, I'm not so sure I do either.

"Spencer…" *Say it. Say it this time. Beg me not to go. Don't let me go.*

"Alright," he says without looking at me. He grabs the keys, and opens the door, looking anywhere but at me.

But I look at him. I notice his jawline, how perfect his chin is. I see the deep brown of his eyes and the fullness of his lips.

His dark eyebrows match mine, and his skin is so perfectly shaded and so smooth that I want to reach my hand out to touch him, to hold him the way he holds me, to tell him that I'll be okay even if I don't believe it myself.

But I don't, and I stare down at my feet as I shuffle out of the apartment that feels like home.

The walk to my house is silent, although it's not the kind of silence that comforts, that fills a hole, that you know will end soon. It's the kind of silence that lets your demons sink in, that makes you feel lonely and broken, like there is no way of going back to that happy place you were in moments before.

I wish I could show up with no problems and leave with no problems. Spencer cares too much, or at least more in a way that no one ever has. I wish I didn't have to see the pain on his face when I say the words that bring me back to where my family is.

I haven't even touched my phone, haven't looked for missed calls. I don't want to know if my dad has been waiting for me to walk through the door. If anything happens, I am not going to Spencer this time. I don't want to hurt him anymore. It's not fair.

An hour is not long enough to prepare myself. It feels too soon when I'm standing on the outside of the pale green door with the discoloring metal doorknob. I watch the shadows converge on the knob as I grab it and it's like they're turning it for me, pulling back the curtain, ready to start the show.

The second I walk in the door, my father starts, "What business do you have at Shady Palms? Finally working?"

"No, it's not a job. A friend lives there." I'm blinking like a liar, but it's not a lie. The shadows are just flickering and the eyes, all of the eyes are watching.

The eyes follow him as he stands up from his chair, arms crossed. There's an empty bottle next to the coaster on the side table. "Old people live there."

"What was I doing there then?" *Don't get smart.*

"Don't get smart with me."

"Sorry." When he doesn't respond right away, I take it as a sign to get out of his sight.

Then his palm strikes my cheek as I try to step past him. He smacks my hand away as I begin to reach it towards my face and takes my face in his hand instead, holding my chin to face him, shaking my head so my hair falls in my face and there's nothing but my hair and his thick breath between us. "You know better than to lie to me."

"I didn't lie."

The shadows perk up, rising.

They know I said the wrong thing.

I know I said the wrong thing, but I can't take it back and now I'm just standing here and he's standing there and why, *why* did I say that?

CHAPTER SEVEN

Strange and Unusual

I take a shower when it's over and he's asleep.

The night turns into a storm, the rain wetting the sill of the open window as thunder breaks the rhythm of the rainfall. I gently rub over the raw skin with a sponge and constantly flip the faucet from hot to cold and back again. The cold is to soothe the wounds, the heat is to never forget them. In the end, the color will have disappeared on both my back and my face.

After my shower, I walk to my room. I am left in silence because I do not wish to see anyone else tonight. I don't have to trouble Spencer. He won't get a call, he won't have to see me.

I lay down on my bed, the current time being too late to care. I curl up in a ball, but I don't cry. I fear that any noise I make will echo towards Spencer and I don't want my mom to know what happened this time. I don't want pity money.

I don't want pity.

I am fine.

Still in a ball, I listen to the storm's winds push against the house making howling sounds like wolves and the rain that makes the gutters overflow and the basement flood.

A bone chilling breeze sweeps into the room and I wake up to find my door open and my window too. How could that have happened? It was storming, my floor would be soaking wet, I'd be soaking wet.

I struggle to untangle myself from the bunches of blankets that had not been in my room when I fell asleep, I didn't even use a blanket at all when I closed my eyes.

I check my blankets and the floor next to me. There's not a single trace of water. It doesn't even smell like rain, unfortunately. I try to ignore the odd happenings so that I get prepared for school, but I can't stop thinking about it.

My window was open, wide open, and the screen had been lifted too. My bedroom door was open, but I always keep my door shut. The only time my window is open is when I sneak out to sit on the dock by the miniature lake in my backyard. I know I didn't do that last night.

What I do notice are brown spots on my carpet. She prints. Muddy shoe prints that leave a trail all over the carpet. My chest heaves with heavy breaths. This is different from the shadows.

I think to myself how simple it would be to look outside to see if perhaps it was just my mind playing tricks on me like it always does. I do not want to look out though, because I know that the figures conjured up in my mind will be all lined up in a half moon around the back of my house like they always are when I am afraid, and I am.

I am scared that someone came into the house and is waiting for me to step out of my room so that they can take me or kill me. I know this has all got to be paranoia and wishful thinking, but I can't help it. I am not ready to die no matter how great it would be to never have to go to school again or see my father. I am too young to die. But that's what they all say.

Afraid, but prepared, I have my hoodie on and backpack on my shoulders ready to continue my day. I step out into the hall and walk down, safe in the skinny stretch of the house. I peer into each door in the hallway. The bathroom, the closet, the spare room, and my parents' room are all empty.

Part of me wishes someone had come into the house last night just to hurt my father, but just like every other time I think of something like that happening, I push the thought away.

I set down my book bag, lace up my tennis shoes and head into the kitchen. Still nobody. I look down the steps to the basement. Nothing. The lights are off so it is solid black down there. Worried for nothing.

That is, until I walk back into the living room and begin to hear laughter, a boyish laughter that unsettles me. I stand, spinning around looking for any sign of anyone being in the house, but still nothing.

With ten minutes to spare this morning, I sit in the corner of the living room to see all possible angles for someone to pop out. I don't put my music in, I don't turn the t.v. on, and I don't get out a book. I sit in the silence, my thoughts my only company. Of course I am paranoid, I know this.

Mind over matter, Elle. If it's going to happen, let it happen. I only get what I deserve. I can't think of the last thing I did wrong. The only thing that I've done is think bad things about my father. That isn't wrong though, is it? If God met my father, He'd understand.

I step out, black rain jacket on and plastic bag over my book bag to keep the rain from getting inside the pockets. I step around puddles in a failed attempt to keep my shoes from soaking through to my socks.

Once I make it to the end of the driveway, the fresh smell of rain and the droplets hitting my face remind me of another time with my grandfather. I sink into the memory to distract myself.

It was mid-spring at his farmhouse. My dad dropped me off on his way to a conference for wherever he was working at the time. My grandfather let Rover off his leash before I made it to the door and he came at me, a red blur jumping in my face. His paws pressed against my shoulders and his tongue tickled my cheek. I was six at the time.

It was close to nightfall and my grandma had a fire going in the backyard, what a beautiful fire it was. I remember staring at it and seeing pictures in the flames. Images of people dancing and laughing.

Excited, I bolted up out of my lawn chair and started hopping around, Rover barking and running after me. As I jumped, I felt rain begin to fall and get heavier by the minute. I laughed and ran back over to my grandfather. He hugged me as Grandma tended to the fire that extinguished in the rain.

They took me inside and I dried off with a towel. I screamed and shouted about how I wanted to go back out and play, but they said that I couldn't. That it was too dangerous in the open field. I was quiet for a while until I decided to open a window and let the rain come in through it, brushing against my face like tiny pellets.

I had been smart enough to set up a blanket of towels covering everything in the room so that my grandparents wouldn't get upset. Rover came over to me and began howling out the window next to me. I howled with him. The loudness of our screams brought Grandma and Grandpa into the room.

At first they were shocked, but then they laughed. We all kneeled close to the window and howled out one loud roar into the wind. This is one of my favorite times with them.

The sound of tires screeching against pavement and splashing rain puddles off of the street calls me back to reality. I sigh as I board the bus. Unfortunately, a man did not murder me at my house and I have to spend another day at Norwood High.

Staring out the window, I think about all the things that I did wrong this morning so far. One, I thought there was a killer in my house. Two, I left the box of cereal on the table. Three, I admitted wanting to die. Four, I let the memories of my grandparents overwash my reality. Five, I got on the bus.

A splitting headache makes my brain pulse against my skull, so I turn my iPod off, leaving my earbuds in my ears so no one will talk to me if they even wanted to. I sit here, getting off of the shaky side of the bus and sitting up right in my seat. I continue to look out the window, but the more I look, the more I see.

There are creatures standing amongst the people, but no one else seems to notice. Taller than all of the others and made of tar, they stare back at me, tracking my forward motion until I can't see them anymore. Just for another to appear ahead, watching me, *wanting* me. I can feel their melancholic hunger.

The bus turns into the school's parking lot and the creatures are gone. There's nothing but the usual gaggles of teenagers just as eager to be here as I am. I sigh and stare up at the ceiling of the bus while everyone else walks off and into the building.

I stand slowly when the last person comes around, but pause when they come into view. Short, black hair, dressed in a little white dress. A child. I force myself to hold my breath and close my eyes, saying in my head, *she's not there, she's not there. She. Is not. There.*

I snap my eyes open and look in every direction for any sign of Lilith. I spin around until I feel a hand grab onto my shoulder and a small scream escapes from between my lips.

It is only Lanni. He must've seen me searching and figured I was looking for him.

"What? What did I do?" He says while quickly letting go of my arm, the veins in his settling back to their usual place just under his skin.

"Oh, nothing." I pull my hair behind my ear shyly and look towards the ground completely embarrassed. "You just scared me, that's all."

"Anyway." He puts his arm around my shoulder and begins to walk me up the steps to the doors. A cool wind blows by us and I can smell the aftermath of rain. "How do you feel about the upcoming dance this Friday?"

"I think it's for people who have money to waste and have no other life outside the small cliques of people they call friends." I open up a bit. Easy conversations, that's all I want today. "It's stupid really. There's no point in getting all dressed up for one night just to end up getting wasted at some afterparty."

"Oh… yeah," Lanni says shyly and pulls his arm back down to his side.

"No, I didn't mean you. I just—I've never gone to a dance." I reach out towards him in hopes he will allow me to hold his hand as we finish walking towards our lockers.

He takes it and eases a bit. "But if that's how you feel about them, I completely agree. I've never gone either."

"You liar." I begin to smile, preparing to nag. "You? You have never been to a dance? You had to have gone with at least one of your girlfriends."

"I have never had a girlfriend either." Lanni rubs the back of his neck nervously and I begin to feel like an idiot. Everyone like him has or has had a boyfriend or girlfriend.

It just seems like a rule, once you're a junior, you automatically have to be dating. Otherwise you are a nobody and with Lanni's looks, there is no way that a desperate-to-fit-in girl hasn't asked him out. I myself think about those twinkling blue eyes and incredibly strong but soft arms every now and then. I never said anything because I assumed he knew that.

"I'm sorry, I didn't mean to—" I knew I waited too long to say something, so when he cuts me off, I'm silent.

"No, it's okay. You didn't know."

"How about that dance?" I ask, biting my lip in hopes he will forgive me and forget about everything I just said.

I begin to skip a little and look up towards him trying to make him see how much I want to make up for my ignorance and how I would love to actually go someplace with a real friend. "I'd love to go. I'll pick you up at five?" He says, accepting my offer.

"No!" I say a bit too urgently. "I mean, I'll just meet you there."

"Al-*right*," he sounds confused, and with good reason. "See you later."

"See ya."

My heart flutters, something I never thought I'd feel. I am actually going to the dance and I am actually going with an actual person. All of this seems too real to be true. I just hope that when he says that he's my friend, he means it, otherwise I have no idea what to expect.

Surely one of my old dresses still fits and I can pick at the old makeup my mother keeps in the bathroom closet. I have never tried to look good before. I need to believe that this isn't a hoax, that Lanni is really here for me. It is strange how someone suddenly seems fake the second they do something unpredictable.

I look up to find no trace of Lanni as if he has just disappeared. I think that maybe 1 had been too lost in excitement to notice his parting, but this has been happening a lot lately, and I begin to have the feeling that he left quickly to get some money from the guy whom he made a bet with to see whether or not he would ask me out.

I always look at the bad side of things, and right now, there is nothing worse in my mind than me showing up at the dance alone.

○ ◎ ○

Everyone's heads turn towards me as I enter the art room after Mr. Feldon's class, and I look away nervously. It's like they'd all been watching Lanni and I exchange impish grins last period and now they want details.

There's an empty seat near the back of the classroom and I pray that no one else is late or absent so that I can get the entire table to myself again.

However, with my luck, Alex arrives fashionably late as usual. He's one of those students with a seemingly unlimited supply of excuses, walking around with a king-of-the-school swagger. Ms. Caarp doesn't mind because he's on the school's hockey team and the people at this school worship the hockey team.

"Hey, Groeman." Alex greets me with those green eyes, the zipper of his backpack swinging off his one shoulder, half undone, but there isn't anything inside to fall out of it.

I swear, he's the only one in this school other than Lanni who knows my name and I cannot for the life of me think of any reason why. He doesn't usually talk to me, either. That one morning was a fluke. Is there something about being asked to a dance that makes people acknowledge you? I respond, short and unsweet, "Hi."

Alex reaches in front of me to grab from my pack of oil pastels, smudging the maroon line I was idly trailing down the side of my paper. The way Alex acts sometimes makes me wonder why I am friends with Lanni, someone way out of my league of people to be associated with, but then I remember how I met Lanni.

It was seventh grade and I had been freshly bruised and taunted. Someone had called me a bitch for the first time in my life and the night before was the first time I was forced to sit and watch my mother get beaten. I didn't want to go to school, but I had to go. I cried in the girls bathroom the entire first period wondering what the rest of my life would look like, thinking of ways to shorten it.

My locker wouldn't open when I had finally gotten to it, so I walked to my next class with only a book in my hands. On my way, one of the girls decided it would be a great impression on the popular crowd if she picked on me like everyone else. She swiped my legs out from under me and sent me tumbling down half the staircase. Again, the other kids laughed.

I pulled myself up and looked around for my book, only it wasn't lying next to me on the ground. The football stars were tossing it around like it was just that, a football. I started towards them, running like an idiot, and reached up for my book.

"C'mon, Leighanna. Get the book," Tyler had said, he was the star of the team at the time. He taunted me and held me down while raising the book high up in the air.

Tyler walked towards the trash can. I looked up at him just before he threw it in and watched it tumble into the gum-filled trash bin. After the little celebration the players had while following Tyler into their next class, I slunk over to retrieve it.

Surprisingly, there were no pieces of gum on the cover. I wiped it off and even sprayed some perfume on it after heading back to my locker in an attempt to open it again. When I got to my locker, someone was standing there with a big boyish grin on their face. I figured he would just be another kid making fun of me. I walked right past him. Whoever he was, I didn't care. I didn't need someone else to push me around.

When I turned around to look back at my locker to see if he had moved, he was standing right behind me. "Hello."

He was just so plain and ordinary. I was thinking he was talking to someone behind me until he said more, "I'm Lanni. I'm new and was hoping I could get someone to show me around."

"Why don't you ask a counselor? You don't want to be seen with me. Trust me," I said and began to head in the opposite direction.

"Please, I was hoping we could miss class so we could hang out," he said with big pleading eyes. His eyes were so blue and he begged like a little kid, I had to agree, even if it meant he would be taunted for hanging out with me.

"Okay, but I'm not the one to befriend for social status."

"It's just an excuse to miss class. I know where everything is," he said as we walked back to my locker so that I could put my book inside.

"Then why'd you ask me?"

"Why not?"

And that is how I got my one and only friend that is my age. He had already been a great hockey player, but he didn't know Alex at the time because he was new and Alex had gone to the other junior high.

This class takes longer than anticipated. The work is all independent, but Alex sure seems dependent on my art to do his. "Take it as a compliment, Groeman. Your inspire me."

"Right." If he thinks he can try anything on me because I'm the only girl who tolerates him, he can think twice.

"It's true!" He attempts to defend himself, but the exclamation only makes me watch Caarp to make sure she doesn't take his outburst as an invitation to approach.

I hunch my shoulders around me as if they're some sort of cape or curtain I can drape around my workspace. When the dismissal bell goes off, I feel as groggy as waking up from an upright nap. But all I hear beside me where Alex had been sitting and staring is a quiet, "Woah. I could totally make that a comic."

"What?" My question is more of a whisper than a real question as I look back to my paper. My fingers are stained all shades of deep, dark blues, the pastels rubbed down to nubs.

On the page, staring up at me, is the image of the creatures I saw lingering this morning. The tall, tar-like, beady-eyed monsters.

I crinkle the drawing as I snatch it off the table, shoving it into my bag and hurrying out of the room.

"Wait!" Alex calls after me, catching up as I get caught in shoulder-to-to-shoulder traffic at the stairwell. "That was *really* good. Why didn't you turn it in?"

"Why do you care?" A gap opens in front of me and I try to take it when Alex grabs the handle of my bag. "Hey!"

"Seriously, you could have your own table at the art show with stuff like that."

I resituate my bookbag as I try to shrug him off again. "You're a sports guy. The arts don't matter to you. Frankly, they hardly matter to me."

We breach the top of the stairwell and Alex pulls me by my bag's handle again into the back corner by the fire extinguisher as the rest of the stream of students continues into the hall. "I care about talent. You've got it, Groeman. I thought you knew that until now."

"Look, this is really weird. We don't talk, and now you're pulling me around the school like we're best friends or something?"

"I—Yeah, I see how that could be weird. I don't know. I've just been admiring you all semester."

"I have to get to class."

"Can I... have the drawing? You know, if you're not going to keep it?"

My eyes dart from the floor to him, to my hands in a cycle of uncertainty as confusion furrows my brow. But I have to get to class. I have to get away. Something tells me he'll just grab me again if I don't give him what he wants, so I swing my bag around, pull out the crumpled paper and hand it to him.

"Thank you," he says, and that statement only confuses me more.

A static-filled silence accompanies me through the next couple of periods, the focus that I can usually maintain throughout the school day kind of disappears. Something else seems to be traveling these halls with me, something that isn't another student or staff of the school. I haven't found my footing since that conversation with Alex. What *was* that? Some sort of joke?

Something's following me. I can sense a heavy presence of something ominous, making everything feel wrong and like any little thing that happens can be a sign for something terrible to come. But I don't turn around, I don't look, I don't need to see Lilith or another one of those creatures.

A pencil topples out of the pouch of a student, the thin yellow utensil spinning as it falls to the ground, remaining in one piece opposed to my expectations. A boy is running out of a classroom, bumping into a girl just trying to get through a crowd of students, but they smile at each other. The second hand on a clock ahead of me ticks like normal until it doesn't.

Boyish laughter echoes through the halls like the whispers from the shadows.

When it stops and I peel my eyes away from the clock, I expect all of time to be frozen, but I find that everyone is still carrying on with their daily business as if the clock hadn't just stopped because no one cares about a broken clock when they have their phones telling them that they have a minute left to get to class.

CHAPTER EIGHT

Someone Gets a Papercut

The smell of tater tots travels through the hallways drawing all students in and making their mouths water. It doesn't feel as awkward going into the cafeteria today to get lunch. With so many people willing to eat what is being served, it is like being that one small little nobody in a crowd.

The lunch ladies move as fast as they can without starting up any small talk in an effort to get the students in and out as quickly as possible. I get my food, squeeze through the lines of students waiting for their trays, and punch in my school ID to pay. Not that it matters, our annual income is below the reduced lunch minimum, so my meals are free.

High school bothers me most days, but today especially. Somehow, the halls are narrower, the crowds are louder, and instead of being annoyed by it for being cramped and deafening, I'm annoyed that I'm annoyed by it. Because it's loud and crowded with life, with normal.

I even had a conversation with a classmate, I got asked to a school dance, and I couldn't react normally to either completely normal thing. Am I the one standing in the way of my own happiness?

Gross.

As the other students finally begin to sit down, I spot Lanni coming out of the cafeteria with a double helping of tater tots and a sliding pile of honey mustard squirted into one of the portion holders. The smile across his face warms me and I forget about being my own enemy for a moment. I do hope, however, that he isn't expecting the dance to be like a date.

Just the thought of us being together isn't one that disgusts me, nor one that hasn't crossed my mind before. It's more like the thought of me being with anyone in general that gives me that sense of anxiety that immediately expels the idea from my mind.

Lanni's plain red shirt sticks to his skin, shaping his torso like it always does. It would be easy to fall for him. But I quickly rid my mind of these thoughts as he begins to speak. "So, we have just three days until the dance. Do you think you're ready?"

"As ready as I'll ever be, but, um, I don't want to ruin it by talking about it, you know?" The truth is, I'm terrified. But I cannot tell him. He's too excited and I want to preserve that. I want him to see me excited about something without muddying it with my usual doom and gloom.

"I get it, we might end up setting expectations too high."

"Exactly," I say with a smile. It's nice to be completely understood without question.

The two of us start eating our lunches and remain quiet. I pay attention to him more than I think I ever have before. For instance, I notice a freckle behind his ear and the way the muscles in his neck work as he chews. There's something intriguing about human mechanics.

I wonder at this very moment if he is doing the same as me, or if he has in the past, and the thought makes my stomach flutter. It wouldn't surprise me to know that Lanni has analyzed my antics or observed certain characteristics. What does he see when he looks at me?

"You know," Lanni begins to say as he swallows one last mouthful of tater tots, "I can't help but notice you staring at me."

"Uh…Shh—um…" Embarrassment makes my limbs do a weird series of motions as a search for words until I finally bite my lip to stop the nonsense.

My arms fling out, knocking over my milk carton, spilling milk all over the table. My knees come bouncing up, each one hitting the bottom of the table resulting in a bruise-like feeling in which my arms reach down to touch. I quickly collect myself and get up from my seat, retreating to the cafeteria for napkins without saying a word.

I breathe one of the deepest breaths I've ever taken wondering if I should have even said yes to going to a public event.

There is nothing reasonable about going to a school dance. They don't feed us, they don't play good music, and they don't monitor students well enough to keep them from drinking. It's basically a t.v. version of a dance club. And I am clearly not coordinated enough to take part in the dancing aspect of it all.

With another breath, I start heading back to the table with a handful of napkins. Lanni has disappeared for a reason I don't really care for this time. Wherever he is, he's probably wishing he could take back his invitation. The milk is absorbed inefficiently as the smallest little drop soaks a pile of this thin paper that they expect us to clean messes with.

Cleaning as much as I can, leaving translucent liquid streaks on the table, the lunch aid behind me clears her throat. The dry sound of it, like rocks against sandpaper, is directed at me in a more judgemental tone than an angry one. I try to look at her in that pissed-off, angsty teenager way that works so well for other students, but I must not get the cowl right, or is it a snarl?

Yeah, that's a problem. If she wasn't judging me before— she was—she definitely is now.

My eyes follow her as she moves across the room and I take my seat. She meets up with some teacher and stands beside him so that they are both turned towards the lunch room while talking to each other, like secret agents in a movie trying to be inconspicuous.

As uncomfortable as the conversation would be, I can't help but wish Lanni would come back if only to help me hide.

Just as I consider turning back to the table to mind my own business, one of them begins walking into the sea of half-seated students. I pretend I wasn't watching and get out my phone pretending to have friends or something so that he doesn't think I'm some freak kid who sits alone at lunch.

But my mind keeps thinking about the man who may or may not be approaching me.

He is portly with a thin speckled mustache like grey fuzz covered in salt and pepper. His black pants are held up with suspenders that seem to be straining to keep them up. The hair on the top of his melon-shaped head is thinning, a rainbow of white hairs ending at cloud-like ears.

"Excuse me, miss…" he walks right up behind me, but does not know my name in order to address me.

"My name is Elle," I let him know innocently while turning to face him. "Is there something you need me for, Mr. Saundler?"

"How are you today, Elle?"

"I'm just fine. And you?"

"Would you mind if I took a seat, my old knees are getting weak."

"Not at all. Go ahead," I say, smiling all the while like an idiot.

He huffs and puffs, exhausted from action like the elderly tend to be. "I'd like to address you about your visit to the guidance office the other day."

I consider saying something to avoid the topic, but my curiosity gets the better of me, understanding that anything in the guidance office is supposed to be confidential. "What about it, Mr. Saundler?"

"Ms. Rayas was rather bothered by your last visit. I believe you told her that you are unusual."

"Because she said so," I can't stop myself from saying it before I say it. The defense system fires up, already feeling offended by whatever he might say next.

"I have to tell you why you were called down. The lunch aide I was just speaking with noticed that you aren't very integrated in the social crowd and wanted to make sure you were alright."

"Wait, an aide got me sent to guidance?"

"She's… taken a special interest in mental health lately, so she has been the head of an initiative to get school officials more involved in the lives of students. You know, 'If you see something, say something.'"

Just as I am about to spew out hateful words in a manner that would land me right back in Ms. Rayas' nauseating office, Alex approaches the table. The apprehension takes over, stopping the words in my throat as he talks to Saundler. "I was just looking for you, Mr. Saundler. There are boys vaping in the bathroom again."

A look crosses Saundler's face, one of an inner battle taking place over which situation to handle. He makes his decision. "I have to handle this, please excuse me. But if you ever need someone to go to, there are adults in this building you can confide in."

"Thank you, Mr. Saundler, but I'm okay," I say in hopes of convincing Alex more than anyone.

"Okay," he says all happy, but not quite convinced while putting both hands down on the table before standing up. He seems to want to say something else but thinks better of it. I watch him as he makes his way away from me the way he came, getting jostled around in the mix of sliding chairs and mobile teenagers.

My attention turns to Alex as he starts to walk away. "Um, what was that?"

"See something, say something. I guess I always took that as a way to get out of talking about things. Besides, you can't tell me you didn't want him to leave you alone."

"Of course I did, but I didn't need you to do that. I mean, why did you?"

"You're alright, Groeman."

I almost say "whatever that means," but something about the way he said it with a mysterious smile and coolness makes me keep my mouth shut. There's nothing left in me to question it. He turns on his heels and walks back to the table he came from, surrounding himself with the rest of the hockey jocks who no longer seem to be the crowd he belongs in.

Mr. Saundler walks out of the boys' bathroom looking confused by the lack of teenagers to bust. I watch him to ensure he keeps away from me. He finds the lunch aide who was talking to him earlier to give her some report of the conversation we had.

As their secret agent-like fashion fades away and they turn towards each other in what appears to be a heated conversation, I am reminded of my grandparents. They would do the same thing after my grandfather would talk me out of a fit.

"That's it, Elle. You know what to do," he'd say, and I always did. His face would be inches from mine, blocking out the images I was seeing, the ones my parents kept telling me weren't there, but my grandfather believed me. He said he even saw them too, something that I know now must have been a lie, but it was one of those lies that are said to protect someone.

He convinced me to make them go away, told me to hide it, and the more I thought about it, the more it worked. The images would disappear and I would be able to go about regular business again within minutes rather than the hours it took when I was alone.

Rover would come to my side and I'd pet him while I regained my breath. Then we'd play a game of tug of war with an old sock. My grandfather would laugh until my grandma called him into the kitchen one time. She'd always seemed so distressed during my fits, especially when Grandpa would calm me down. I never really knew why. I still don't.

I've seen those creatures before. I remember now as I recall a time when I listened to my grandparents talking in the kitchen after seeing a tall dark creature with blank white eyes and long, sharp, black fingers. It had been chasing me all the way from my house to theirs, so this was after they moved back into the state.

The creature appeared as my dad started on us worse than usual. Its teeth were razor-like, fingertips likewise, and bloodred saliva dripped from where its lips should have been. Its entire body was dark, like a shadow when seen at night. Only, it had appeared to me in broad daylight, sunshine directed onto it through the large window of the living room.

In the light, the creature was muscle, black muscle, a finely tuned specimen of fit proportions, skin seeming unable to contain the veins attempting to bust through the surface. Its eyes, although nothing but white, stared at me, observing me. It licked what should have been lips with a long and slimy, black tongue. It kept creeping closer to me, the air turning blue and shiny as I began to cry.

Other people appeared as ghastly figures around the room, children with blank expressions, arms limp, and bodies translucent, fading into the wallpaper. They spoke without opening their mouths, incomprehensible whispers. The creature snarled, teeth bared, and I screamed.

I covered my ears and shut my eyes, turning myself into a ball to keep my limbs together and less accessible. My grandparents came rushing down the stairs. They had no idea I was there, so my grandfather had his shotgun.

Once they saw it was me, my grandmother wanted to come straight to me, but my grandfather stopped her, placing an arm across her path while setting down the gun. He approached me slowly, probably noting the blood on my hands and head from my father's beating.

Somehow he knew, he just knew. He immediately started to remind me of the forest, "Send it away, you know how. You've done it before and you will do it again. All you need to do is hide it away somewhere you won't ever go."

As he spoke to me, the whispers stopped. I opened my eyes, watching the children who were barely even there disappear. The creature lingered, crouching there, breathing as calmly as it could as if it knew I was sending it away. It began walking away and fading into nothing as my own breathing steadied.

Just when I was about to hug him, Grandma cleared her throat, the sign we both knew as a demand to speak to my grandfather alone.

With a smile and a pat on the head, my grandfather went to his wife. I listened to them, desperate to know what she always has to talk about. My grandfather spoke first, "She's hurt, Mable. Let's help her first."

"You know you can't keep doing this to her. You need to stop—"

"Stop what? Helping her?"

"Feeding her delusions, Louis."

"You keep telling me you understand, but clearly, you don't."

"I was more than willing to go along with your nonsense, but you are creating problems for our granddaughter."

"I did not give her this, it is a part of her the same as it was a part of John. I won't make the same mistake."

"John had an active imagination that went away when he was a teenager."

"When he met Jenise, right? And the alcohol?"

"Oh, you wouldn't know, you were never home. Always taking care of your own personal matters."

"Which is exactly why I am doing what I am doing now with Elle. I need to be here for her the way I should have been with John."

"Things are only getting worse, Louis."

"And she needs me. Trust me, Mable, I am only giving her what she needs. She is going to go through more than anyone realizes."

There was some rummaging in some drawer and my grandfather came back into the room with a first aid kit.

To this day, I can't figure out whose side I'm on. My grandmother only wanted my grandfather to stop filling my head with the idea that the things are real, but my grandfather made it all go away. I favor the bad things disappearing, but if my dad saw it when he was a kid, then it would probably go away for me.

Whether or not what my grandfather did actually impacted me is a question that will never be answered because those are the trivial kinds of things that will forever remain ambiguous.

After everything I have tried to process today, I have no energy to add this to the list.

I almost wish I could tuck it all away, pretend it never happened, and just keep on going through the motions. Either that, or stop altogether. I don't have to remember anything. I don't have to be anything.

My grandparents wanted me to be fearless. My parents want me to take care of myself, quietly. Lanni wants me to be the girl next door who gets excited about dances. Even Alex has wants for me, saying I should pursue art. Everyone seems to have some idea about how I should live my life except for me.

DING- DING- DING

In the blink of an eye, the hallways are empty, vacant, deserted. It's almost like I am here after hours, after sports practices are over on a day when the school isn't holding any sort of event. It is so silent and barren that I have a hard time believing that it is still a Wednesday in the middle of the school year.

This emptiness around me is so absolute that I could convince myself that I am the only person alive for miles. To stop myself from testing the theory, I continue walking in the same direction that I would be going for class.

When I turn the corner, she is there, the little girl whom I now know as Lilith. She's standing upright, arms down at her sides. Her legs stuck together, unbent, and feet pointing straight forward.

Her black hair blows in a nonexistent wind, covering her face. The breeze that only she can feel grows faster, apparent by the increasing force of her hair whipping in and out of her face. If the wind would hit anything else, I'm sure posters would fall and the windows would be shaking. Just like I am.

Her little fists clench as her white dress whips against her legs. Her jaw falls, mouth open, and a high pitched shriek makes its way to my ears at a volume louder than the thoughts in my head. My ears begin to ring, but the screaming persists.

The miscellaneous students, the indistinct girls that aren't real, the images that have grown up with me, line the edges of the hallway. Their eyes are white and their mouths are open too, each face having a gaping hole larger than what should be possible. My heart jumps into overdrive.

I do everything I can not to cover my ears or shut my eyes. Their screaming is like a wind stopping me from moving forward. I continue to place one foot in front of the other, aware that the hallways are not at all empty. I cannot see them, but the other students are still hanging back, still waiting to walk into class.

Each and every one of them will put their eyes on me the second I act like anything other than normal is happening. I have to hide them away, make them go away. Starting with Lilith. She is just another thing I can put back into my mind where it belongs, sitting back there as a thought and not a person.

The pressure fades, the screaming silences, and the people are replaced with actual students with normal mouths and normal stances.

Just normal, slouching, waiting, stupid people.

CHAPTER NINE

Blaming the Victim

Almost too soon, the bus stops at the house.

There are no cars in the driveway. No one's home and I'm not driving anywhere. That was to be expected. I fall into the routine of coming home from school, unlocking the front door but locking it once I'm inside and discarding my bookbag in my bedroom before heading to the kitchen to do the dishes before anything else.

My mind wanders back to that isolated hallway, trying to analyze the meaning the way my grandfather never made me do before. Something from English class got me thinking that there is no possible way that anything from one's subconscious is just nonsense. As much as my grandfather insisted I push it down and tuck it away, I can't stop wondering.

The kids crowding the halls amidst a flickering in the cool-toned air were probably some strange hallucination of the crowd of students expected at the dance. That's what it had to be about. Something in me does not want to go. It's nothing more than that. It's nothing real.

I have to stop thinking about it.

He's not a distraction, he's a friend. I repeat this in my head as I dial Spencer's number. Something about his presence turns everything awful into something irrelevant. Maybe, just maybe, bringing him here will lighten this place's desolation. I just hope it isn't so tainted that he refuses to come anywhere near.

The phone rings forever and I begin to doubt that he will answer until there's a click and an eager hello from the other side. "It's me. Elle."

A small laugh breaks through the receiver and as he responds, "I know, you're in my contacts."

"I was wondering if you'd like to come by my place?" I say it slowly, like a question, and bite my lip in anticipation for his response. The shadows perk up at the sound of conversation, listening as the house's eyes widen, watching.

"Aren't your parents home?"

"I wouldn't be asking if they were. They're at some bowling thing for work, sucking up to their boss or whatever, so I don't think they'll be home for a while."

"Oh, well, I guess I could come by, why not? Got any movies or cable?" He chuckles a bit after saying that.

"Ha ha, you're very funny," I say sarcastically. "Bring whatever you want, I think we have some stale chips in the cupboard for snacks."

"Don't worry, I'll stop at the store on my way over. I'll pick up some chips, candy, and junk."

"We must clean up afterwards as if we're clearing a crime scene." I try to make a joke of it, but I'm the only one laughing. I'm not built for comedy.

"See you in a bit then."

"Alrighty, bye."

"Bye." The final click and buzzing marks that he has hung up the phone.

After cleaning and taking a shower, there's a knock on my door. Expecting Spencer to be there, I open the door right away. I start walking towards the t.v. to turn it back on when I realize that no one has come inside. I take a look at the doorway and no one is there. Starting to worry, I step outside and take a look around.

No car was parked in the driveway, but I hear a sound near the garden. I take a few more steps so that I can get a good look around the house to see it, but all I see is a girl with long silky black hair. She's in a white dress with a red ribbon around her waist. It's Lilith.

I pinch my eyes shut, hoping to get rid of her. One blink and she's usually gone. She has to be gone.

I open my eyes. My heart jumps to my throat or drops to my stomach. Either way, it's not where it's supposed to be.

Lilith is standing in front of me, so close that if I reached out my hand, I could touch her.

No, you couldn't. She's not real. Even so, I don't move. I only stare.

Her eyes are large and all white. No irises, no pupils, just big white eyes. There's a mess around her mouth. Red like wine… or blood.

I blink to make her go away, but now her entire body is covered in streaks of that violent red as her black hair blows in an imaginary wind. Her mouth hangs open.

The sound of tires crunching on the loose gravel at the end of the driveway takes my attention away from her. That seemed to do the trick. I whip my head back around to face her, but she's gone.

The car door slams and I'm still staring at nothing when Spencer reaches me, engulfing me in a big hug. It's exactly what I wanted, exactly what I expected getting him near me, to make me smile, to make it better.

"Well, hello," I greet him, turning out of the embrace to face him.

He's tall and the bits of hair that always stick out are shaking in the wind. T-shirt and jeans, like always. Just so *real*. And he talks *real*. "Should I have announced myself?"

"The driveway did all the announcing for you." He turns to look at the trodden gravel, but all I want to do is look at him. "Come on, let's get inside."

I look back at the garden one last time before I lead us both inside.

Instinctively, I wave my hand behind my back as if that will make the shadows keep their distance, but I've piqued their interest by bringing a stranger into the house. Their eyes grow wide, watering like mouths salivating for a taste of what new drama is about to present itself.

"So, what movie do we have first?" I ask him anxiously while settling myself onto the rickety pleather of the sofa.

"We have," Spencer takes a dramatic pause as he flaunts the DVD like a model showing off a product, "*The Sixth Sense* and… *Unbreakable.*"

I laugh, "You sure like your Bruce Willis."

Excited, Spencer makes his way towards the t.v. stand to look for the DVD player.

"It's— you have to— pull out the— There you go."

After a minute, he finds it and puts the disc in. He moves around the house, making himself at home and I watch in amazement because I've never seen anyone look so comfortable here. It's confusing, but before I question it too far, the movie begins and Spencer pulls me in real close.

"It's scary," he insists while pulling the blanket off of its draped position on the back of the couch. No one ever moves this blanket. But I'm not going to talk about it, or anything like that, anything to point out why he shouldn't make himself at home. I swallow my nerves.

Partly through the movie, after the boy with the gun and just to the crowd of people hanging in the halls, my mind falters. For the first time, I wonder whether or not this movie is based on a true story and how what I see may actually be real things that aren't just in my head. My thoughts get to me and I can no longer keep them to myself.

"I have to tell you something." *Am I really doing this?*

"What is it?" He asks with a hand in my hair.

Can't go back now. "I'm insane."

"You're not that crazy." He sticks his hand in the bag of potato chips he brought over and licks the residue from his fingers. "All teenagers go behind their parents' backs."

"No, not about that." *You're still a teenager, so save the sage wisdom,* is what I actually want to say, but there's a certain calm I have to keep if there's any hope of him taking me seriously. I take the remote and pause the movie as Bruce Willis sits across from his wife at their anniversary dinner. "I see things."

"Dead people?" He jokes, but his laugh is dry.

"Not exactly? I mean, I don't know." The blanket falls to the floor as he turns himself to face me and we're sitting on the couch, legs criss-crossed and hands in our laps. "I see shadows with no source and eyes in the walls. Right before you got here, there was a little girl playing in the garden. And sometimes…"

Okay, maybe he doesn't need to hear about the creatures made of black tar with liquid white eyes.

Spencer doesn't say anything, just kind of inhales deeply. It remains like that for a while, just pure silence, you can't even hear the cars on the street or wind blowing against the house. Even the shadows hold their breath.

He wants to leave. I don't blame him. I'd walk out the door myself, let it blow over, take it as some weird joke I didn't understand and wait a while before hanging out again.

But he doesn't leave. He doesn't get up. He brings me into a hug again. A nice and warm one that almost speaks for him saying, "It's okay."

I want to believe in those words, the unspoken comfort. "The thing is, I'm not convinced it's not real."

"You've got some pretty messed up shit going on up there." He touches my head with his finger.

I grab his hand out of the air and hold onto it. "So you think it's all in my head? Nothing's... watching me? Nothing's making me stop, stare, and act weird? It's just... me acting out?"

"Hey. Look at me." His eyes are serious as he brings his other hand in to hold mine and stop its fidgeting. "What your father does to you is not your fault."

We stay sitting and silent because I don't know what to say now. I didn't expect the conversation to go this way, for him to say that. And I can't tell him that I can't believe him.

Just like he always does, he brings me back out of my head. What's been said is all that needed to be said and it's time to just be two teenagers hanging out again. His hands pull away from mine quickly before tapping the top of my head and he shouts, "You're it!"

"Tag? Really?" I ask, but I'm smiling as I follow his awkward path into the kitchen where he's backing himself into a corner.

Only, when I lunge for him, my hand meets the wall as he jumps onto the table and then down to the other side. My mouth falls open wide, silent at first, but then I am laughing. Still, I chase him back into the living room, into the skinny hallway, and up against the bookshelf at its end.

With a single finger, I poke his chest, feeling his beating heart beneath the touch. "You're it."

"I don't think so," he taunts. His hands grab me before I can turn back and I squeal as he lifts me off my feet, throwing me over his shoulder as he walks us into the nearest bedroom. My bedroom, where he throws me down on the bed as laughter steals my breath.

"Wait, wait, wait!" I beg, one hand holding my side and the other pressed against his chest as he leans over me.

Then, a single sound makes my entire body still. For the second time today, someone's pulling into the driveway.

Please just be turning around, please just be some random person turning around. "Shit."

Spencer follows me back out into the living room and I wish I had told him to stay put or to leave through my bedroom window, anything other than follow me.

My dad practically falls over on his way inside and stops himself. He stops in his tracks when he sees Spencer standing beside me.

I don't know what to do. I can't think of a single thing to do. The shadows have me. They have the floor, the room, their eyes just watching.

What will he do?

What won't he do?

His voice is deep, tired, the same as I've always known it. "What the hell is going on?"

"Dad? Please, I can explain," but before he lets me, he grabs my hair and pulls on it.

"What is this? Who the fuck is he?"

"No, Dad, please, listen—" He cuts me off again by throwing me to the floor like I'm just another object in his way.

"Stand up!" He shouts at Spencer.

"Dad, please, stop." I begin to cry as my father threatens the only person I care about.

He turns his attention back towards me and starts, "I can't believe you would do something like this. Every hour I spend at that damn warehouse is to pay for *your* schooling and *your* food and *your* clothes. And you haven't even been to school, you won't eat, you won't grow up."

Through my tears, I see Spencer trying to make his way out of the house, but my father stops him, pointing at him as he travels to the kitchen, "You're not going anywhere! You think you can come to my house and screw my daughter?"

I dare not watch him and instead stare at Spencer who doesn't say anything, just stops in his tracks again. He makes gestures towards me, but I can't tell what he's trying to say. His two fingers move towards each other and apart again. I swallow. My dad got out the scissors?

My dad got out the scissors. And his heavy footfalls step towards Spencer. "Dad! Please stop!"

There's a sharp pain in the back of my knees as my dad knocks me to the ground again. I watch as he walks towards Spencer, pointing the scissors at him.

My voice comes back to me, "Dad. Dad, that's enough!"

With my newfound adrenaline, I rush to the living room and step in front of Spencer as my dad holds the scissors in the air, grunting, "Get out of the way!"

"No!"

"Who even is this guy?" He asks while trying to get around me.

I move with him like a basketball player does his opponent. *Reason. He has to listen to reason.* "He's my friend and an adult. You can go to jail for this, Dad. Put the scissors away."

He doesn't listen. Why would I expect him to listen?

He swings the open sheers in front of him like a man stranded in the wilderness whacking at leaves with a machete. But I stay between him and Spencer, raising my arms to the slashes so that he's only hitting me. The blades strike my skin and I bite my lip against the burn.

I stand my ground and call out behind me, "Spencer, leave! Just go!"

Each hit feels new and hot, I tell myself it feels good so that it doesn't hurt as much. I push Spencer towards the door and he starts running out to his car. I turn to slam the door shut behind him and my dad tries shoving me out of his way, making a deep cut in my arm while doing so.

I don't stop struggling until I hear the sound of Spencer's car pulling out of the driveway.

"Goddamn you, child!" Those are the last words I hear tonight other than my pleading for him to stop.

Lilith shows up in the corner of my vision with a pair of scissors in her own hands. She makes stabbing motions with them. Some other figure appears, although its features are unrecognizable, and Lilith hands them the scissors. I stop my struggling to watch her performance.

She grabs the scissors from the unknown figure's hand and stabs it with them. The figure fades away as if someone was blowing at a pile of dust. I imagine she's telling me to kill my father, but I'm not strong enough, because I would if I could.

I feel the blood drip down my face and he walks away grabbing a beer out of the fridge and going downstairs. I'm too bruised to move too much, but I force myself to the bathtub. Unclothing myself and pulling gently over my new cuts, I fill up the tub. For hours I sit in a pool of my own blood mixed with water. It's filthy, I know, but the sting feels too good.

The cuts are not as deep as I thought, each mark appearing as a pinkish strip with only a few bits of skin barely penetrated. I don't want to move. I rub over my raw skin, feeling every bump and cut, almost enjoying the pain trying to keep my mind off of it and Spencer. I can't believe he would stay here, I can't believe his stubbornness. I wish he'd put up more of a fight.

And now comes the self-deprecation. I believe the female stereotype that women are confusing. We say one thing and mean another. Telling him to leave was me begging him to stay and help, but he was too frightened, too confused.

I would never ask him to stay through something like that, I would never ask him to risk helping me in the moment. Those aren't the kind of things you ask of someone, it's just what you expect them to do on their own. Only, I didn't really expect him to do anything, not really.

Spencer has spent his whole life running from person-to-person confrontation. He does things that could get him in trouble and flees at the last second. He's been doing it for years. I don't hate him for it, I've always admired his strategy. But this isn't the streets, this wouldn't get him in trouble.

I know why he fled. I just wish he hadn't, and it's unfair, but it's the truth.

Stepping out of the shower and into the steamy bathroom, I wipe away the fog on the mirror after getting dressed. I despise my reflection. I am disgusted by the person I am looking at.

Someone could try to convince me that I am a hero for standing up to my father to protect someone else, but I am no hero. Spencer shouldn't have been here in the first place and it is all my fault. I've become so broken to the point where I give my father reasons to hurt me.

What your father does to you is not your fault.

How am I supposed to believe that?

CHAPTER TEN

First Dance Ready

It's Friday morning, but it's not just any Friday morning. It's Friday morning on the day of the Homecoming dance. Only a couple of days after watching Spencer run away from my crazy.

My face is as it usually is, eyes grey and face pale from exhaustion. But today, I have to look decent. Today, I have to be pretty. Somehow.

The smell of everything pollutes my bedroom the second I remove the lid to my old makeup box. Although nothing has cracked or burst open, makeup has a way of getting its stench everywhere.

Some weird feeling courses through me as I sift through the eyeliner, mascara, and contour. I feel almost normal as the anxiety about looking nice fills me, a normal anxiety.

Waking up earlier than normal doesn't feel so bad when I keep my hands active. Looking back in the mirror, I hold up the different items to my face to figure out what would look best.

The smell is intoxicating, so I get out a spray that I haven't used in a while. The liquid is down to its final drops, but I have to mask the dry stench of powder with something more floral.

I cannot wear the old dress I'm going to borrow from my mom—steal from her closet—to school, so I put on something close to it, colorwise. A pair of dark skinny jeans and a baby pink and flowing, country-girl type of shirt that has a few small stains, but it doesn't matter.

Something pleasant flutters in my chest. I'm going to a school dance *with a date.*

No, not a date. It can't be a date. I don't want to date Lanni. At least, I don't think I do. I am too into Spencer to want to date Lanni.

By the time I walk outside to wait for the bus, I don't feel any different. The music from my iPod is just noise, not something I'm actively listening to like usual. This time, today, to stop thinking about the status of my relationships, I feel like making observations. I wonder what other people think the family in my house is like as I put families in the houses around me.

The closest house to the left is much larger than ours and painted blue recently. Dark blue painted brick and pale blue painted paneling. Their driveway is complete and a strip of sidewalk extends on either side of it, but connects to nothing. They even have a garage. They look like the ideal young couple in their first home together.

To the right is a lot currently being cleared out for the recent buyer, so there's nothing there but chopped up trees and shrubbery. In front of me, though, is a nice wooden home set back among the trees. A car goes in and out of the driveway, but only a few days a week. They are probably those really independent types, him especially, stubborn too.

The rusting yellow machine pulls in front of me suddenly, I hadn't heard it coming down the hill. Its old brakes squeal at the request to stop the vehicle's motion and a large puff like a wheeze sounds as the doors open for me. My heart drops.

The entire inside is glowing blue, faint twinkles of light glowing among the crowd. The students are all standing, faces painted blue, bodies see-through. They're all facing me with blank expressions, no hint as to what they want from me or how they want me to react.

The bus driver clears his throat in annoyance and my feet move before I can stop them. My hand grabs hold of the rail that no one ever actually uses, but I'm finding that I need the stability because this can't be the bus, not the *real* bus. It's a bus I'm seeing like all the other things I see.

But it is my bus, just altered, showing me something else, something I'd normally walk away from. But this is my bus. I have to get on.

The blue air swallows me, turns me into one of them, and they all turn in accordance to my movements, following me wherever I go. As I sit in my seat, I can sense them moving, coming closer to me, hovering over me. They are crowding me, a fraction of the amount of people that will be at the school later tonight.

I shouldn't, but I can't stop myself from closing my eyes. The air becomes like liquid, clogging my ears, washing out the music I wasn't paying attention to anyway. Whispers replace the sound that should be coming from my iPod. Indiscernible murmurs of something probably a lot more vital to understanding their purpose than I think.

They aren't real, I have to shut it out. Shut everything out. I can just make it go away, send it away, so that I follow through with these plans. I can't let anything make me back out, not on the day of the event. Shut it out. Shut everything out.

The driver clears his throat in impatience. I open my eyes and unclench the fists that I hadn't realized I'd been making. I am the last kid on the bus. We have been stopped and he has only now turned to me to get me off. I would say thank you, but he wouldn't understand, so I don't bother.

Walking toward the building, I wonder about what Lanni might say when he sees me. I wonder if he has been thinking about tonight as much as I have. Most of all, I wonder if he is going to back out at the last moment, and knowing him, if this is true, he will ignore me all day to avoid having to tell me directly.

The fake face I have on seems to be melting in the unforgiving light of the hallways. Instinctively, I look at other girls, evaluate their faces, and try to catch anything not quite right like a smudge or cakiness to make myself feel more secure. It works and I think I am just about ready to ignore it for the rest of the day when Lanni walks across the hall adjacent to mine.

He looks left and right like a young boy listening to his mother before he spots me and hurries over. Quickly, he says, "Elle, about tonight."

"You don't want to go anymore."

"No! It's not that at all, actually. I wanted to ask you what you are planning on wearing, but I can see that you've already thought about it."

I can feel him looking at my face and not me. "It's bad, isn't it?"

"No, you look… beautiful."

Everything I've ever told myself about not turning our friendship into something romantic bursts to the front of my thoughts, threatening to spurt out of me in an inconsiderate fashion. I manage to keep my mouth shut and blush instead.

I don't think anyone's called me beautiful before, and it's… beautiful.

We go to class at the sound of the bell and the rest of the school day goes by in a flash. There are no outbursts of translucent students, no inconvenient calls down to the office, and no embarrassing confrontations. If I didn't know any better, I'd say the day is normal.

When I arrive home, I immediately get ready, wanting to be in and out of the house as quickly as possible so that my parents don't even have a chance of coming home early. The probable shouting dialogue forms a scene in my head already. My dad would start with something about my mom until I walk into the room.

He'll see my face and yell about the makeup and the dress, telling me that it belongs to my mother and I have no right to wear it. He'll ask me where I think I'm going and when I tell him, he'll say that it won't happen. He'll say I have no one to go with, that I'm mental for thinking anyone would want to do anything leisurely with me. Then my mom would beg him to leave me alone and he'd push her to the ground while I stand back and watch, awaiting my turn.

I won't give him the chance. He can do whatever he wants tonight and I won't be there. He can wonder all he wants about where I am or continue not to notice. Either way, whenever I come home, he'll have something ready for me and I will take it just as I have taken everything else.

For now, I'm going to attend a school dance with a school friend and do normal school things.

And for the first time, I'm not afraid of it. Nervous, sure, but what teenage girl doesn't get nervous about her first homecoming dance?

The dress is folded neatly in an old box that my mom keeps on the top shelf of her closet beside my father's gun. She keeps it there to know whether or not he goes up there. The dress is the same one she wore to her prom.

The black faux-satin trails down to my ankles. There's a slit in the left leg, but nothing too revealing. The chest and arms are a floral patterned lace extending all the way to the wrist.

Using bobby pins to hold back a pulled over sort of bangs look, I hairspray everything down to help keep it from falling out. Once it is all sprayed stiff, the smell of hairspray impossible to get rid of, I fix any of the makeup that might be washed out from wearing all day.

To add a few extra details, I rub on body glitter on my cheeks and neck after emphasizing eyeliner in a winglike fashion and darkening the tones of my contour, a skill I have yet to master through the use of tutorial videos.

The person in the mirror is a stranger. A smiling, sparkling, *alive* stranger. I'm excited to be her.

The only question lingering is about what to do with my time. I could go to see Spencer and ask him about how I look, about whether or not I should even bother showing up. He is my decision-maker for things like this. I can only trust him to know what is best for me. Plus, it will be another visit where the reason I'm showing up has nothing to do with my parents.

So, with a destination in mind, I turn on the car and head for Shady Palms. As long as I keep moving, I can't think so much. And if I'm not thinking, there's no room for shadows or figures or anything else that might want to stop me from going through with the night.

As long as the day continues to be void of interruption, I will have a good time, as scary as it sounds to do anything unprovoked in public. I park the car and walk into the building, the little buzzer buzzing to let me in. I pick up the dress to get up the stairs, glad I'm wearing my tennis shoes, and knock on Spencer's apartment door.

When he opens it, he seems upset. I didn't see him yesterday and the last time he saw me, I was getting a beating. An apology seems to want to escape him, but when he looks up at me to say it, the words get caught in his throat and are replaced with just one, "Woah."

I breathe an airy laugh. "How do I look?"

"How do you look? You shouldn't even have to ask. The real question is why you look?"

"I'm going to the school dance," I say, cringing at myself because *I'm going to the school dance.* My face turns to the ground, staring at the dirtied tips of my shoes.

"Oh," he sounds rightly surprised. "With someone?"

I get a bit embarrassed and feel guilty over the realization that I haven't told him about Lanni. "Yeah, actually. Lanni. I kinda keep school stuff at school, don't I?"

"No kidding. Is this like, like a date?" Spencer sounds more like a parent than ever as he asks me these questions.

"We're going as friends." I hope it's not obvious how uncertain my answer is, because the truth is that Lanni and I never actually discussed it.

"And your parents are okay with this?" Does he want the answer to be no? For me to go back home?

"My parents don't know," I slow my speech thinking of a question, my shoulders sagging as the excitement wears off. "Are *you* okay with this?"

"What?" His shoulders relax and he does one of those arm waves. The look in his eyes is the frightening kind of concern like he knows something that I don't. "Of course, I am. Just, um, be careful."

"Um, okay, of course." Is he telling me to leave? Should I tell him I have time to stay? Should I offer not to go and stay here instead? None of those questions are what I say. "I'll see you soon?"

"Yeah."

"Okay," I mumble, stunned and trying not to notice how he stopped looking at me, how dejected he seems holding his door open for me to leave, or walk away. I haven't even technically gone in.

When the door shuts behind me, I don't walk away. Spencer's inside on a Friday night, hadn't seen me since I invited him to a front row seat of a Groeman family event until just now, and what am I seeing him for? Not to check in on him after what happened, not to thank him, not even to tell him in the words themselves that I am okay.

What was I thinking? Why did I think showing up at Spencer's all dressed up for someone else was a good idea? I mean, I'm not dressed up for Lanni, I'm dressed up for a dance, for something I've never done before and never thought I would do.

But how is he supposed to think that? If I wanted to go to this dance, why didn't I ask Spencer to go with me? Why did I think Spencer would want to see this?

I didn't think. That's the answer. I never think. Just like I never think about how it makes him feel when I show up after being hit. I don't think.

My knuckles rap on his door again and I hear his question through the door, "Elle?"

It opens and he's standing there while I'm standing on his welcome mat. This time, though, I try to say the right thing. "I'm sorry about Wednesday and for showing up like this instead of so much sooner and not like I just walked out of a totally regular teen movie from the 1980s."

"Slow down."

"No. I'm sorry you saw any of that and that you always see these bad things and that I don't tell you when I'm okay. I should have come over yesterday at the very least to smooth things over with you and told you about the dance and about Lanni. I should have told you all of that on Wednesday instead of getting all dark and serious about my hallucinations. You don't need that. You don't deserve that."

"Breathe." Although he's tired of me, his smile returns and I feel selfish again about how relieved that smile makes me. "I told you before. I am glad you share your life with me. I am happy to see you whenever I see you, no matter the reason or the timing."

"How can you say that and mean it?"

His eyes are still afraid, but he just shrugs. "You just have to trust me."

But me trusting him has never been the issue. It's only now that I realize he might not trust me. How many times have I said I'll be okay and it was a lie?

Just as I think about staying, he says, "Now, I'm not making you leave because I don't want to see you. I'm telling you to go because I know a part of you is hoping that if you're here long enough, you'll be able to justify standing up your not-a-date."

"It's really not a date." *Stop blushing and maybe he'll believe you.*

"I trust you."

He's unbelievable. And I'm the worst. "I'm—"

"Don't you dare apologize again, Little Fawn."

"I should have invited you…" I swallow, but it's got to be said. "You should be my date."

"I appreciate the sentiment, but you don't need to be bringing an alumnus."

"So you did graduate?" I joke and when he laughs, I know we're back to us.

Still, his chest heaves a silent, heavy breath like he's holding something back. Nudging my shoulder and holding the door open much more casually than before, he says, "Now go meet up with your friend. I'll be here to hear all about your first normal high school experience. *That* is how you make it up to me."

"You got it." For a moment, I get another itch to touch him, to maybe even get up on my toes to plant a kiss on his cheek, but as I'm off to a dance with another guy doesn't quite feel like the time so I just leave.

CHAPTER ELEVEN

Disappearing Act

Lines of students shuffle into the building, waiting to be tested for alcohol levels before getting into the dance. As I head to join them, I find Lanni standing quite impatiently for me.

His eyes fall on me and he perks up like usual. "Thank God you showed up, and quite ravishingly too."

Who needs rouge when any semblance of a compliment makes you blush? "Of course I did, why wouldn't I?"

We laugh and start into the building, awkwardly blowing into breathalyzers for the policeman by the door.

The only lights on in the building are the ones in the first hallways, but the second we cross the threshold of the lunch room, the only light comes from candles set up as center pieces for the tables.

I hadn't noticed my body tense up until Lanni touches my shoulder. "Relax, take my hand."

His hand is laying in the air, palm-up inviting my hand to complete the form. I put my hand in his and he guides me to the gymnasium. Once inside, I try to take in everything that is happening. A single row of the bleachers has been pulled out and the dance floor seems to be following the boundaries of the basketball court.

Lights bounce off of the stage, changing color and direction, each one shining through a blue film. They'd somehow attached a disco ball to the ceiling, showering the students below in twinkling light as every pop song from the last five years takes turns playing through the speakers.

My feet stop just a few feet short of joining the crowd. Lanni looks at me prompting me to look at him. He squeezes my hand and nods, neither of us bothering to try to speak to one another in the noise. This is it. I'm okay. We got here and that's all there is to it.

Am I already wishing the night is over? Would I really be content to leave even though we just got here? What sucks is that the answer repeating itself in my head is a resounding *yes*.

But Lanni starts to jump, one fist in the air, in accordance with the movements of the other students until we are buried deep within the crowd and I can't leave him, can't leave *this*. This is the experience I'm supposed to tell Spencer about.

I recognize the other students in the mass, people I've sat next to in class or awkwardly shuffle behind in the halls. Everyone's dressed up, even the hockey team traded their Norwood jerseys for dress pants and jackets. Some of them have t-shirts on underneath, one of them even sports one of those black tees with a tux graphic printed on it.

And everyone is jumping. Girls are barefoot and if the boys' sneakers are squeaking on the court floor, it can't be heard over a blaring mix of Ellie Goulding and Flo Rida.

Then Lanni starts doing the strangest things I have ever seen someone do. With an arm and a leg wiggling in the air, he spins around in an effort to get me to move and stop him from embarrassing himself.

Next thing I know, I'm moving my own limbs. It's not pretty and I know it. I'm double-jointed and sore all over. My arms can't lift above my head and the best I can do is bounce even though my legs scream in protest. Nonetheless, I don't stop moving. The crowd, the music, the lights, all of it creates a blur that I fall into effortlessly, carelessly.

Then the beat softens. A slow song. Lanni holds out his hand to me as the opening notes to Eric Clapton's "Wonderful Tonight" fills the gym. Couples pair up, and we fall into step with their swaying when I take Lanni's hand and let him hold my waist while I drape an arm around his shoulders.

In the sixth grade, I danced just like this with my dad. It was a father-daughter dance that one or both of us insisted we attended, or it might have been my grandfather. Either way, we went and we danced. We danced to this song. And if I close my eyes, I can easily swap out the glittering blues of the school gymnasium for the shimmering reds of shiny heart decals and balloon arches in the rec center's ballroom.

I remember feeling like I could fall asleep in my father's arms that hugged me then. He didn't squeeze, he didn't pull, he didn't try to get us to leave early. We danced, my feet on his when I was getting tired, and when this song played, he just held me.

Not unlike the way Lanni holds me now. And as far as I'm concerned, the rest of the room can fade away.

That is, until the room does fade.

When I look at Lanni, all I notice is the stillness of the room around him. Everybody else has stopped dancing. The students are looking at him, faces blank with unimpressed expressions. The entire room has turned inwards to face us like some dance circle, or jury.

I spin around, their blue lighted bodies staring at me, lips turning upwards in ridiculing smiles. This is it. The people I saw on the bus, the blue air, the flickering of it all and those blank, watching stares.

"Who does she think she's dancing with?" Someone sniggers and others pretend to stifle laughter.

I look at Lanni as the laughter swells, but he's no longer looking at me. Without warning, he breaks into a sprint, pushing through the crowd. I follow suit, chasing after him.

But as I start to run, the faceless crowd closes in on me. I run into their shoulders, getting knocked around by the now laughing crowd, their laughter so loud that I can't possibly shut it out.

Every collision bothers some bruise or another and I try not to freeze when I see Lilith. Her black hair, white dress, and short height stands out in the crowd of teenagers. She appears as if in sunlight, unaffected by the strobing blues.

Just when I think I am about to break through the last of the students, away from Lilith and the blue bodies, a hand takes hold of my arm and I am forced to stop. I turn to beat them off of me, but he only grabs my other wrist before I can push him back.

It's Alex. He's taken a hold of me, keeping me from following Lanni. His face is a whole head above mine and I look up to him to try and read his expression. He's cleaned up quite well in a pair of dress pants and a jacket, but it's unbuttoned and I can see the t-shirt he's wearing underneath.

Without a word, he keeps a hand around me and guides us out of the gymnasium and away from the noise so that I can hear him when he does speak.

"I didn't expect to see you here," he says as if that is his explanation for pulling me aside.

"I didn't expect to be here." I speak quickly, looking around him for a sign of Lanni.

"Are you looking for someone?"

"Yeah, Lanni. He just ran out without telling me why." Ignoring his perplexed expression, I free myself from him.

He follows me as I walk around the school and continues to talk, "I was hoping you were alone. I've been wanting to ask you something. I mean, you're weird, I can't act like you're not, but there's something about it that, well, I don't know, I guess maybe I—"

I spot Lanni pushing through the exit doors and cut Alex off, "I have to go."

Without any more words or waiting for what he might say next, I follow him, imagining how much more difficult this would have been if I wore nicer shoes. The chaperones, mainly consisting of the daily lunch aid staff, turn their heads in surprise and confusion as I rush passed them and out the door.

The chill of the air hits me immediately, the cold of autumn a thing I forgot about.

I disregard everything when I catch another glimpse of Lanni rushing into the woods. The leaves crunch beneath my feet, branches bare and dry from the progression of the season. My dress gets caught in a gathering of dried vines on the ground, a thorn sticking itself into the fabric. The skirt tears as I push forward. I can move better, run faster.

"Where are you going?" I shout for him.

"Come on!" I hear him shout back, but he doesn't slow down for me to catch up.

I find myself laughing as I follow Lanni for quite a while until we reach the more dense part of the woods. He's an athlete, jumping over fallen trunks and ducking low-hanging branches swiftly. I try to copy him to not fall too far behind, but my speed is no match to his.

The woods smell beautiful, the trees are still damp from the rain and I amuse myself by peeling at their trunks. I can't run like he can, I have to take breaks.

I stomp on worms and run my fingers along the tall, leafy plants as my run turns into a brisk walk. Sometimes, I stop in my tracks and stand there feeling the wind blow by and listen to the sound of the leaves rustling above us. And I wish he would stop. How much farther can he want to go?

Then he finally stops before a pond and calls to me again, repeating himself and waving his arms, "Come on!"

Now that he's stopped, I bend over to catch my breath. My lungs are in stitches, but I pick myself back up to close the distance between us. But when I lift my head, he's gone again. I look around in each direction trying to spot a quickly moving teenage boy, but it's nearly impossible to see anything in the dark of night.

I cup my mouth to somehow make it louder when I shout his name. I hear my voice echo back to me and birds fly off of some branches, but there is no human reply. I end up staring into the pond in defeat, right where he'd been standing. The water reflects the earth around it spectacularly and I don't want to take my eyes off of it in fear that it will disappear if I do.

While I stare into the still pond, a glimmer enters my vision. A small white orb of light bounces into view, bobbing up and down like a living creature, beckoning me to pursue it.

It hovers over the water. Something in me wants to touch it. The pure light lures me in and I step into the water slowly, so slowly that I'm not even sure it moves.

Once I'm at the center of it, inches away from the small orb on its surface, I stick a single finger out to touch it. My finger stops the second it touches the water and for a moment, everything is quiet.

Then, it's like the air is sucked out of itself and ripples explode in a delayed burst from my slight touch. They expand into larger and larger circles, beginning to glow brighter and brighter until I swear that it moves.

Up and up they go, surrounding me in the blinding rings of light. They grow brighter still and I can't stop myself from shutting my eyes. All I can see is a bright light before my stomach plummets and everything takes a sudden stop.

CHAPTER TWELVE

It Isn't Real?

I open my eyes to an inverted version of the forest I was in just moments ago. The sky is as dark as night, the entire atmosphere takes on a bluish hue.

The air is cold and I've got nothing to cover myself up with this time. I pull my hands inside my sleeves as best I can and hug myself. The woods around me are empty, I can feel it. Slowly drifting frays of white blur my surroundings, but there is no one hiding in it.

"Goddamnit!" I scream into the air and watch as my cloudy breath floats and dissipates.

"It's okay. You're okay." I hear a voice almost like Lanni's, but I refuse to believe it, refuse to believe anyone can be here in what has to be some sort of truly off-the-deep-end hallucination. I've officially lost my mind, but it's better to pretend it's real this time. I think I'd freeze before I'd be able to make it go away.

"Who—who's there? Where are you?" I spin around in circles trying to find the source of the voice, carefully looking passed the trees.

"You can't see me, so stop looking," he tells me, but I continue to search the forest for a sign of anyone.

"What is this? What did you do?"

"I'm sorry, Lilith told me to lead you here, said you needed to know the truth." Its voice is full of regret and, as if I had once felt its presence, I feel a sudden absence.

But I was right, none of this is real. Lilith isn't real, so no voice saying her name can be. I shiver and begin to hop around where I stand, I don't know what I'm doing, I don't know what to do.

The pond is almost an exact replica of the one I was standing in front of before, I see multiple footprints revealing the presence of more than just one person. The slowly drifting flecks of white resemble snow, or maybe that's just the cold making me draw conclusions.

Unlike earlier, I don't see any squirrels or chipmunks running across the forest path, no sign of any living creature. I am truly alone and afraid, and as I take a seat by a discolored oak tree, I hear a different voice calling out to me, "Elle?"

"Who's there?"

"Elle? Elle!"

"Spencer, is that you?" I get up and look up and around looking for the body that matches the voice, but yet again I find nothing. No one replies to my question, just repeated shouts of my name seem to come from every direction. I put my head down and begin to cry, wiping the tears away with my sleeve to prevent them from freezing to my face.

A bone-chilling breeze reaches me from across the water and I shiver. The not-snow sparkles in the air and I watch their descent in an effort to take my mind off of the situation. I always deal with whatever's going on, but nothing like this has ever happened and I fear that I will not return. That if I leave where I sit now, I will be lost in here forever.

I play with the dry leaves on the ground, crushing them in my fist and then blowing them out of my hand to watch the wind take it away. I watch until they disappear from view. If it hadn't been for Lanni and Spencer, I would probably start enjoying my time here, but Spencer's repeated cries of my name makes it so that I can't stand the thought of leaving him all alone.

Although, it isn't my fault; I didn't come here willingly, I didn't know I was on my way to trap myself.

What was Lanni thinking? Where was he running? Will he just keep running or will he come looking for me? Would he even be able to find me if he does?

A soft sound comes from somewhere behind me, the only sound I've heard since arriving besides the voices. It's animal-like and I listen closely, focusing all of my energy on that noise.

My heart races inside my chest and I'm waiting for it to track me with it, like I'm a sitting duck. Do I really want to see whatever my frantically spinning mind wants to throw at me in this state, in this complete breakdown?

Preparing myself to run, I get up off the ground and glance around the tree to see where it might be. A loud snap makes me pause in my tracks. This time when I look around, I see the corpse of a deer, slaughtered and bloody, disemboweled. It's like the one my father hit with the car on our way to a campground once.

I can't remember anything else, not with the viscera spilling out in front of me. Bile rises in my throat, but I swallow it down to follow a snapping sound.

A creature, tall and slender, dark as night, is creeping around the dead deer. It's crouched down, ripping open another animal with its teeth. That must've been the sound, the animal being brought down onto the ground.

I would move, but I remember how in almost every horror movie when the person moves, they make a sound and the monster attacks.

Paralyzed with fear, I do my best to breathe quietly, but the more I look at it, the more I know it. The black, sloughing, tarred texture of its skin and those empty, blank, white eyes had stared at me just the other day in huddles of people outside the bus… on my desk… drawn up by my own hands.

As I watch without blinking, I see a new figure appear next to the creature. It's Lilith, she begins making the same scissor hands she did before and points to the creature, but then she points to me and then at the deer that is currently being devoured.

What is this place? What is this hallucination? Why isn't anyone snapping me out of it? No one has ever done it before, not since my grandfather died, but Lanni has got to be wondering where I am. He's got to be looking for me. He has to find me.

But I can't sit here and do nothing until he does. "What do you want?"

Lilith only shakes her head and then puts her finger to her mouth. I glare at her and then notice that the creature has ceased its eating. It is now sitting there beside the water, and I can see its face in the reflection. Strings of torn tendons and veins drip red from its large toothy grin. It stares into the water as if it's waiting for something, as if the pond is going to feed him more.

There are so many different directions this situation can go. I could begin running, but I would probably end up right back where I started, I could end up getting chased and more than just that one monster could follow me. I think more and more while also trying to figure out what the creature is doing.

Why stare into the water like that?

What is it waiting for?

I look at the freshly limp deer that is as bloody and gutless as the deer I saw earlier. It is soaking wet, a hideous mass of blood matting its fur and water dampening everywhere else. I look down at my own feet and see that they are still wet from standing in the pond. That deer must've been in it. Could it have come from it?

The creature sits and waits like a dog. It glances at the deer but then right back at the water. It's definitely waiting for something to come out, something that is not a fish.

I begin thinking about how I got here myself and it hits me. The water brought me here. Somehow, I have transported myself to some messed up dimension by stepping into the water.

This is how to make it real so that I can finally do something about it, to create a diversion so I can escape.

Picking up a huge rock from beside my feet, I toss it over in the opposite direction of myself and the pond. Once the creature's pointy bat-like ears perk up and shift towards the noise, I stand completely still to make sure I don't stop it from following the sound.

It runs over to the noise on all fours. Its unbeatable speed frightens me to stiffness. If I make any sound, it will turn its head, find me, and attack. There's no doubt. But I have to do something.

So, I take a single soft step towards the water. Something hiding under the leaves cracks, the sound hardly noticeable to anything that isn't listening, but something tells me that the creature has more than just a heightened sense of hearing.

It turns its entire body towards me, large muscular arms in front of it in a gorilla-like fashion and its hind legs preparing to propel itself forward. Something's stopping me from moving, call it fear or whatever, and I just stand here as the creature bounds towards me as a quick shadow.

Its clawed hands grab a hold of my shoulders, knocking me to the ground just beside the pond. One of my hands feels the water, but something tells me that's not enough.

The creature's long black tongue drags over my face, the slimy blood-ridden spit wetting my cheek. I stare into its face, knowing better than to close my eyes. Its white eyes are anything but comical. They are enlarged human eyes stripped of its color and pupils. I wonder if it can actually see me or if its flaring nostrils are its only sense of what it has pinned down.

My hands feel the ground around me, my fingertips touching rocks.

I pull a hefty one loose from its place in the ground as the creature crushes me further into the dirt. With as much effort as I can gather, I lift it forcefully in a swinging motion at its head. It's slightly knocked off focus and I manage to get my feet out and run back into the water.

The water doesn't move in the wake of my steps as if I'm not here. How am I supposed to make it ripple if it doesn't react to my touch? Frantically searching for a clue on how to get back, I barely notice the creature regain focus and jump towards me.

Once again, it has me pinned to the ground, but my head falls beneath the water. The way it refuses to move, no splashes or sounds, I expect to not even get wet, but my hair floats around me the way it would underwater.

When my head smacks the ground, my mouth opens for air but only finds water. I'm thrashing my arms and legs, but the water refuses to move. I close my eyes against the water, not wanting to see the creature's teeth looking for me.

I grab its arm, look for its face with my hands, and try to find its eyes to scratch them out or anything, but its grip on my shoulders won't give up. It's pushing me down and down again, trying to force me beneath where the ground is stopping me.

My breath stings my lungs as I hold it in with the water that I have already taken in. I breathe out, a stream of bubbles of air flowing out of my mouth. The creature is pushing me, forcing me down, and something beneath me seems to be pulling me in, sucking me under.

I begin to scream wondering if this is where it ends, someplace that I do not know by the murder-crazed creature from my mind that most-likely doesn't exist. Either my thoughts or the lack of oxygen dulls my senses. I'm almost calm, succumbed to the end.

My hand wavers above the surface, gently touches the water, and I'm surrounded by light.

Someone has their arms around me, their hands rubbing up and down as if to warm me. Then, they smack me in the back, the pounding kind like someone casually forcing a cough out of someone. Water spills from my mouth as the person turns me over to expel the liquid onto the ground.

Once it stops, I lay myself flat on the ground. I'm completely soaked. As I lay down, my shoulders loosen.

But I can't relax. I can't assume I'm safe.

My teeth chatter and I hug myself, rubbing my hands up and down my arms. Warmth, I need warmth. It was so cold over there, colder than winters in Norwood. The cold seeped down into my soul, creating darkness. There's a darkness inside of me. No, the darkness is just my eyelids. I have to open my eyes, forget that place, leave it.

My eyes open slowly and I get a glimpse of a normal sky. The air's no longer blue, nothing's shining. I'm back in the real world. I have to believe it. The air feels warmer and I let myself absorb the heat. The real world returns to me, its plain state of reality somehow reassuring, like waking from a dream and knowing that you've actually woken up this time.

"Elle, it's okay. Calm down." The person who pulled me out of the water embraces me in a warm hug and I almost instantly stop shivering.

"What the fuck, Lanni?!" I shout into the air whether or not it is him who has me in his arms.

"Woah, woah, woah, just breathe."

I do just enough to break away from him and sputter, "Spencer? How'd you—? Why are you—?"

"I saw you running this way. I hope you don't mind that I was watching you."

"Watching me? Like stalking me?" I must be talking faster than I should be, but it's the only way I can get the words out without a stutter. I can't process the words he's saying and everything that just happened at the same time, but my mind needs answers, "Did you see him?"

"You weren't chasing anyone, Elle," his voice has returned to that tone of someone who knows something that I don't. He seems concerned for me, but not the obvious kind, more like the kind where he knows something but is never going to tell me. But then he says, "You weren't chasing anyone."

He sounds so sure of himself. "No, Lanni was—"

"There is no Lanni. Not at your school, not in the city, not anywhere."

His words mess up my head even more. He doesn't know what he's talking about. "You probably just didn't notice him. He was ahead of me."

Everything that's happened in what has probably only been a couple of minutes is getting stirred around in my head so that I can't make sense of it even if I try.

But as Spencer's gentle touch continues to try to hold me together, I feel the bruises and cuts from running and fighting, realizing everything that is happening isn't a dream. This is real. "Help me."

Spencer pulls me into his chest as a choked sob claws its way out of me. If he wasn't holding me, I would probably fall. Spencer moves to stroke my hair and I feel safe in his arms, his warm arms.

Although, with my eyes closed, I can see the creature and the rigid body of the dead deer. I see Lilith in that demonic form. I take big gulps trying to stop myself from being too loud, trying to breathe.

"God, you're freezing. How is that possible?" He asks, but it doesn't seem directed at me.

"I was somewhere…" I try to explain the unexplainable between sobs. "It was dark, and there was this… this… thing, and—"

"Shh, let me take you home."

"No!" I stop him before he turns around and leads us out of the forest. "I don't want to go home."

"You misunderstand, Little Fawn. We are going *home*." He takes my hand and begins walking out the way we came.

After that, I decide to no longer let myself think. I instead trust him and let him guide me. It's one of those moments where I can pretend to be a little kid, one who doesn't know fear.

I don't say anything else as we walk to his car, as we drive away from the school, nor as we walk even more slowly up the steps to Spencer's apartment. I can feel the stutter still in my throat, like the water's phantom presence.

When we get inside, he sets me on the couch with a blanket. "I'll get you some hot tea or something."

After putting myself in child-mode, I am more like a statue, stiff and silent. I keep trying to shake the cold away, but it seems to all be in my head. I can touch my skin and it is warm, but my body continues to shake and if someone tries telling me that I am warm, I will correct them.

I only move slightly, remembering that sudden movements may draw the monster closer. I know I'm out, but I feel like it followed me, like I am not free from the frozen forest, from my mind because it had to have been in my head. Everything else is in my head... the shadows, the blue air. Lanni...

I don't realize myself staring until Spencer points it out. "Elle? What happened?"

"I don't know." I close my eyes and shake my head.

He gets up on the couch next to me, handing me a cup of tea and it seems he was only content to not ask questions before we got here. Now, he wants to know everything, and I can't blame him. Yesterday, I told him I have hallucinations, and today... this happens.

"You seem very out of it, so I know I probably shouldn't ask, but..." He worries his lip. "You disappeared right in front of me. I was watching you, but then there was a light and you were gone."

"I was somewhere else... sort of," I try to explain, but it's hard to form the words in my mouth. "Th-the air was shiny and blue and cold, v-very cold," and now I notice I am stuttering from my confusion and chattering.

"What happened? You look like you saw a ghost."

"Not a ghost. A—A *creature*. It was... eating a-and—" I see it all playing back in my head and I begin to shiver vigorously again, pulling relentlessly on my sleeves.

My emotions are mixed, I'm confused, afraid, shocked, and can't stop myself from thinking about what Lanni had said, and what Spencer said about Lanni.

I whisper, "I had to learn the truth."

"What? What does that mean? What are you talking about?" Spencer's concern is written all over his face and nothing I'm saying is helping. I don't know if I can help. He looks at me and lets me move the way I want and talk however I can, though I know he wants me to just spit it out.

"I—I'm sorry." My voice breaks and I try to swallow my tears before I start sobbing again. The threads of my sleeves break as I tug and tug, until I'm twirling and pulling the loose strings. It's all too much in my head to explain. I can't explain it, as much as I want to try. I just can't.

"What truth?" He prompts, but…

"I—I don't know anymore, I don't know." I lean on him and say more softly, "I don't know."

Spencer doesn't say another word or ask another question, he only continues to stroke my hair and we sit in silence. I eventually stop crying and lay there, idly wrapping and unwrapping threads at the ends of my sleeves around my finger.

I try to forget about everything that had just happened, but it is too hard to unsee the feasting creature, to ignore the words that were spoken to me, "Lilith told me to lead you here, said you needed to know the truth." What could possibly be meant by that? What truth?

Spencer's words echo back to me, *There is no Lanni. Not at your school, not in the city, not anywhere.* Only, Lanni was right there. If Spencer was following me, he was also following Lanni. But Spencer wouldn't lie to me, especially when I'm broken down like this. He told me that we were the only ones there, that there was no third person and there never has been.

I think about all the times I have seen Lanni, at school, after school, before school. I realize now that we only see each other between class periods and that no one else ever seems to mention him despite my assumption of his popularity. How I've never mentioned him. That he never touches anyone else and always seems to disappear when we say goodbye.

Lanni isn't real.

Lanni is in my head, just like every other demon.

I'm not sad, now I'm just angry at myself. For three years I thought I had a real friend. Now I know that people always stared because they probably saw me talking to a wall. That's why I was sent to the guidance. I could never have fit in with that crowd. Now the truth seems pretty obvious, I am crazy. Crazy and stupid.

"You finally figured it out. Another piece of the puzzle," I hear, but it's not Spencer, so I know it must be in my head. There's a little girl giggle and then the feeling of having someone else in the room fades away. Like the presence that faded before on the other side of the ripples.

This confirms my insanity, and maybe it ties to what the voice said before. The fact that I am out of my mind is part of the truth I had to know.

CHAPTER THIRTEEN

At Least Once

When my eyes flutter open, I can see bare trees above me, trembling in the wind. Leaves from the ground sticking to my hair and my clothes and surrounding me with crunching, crumbling sounds.

In any direction I turn, there is nothing to see but the dull grey and pale orange colors of a fading forest. Standing up to go anywhere but here, a loud snap gives me pause.

My entire body is suddenly paralyzed. I can barely even turn my head to see what had made the sound. Once I catch a glimpse, I recognize the creator of the sound as Spencer. He must have been looking for me, like he knew I was alone and needed saving.

Something's wrong. I still can't move and Spencer doesn't look right. His eyes are locked on me but his expression is different, void of worry or relief or anything but a menacing determination. As he gets nearer, he raises an arm. It extends it towards me, but not with an open hand at the end. Instead, his fingers are clenched around the short handle of a handgun.

My eyes widen and my heartbeat quickens, panic engrossing me into a fleeting fear, but I still can't move. The end of the gun is pointed straight at me. Spencer only looks sure, his stance strong and entire body still with certainty. The second I try to scream at him, a gunshot vibrates the air, and a brief flash of light blinds me until it all turns black.

I wake up alone on the couch with two blankets on top of me, gripping the side to feel something, to move, to feel okay. My eyes fall on the coffee table in front of me where a bottle of aspirin is sitting beside a glass of water. I look past them and consider opening the tabletop to check that the weapon is still there.

The smell of food from the kitchen distracts me and I pick my head up to look, but a tightening sensation follows like stretching rubber bands as far as they will go. I hold my head in my hands and finally grab the bottle of aspirin from the coffee table. Swallowing the pill, dry, I manage to turn my head to see what's going on behind me.

Spencer is in the kitchen, hovering over the stove and seeing him like I'm used to seeing him, I forget about the panic that consumed me only moments ago and ask. "What's cooking?"

"Breakfast," he replies and uses a spatula to flip what looks like eggs.

"It's morning already?"

"Yeah, but don't worry, I drove by your place."

"You what?" I get up, suddenly more awake and realizing I am wearing one of his sweatshirts.

"I just checked to see who was home."

"What if they saw you? What if—"

"They weren't there." His face is as serious as mine, but I'm not convinced. "Don't worry about it."

"You should've woken me and taken me home." I flop back down and groan, pulling my hands inside the long sleeves and leaning on them.

"There's no way that would help anyone. You weren't okay. I couldn't just wake you to take you there." His jaw clenches and I watch him swallow his anger before going on, "I let you sleep and you seem a bit better now?"

Sometimes I hate how much sense he makes all of the time, so I ignore the fact that I've spent the night out for the second time in a week without any contact with my father.

In response to his statement, I say, "Yeah, 1 thought about it."

"Oh yeah? And what did you come up with?" He sets plates down on the table, so I get up and go over to him.

"That Lanni was in my head the whole time and that I must've walked around to the other side of the pond and hit my head or something."

"C'mon, that's not right, and you know it." He tries to encourage me to have bizarre thoughts instead of letting me shove them away. "I saw you disappear. There was a bright strobing of lights and you were gone, right in the water. I looked around, you weren't anywhere. Bubbles in the water appeared before you did, I reached in, and the next thing I knew, I had you in my arms."

"Well, what do you want me to believe?"

"That something crazy is actually happening here, that you have some sort of superpower that allows you to talk to demons and travel in different dimensions."

"This is real life Spencer, not some crazy comic."

"Fine, I guess you're right, there's no possible way that you disappeared right in front of my eyes. I must be crazy too." He sounds sarcastic and upset that I shut his absurd idea down. He plays with his eggs before shoveling them into his mouth with a fork.

I can only think of two reasons why he wants to believe I'm not crazy, but only one of them makes sense. There is the possibility that he is bored and is one of those people who has waited his entire life to find out that the things that happen in books and movies can actually happen. The more likely reason is that he is desperately clinging onto the idea that I don't have more problems.

Appreciating him for wanting to believe in the best possible solution, I start to eat. Only, I'm not hungry because everytime I think about eating, I see the mutilated deer laying down on the side of the pond. I want to gag, but I need to prove that my own mind doesn't scare me. I need to prove this to myself if no one else.

Something makes me want to return, to go back again, but in control this time. I need to go again to get answers. Maybe I can prove that nothing happened. Besides, something has to detach the scene from the bad memory, otherwise, I will never be able to be near a pond again.

After finishing our food, we move into the living room and start talking again, "What do you want to do?"

I let him distract me. "Like what?"

"Anything, you know, within budget."

I think really hard, trying to figure out the last time I got to go out and do something with someone, someone real that is. "Skating?"

He looks taken aback. "In which form?"

"The roller kind," I mock him. "You said once that we should. Is that within budget?"

"Yes, in fact, it's free. Andrew has a space he used to let me use to practice and I happen to own a few different sizes of roller skates given I used them to get away from cops before I could drive."

"You weren't the skateboard type?"

"No, I always seemed to stop too short." He laughs clearly out of reminisce. "Let's go."

"Now?" I ask and follow him to his bedroom.

"Yeah, what else do we have to do?" He takes off his shirt to get dressed into a new one and I just stand there watching. I've never been in his room. At first I notice the blue walls, large plain colored bed with a wooden frame, posters of bands, and calendars with majestic ocean animals, but none of that is distracting enough to pull my eyes away from his bare skin.

I stop myself, turn away, and blush out of embarrassment hoping he didn't notice me staring. Before I am able to leave, Spencer comes close to me and I catch my breath. He grabs me by the waist and pulls me in even closer so that our chests are almost touching. My heart skips and I don't move. I have a weird feeling inside of me, like I need him now more than ever.

He whispers in my ear, "I thought about waiting."

"For what?" I whisper back.

"To tell you…" he doesn't exactly finish his thought and I realize he meant to cut himself off when he moves down to kiss me. His lips are warm and I close my eyes. He whispers, "I love you."

Everything stops. But it's nothing like how it did in the woods last night.

It's sudden, but beautiful, this feeling. I had told him yesterday that I should have asked him to be my date and now I really wish I hadn't gone at all, that I had stayed here instead and had *this*. This kiss, this silence. Because this is the good kind of silence.

"I love you, too." And it's true. It's the only thing through all of this that I know to be true.

I think about him all the time, his structure engraved into my mind. He is my feeling of safety, of complete trust, and everything he has ever done for me has been out of affection, not out of duty. The way he is and the way I feel about him both seem so strong and there's no doubt. There's nothing and no one else.

He kisses me again, but slower and even nicer than the first time. Then he pulls back again and finishes getting dressed. After that, he ruffles my hair. "Get ready."

"This is all I've got." I gesture to myself with his sweatshirt draped over the dirtied and torn dress that I can't wait to discuss with my mom.

"Well that's a problem isn't it?"

We both laugh at that and I help him clean up the kitchen before we leave the apartment. When he opens the door to let me out, my eyes linger on the coffee table once more, wondering if the gun is still there, or if it ever was in the first place.

Before I stare too long, I leave, Spencer coming out behind me and locking the door. He takes my hand, but not to support me, simply just because.

The first stop is at my house. He tells me to gather my things and I am unsure about what he means. "Keep your stuff at my place."

"All of it?"

"Yeah, you're not coming back here, I'm done letting them hurt you," he says and he takes my hand and squeezes it. "Now go on, they're not coming back for a while. I'll be right here waiting."

"Okay. Don't disappear on me." I play it off as a joke, but my stomach turns because that would be just the sort of thing to happen right now, for him to vanish into thin air like everything else. If I wake up in a white room soon to find out none of my life has been real, I won't be able to say I'm surprised.

"I could never."

"Good. I wouldn't want my first date to end before it started." The word "date" tastes sweet on my tongue.

"Oh, so that's what we're doing." He makes another joke and I go towards my house while laughing. I look back at him multiple times, always double-checking myself to make sure he doesn't disappear.

Thinking this is the first time that I've actually been happy walking into my house, I stop myself once I step inside. It feels different and strange. I don't think much of it because I know that this will be the last time I step foot in here, hopefully. I can't imagine the next time I return being anything but disastrous.

The eyes follow me. Do they know this is the last time I intend to step foot in this place? I throw my middle finger up at them and laugh. Screw the shadows and the monsters and the endless nights of wishing for something to change. Something is changing now.

I change clothes to leave my mother's damaged dress behind. I pull back on my jeans and replace Spencer's sweatshirt over a plain black shirt. Then, I find an old duffel bag and shove everything I own inside.

The kitchen is a mess and empty bottles are strewn across the living room. Thank God my parents have to work Saturdays so that I could do this, so that I can look it all over and leave their mess behind.

Grateful for my escape and almost full of relief, I get out and rush back into the car where Spencer looks completely relaxed. He moves his feet off the dashboard when he sees me lock the door. I smile at him and hold the bag up high as if it's some great trophy or something.

I still haven't told him that I want to venture back to the cold place through the ripples. I'm afraid he won't think too fondly of my idea. I'm pretty sure he wants to try to completely forget about the entire event. But I don't want to sit still wondering "what if?"

After closing the car door, Spencer puts the car in reverse and starts heading out of the driveway and I decide to tell him so that I don't prolong the good moment too long. If a good moment's going to be ruined, might as well get it over with.

"Spencer?" I ask him once we get onto the street.

"What is it?" he seems like he is focussing really hard on driving.

I bite my lip and tell him slowly, "I want to go back."

"Back? Did you leave something?"

I guess I really have to think more before I say things since I seem to be too vague. "No, back to the pond."

"You can't be serious." He doesn't seem to be paying so much attention to the road anymore.

"I am, I was thinking about what you said, about it actually being real."

"I was joking, trying to make you smile." He shrugs his shoulders and keeps a straight face.

"Well, I'm going to try whether you'll be there or not."

He takes one hand off the wheel and grabs mine with it. "Of course I'll be there, who do you think I am?"

I smile and move my thumb over his hand as they remain within each other's grip. I'm glad to have someone who cares about what I want to do now that I have something to get into.

We both continue with this until we reach the warehouse. A green SUV sits on the side of the dirt road. I figure this is Spencer's friend and we park beside him.

He's shorter than I remember, but maybe that was the perspective of a trailer, and there's a cigarette hanging out of his mouth. His dark skin moves fluidly as he pulls on a grey jacket over a white t-shirt that almost goes down to his knees. He wears a baseball cap backwards on his head and has a bow legged stance.

"Elle, you remember Andrew," Spencer re-introduces us as if it's been years.

"'Sup?" He asks, giving me an up and down look. "Looks like someone's feelin' better."

"My eyes." I point to them. "They're up here, pal."

"Damn, you told me she had humor, I don' think you mentioned the sass." Andrew gives Spencer a playful punch.

"Yeah, I guess I never noticed," Spencer adds, looking at me like I'm someone else.

"It's not strange, you just aren't used to me being around people," I tell him as a fact because it is. *I'm* not used to me being around people. This is all uncharted territory.

"You don't like people."

"Touché," I tell him.

The three of us laugh awkwardly for about two   seconds until Andrew speaks up, "Now that I've really met her, I like her. I'mma open the doors now, there might be a few things to move outta your way, but you guys can handle that, I suppose."

"You're not going to join us?" I ask being polite since he's one of the rare few that I don't despise.

"Nah girl, it's cool. You two just have some fun. I'll be back in an hour," he says after pulling the doors open. I watch as he walks back to his car and tell him thanks for letting us use the place. He seems to have somewhere else to be by the way his tires screech to get back on the street.

When we get inside, Spencer goes over to turn on the lights. When they turn on, it goes from a small darkened building to a large and bright basketball court sized room. I squint at first until I get used to the light. It's a plain, unassuming building from the pale grey floor to the beige walls. Pillars are placed here and there as a support system and I imagine spinning around them.

We sit beside the wall and begin lacing up our skates. I don't believe I've ever skated since the last time my grandparents took me, almost exactly a year before they died. Loud music was playing and disco lights were flashing, but I like how much larger this place is and how I can hear the echo of every little movement.

"So you guys are pretty close, huh?" I ask Spencer while trying to balance myself with the support of the wall.

"Me and Andrew?" Spencer stands up with no problem. *Show-off.* "We used to go on killing sprees together."

"Funny. You don't actually expect me to believe that, do you?" I laugh and almost fall down, concentration broken.

"No, but I wanted to see if you could handle a joke and skate at the same time." I stick my tongue out at him in response. "How long has it been since you last skated?"

I try to think how long ago it was, thinking back to the colorful room and seeing my grandparents happy faces as I fall down and get back up to try again. "About ten years."

"Do you remember how to skate? You were what, six?"

"Yeah." I laugh at this remembering the age difference between the two of us. "It's like riding a bicycle. You don't just forget how to ride, you're just a little rusty."

"You're pretty rusty alright," he says while skating over beside me to get me off the wall.

"I need that," I tell him while trying not to fall even though it may be impossible with the way he's holding me.

"What, you don't trust me?" He slowly pulls one hand out from around me and I immediately put my hands out trying to balance.

With his other hand, he grabs mine and starts skating towards the middle of the room. I let the skates wheel me over, resisting to pick my feet up off the ground. I watch as Spencer's feet move outwards and he sways along with it.

Without warning, Spencer completely lets go of me and I continue to slide forward. When I begin to slow down, I bend over to put my hands on the ground to stop me.

I stand up slowly and look over at Spencer who starts to laugh. "What?"

"Nothing, nothing." He skates almost gracefully over to me and gives me his arm to steady myself on. When I stand up straight, he moves away from me again. I don't like him leaving my side, so I do my best to skate back to him, surprised at how easy it is to make the movements that I saw him do.

It almost all comes back to me, my hair flying back as I make my way down the long side of the rink, seeing my grandparents' big smiles before going for another lap. I remember myself skating to the middle and just going around in tiny circles there. I push myself now with more speed and pass Spencer laughing. Again, I feel like a child and it makes me feel invincible.

"That's it!" he tells me while catching up. When he gets to me, he spins around so that he can skate backwards.

I look at him with wide eyes. "Were you some sort of professional skater?"

"No, just made sure I knew how to skate really well so I could avoid going to jail."

"And you had to skate backwards for that?" I ask in a very surprised tone.

"I never had to, but I might have, so I learned." He starts going even faster and I push myself to match his speed.

I think about the music that played at the old roller rink, whatever people had requested. I hear it in my head and begin humming the first song that comes to mind. I start singing softly like how I would in my bedroom. The words are just air and high pitched, controlled, until Spencer notices and joins me.

We continue, laughing and taking turns singing lines back and forth to each other. It feels like when people dance in the rain. I feel alive and free, and no one is here to care that our voices aren't perfect.

We stop when Spencer hits the wall behind him. I do a running-like skate over to him and fall down on my knees to be closer to his height, but when I sit, I seem to be even shorter than him now than when we were standing.

He laughs at his own clumsiness and I laugh with him. I move over so that my back is also against the wall. Looking at the empty space, I play back the entire event in my head. This one is much more pleasant than the last one that was stuck in there.

Then, Spencer asks me a question, "So you're going to need people to witness, right?"

"Witness what?" I ask half-knowing what he might be talking about.

"You going back," he says this with a pained sigh.

I look at him feeling bad for making this decision, but I have to go through with it. "I guess, and don't act like that, I'll be fine."

"You weren't so fine the first time," he says to the floor.

I sigh. "I wasn't expecting that to happen, I didn't know what was going on. I know what I'm walking into now, I can prepare myself."

He looks back to me, that same pained look in his eyes that he had when I saw him before the dance. "You promise you'll be safe?"

I put my hand on his shoulder, wishing it could be enough to reassure him. "Would you expect anything else?"

"Okay, then I'll gather up some of my jail mates." He lets go of his saddened mood and stands up.

"Stop with that. You had skates to get away from cops. You weren't in jail, just belonged there," I say ruffling his fluffy hair.

"Gee, thanks," he says and we hold hands while skating in more circles.

Our palms get sweaty, but we do not let go. He leads and we skate around each of the pillars. No good moment can ever stay good though. I see Lilith. *Predictable.*

She has white eyes again. Her long black hair looks tangled and her dress is torn and dirty as if she had fallen down multiple times. Although everything else about her seems like she is struggling and in fear, a wide smile dances on her lips...

Staring into those eyes not paying attention to anything else, it's my turn to run into a wall. I hit it head-on and almost fall but stop myself. "Woah."

"You okay?"

"Yeah, just spaced out a second I guess." I rub my forehead real quick and then put my hand back down to my side because I'm not physically hurt, it's just that that image is giving me a headache.

"You think we're about done?" He asks me while breathing a bit harder than before.

"Sure." I realize just how exhausted I am as well and we both head towards the exit before sitting down and changing back into regular shoes. We both breathe a sigh of relief when we remove the skates off of our feet. The release feels just as good as the grip.

Lilith isn't anywhere to be seen anymore, but the fear she instills lingers like a shadow, a phantom. Everything, *everything*, has to be tainted. She'll always be there to make sure of that.

Once I step out the doors, Spencer turns the lights off and I look back inside. It doesn't look as lively as it felt when we were skating. I almost want to go back in and skate more just to bring life back into it. It revived me and I want to do the same for it.

That is stupid though because it is just a large object, it has no feelings. I still feel a pull towards it all the same, like now it's a part of me.

I immediately forget about all of that when I see Spencer is already all the way back to the car. I feel alone even with the bright memories of the last few hours replaying in my head making me feel happy. I need to be near him so I finally close the doors and go back to the car.

Andrew is back just like he said he would be, and I watch him close and lock the doors. It gives off a very suspicious vibe as if we had some very secret military or scientific business going on inside.

I roll the window down to shout at him. "Hey!"

"What are you doing?" Spencer whispers to me.

I ignore his question as Andrew replies, "Yeah?"

"Well," I take a breath remembering what Spencer said and wanting to go right away, "want to come with us somewhere?"

"Where are we going?" Spencer keeps whispering questions to me and I keep putting them aside.

"I got nothing else to do," Andrew confesses and starts walking to our car.

I hit the side of the car in celebration and get comfy in my seat. "Got anyone else you want to bring?"

"Umm, I don't even know where we're going," Spencer says to me, starting up the car anyway.

"Yes, you do." I laugh thinking about how crazy this is and how crazy it sounds. Lilith will not get the final laugh today. "We're going to the ripples."

Without another word, I suppose understanding, Spencer starts driving. I almost bounce up and down in my seat like a little kid. I want to meet the creature this time, I want to confront it. My only need is to stay in the water so that I can leave as soon as there's a possibility of something terrible happening.

I'll be fine.

CHAPTER FOURTEEN

An Audience

The terror and anger that had shocked me so terribly the first time around are still in my memory, but it is like being in bad situations so often has made me immune to the long-term effects. But my entire self is drawn to the pond almost magnetically.

Like I told Spencer, I didn't know what was happening the first time I entered, so now that I can prepare myself for what may lay beyond, there is no reason to be frightened. This seems so simple in my head and I go over different ways to go about this entire thing before we stop in front of an old brick building that stands on the outskirts of town.

The street and even the house itself seem deserted. There are cracks in the structure and abandoned factories on either side of the house emphasizing its antiquity and solitude. It's hard to imagine people actually living here, and maybe they don't, maybe they only meet up. I don't know and the closer we get, the less it feels like my business.

As we get out of the car, the sound of the door slowly creaking open fills the quiet street. Three guys come out of the house looking either threatening or high. One is dressed in all black, maybe Spencer's age, and donning a lot of silver in his face. Another looks more like Andrew but taller, and smells of a different kind of smoke.

I do a double-take when I see the last one shuffle forward because this is the last place I expected Alex to be.

I watch as he keeps his head down and kicks the rocks that make up the driveway just like my own house, my old house. Spencer introduces us, "Elle, Andrew, this is Kyle and Ian."

"And Alex?" I ask, but when I look at where I'm pointing, there's no one there.

"Oh, she really is crazy," Andrew says.

I mimic what the apparition of Alex was doing and put my head down playing with the rocks beneath my sneakers.

"She's not crazy, she's…" Spencer tries to come up with a word for my not-yet-determined ability, "unique."

I actually laugh out loud at this, finding it hard to believe that's the only word he could think of. I say, "Yeah, I think crazy is a much nicer way of putting it."

"Well," Spencer gets into what we came here for, "we don't know that or not. See, what we wanted to ask you guys was if you wanted to see something 'unique' to prove to her that she's not insane."

"Sure, whatever," Ian says and I notice his lip piercing when he licks it and plays with it with his tongue.

"I guess. Let me get Izzy," Kyle says and runs back into the building.

"Izzy is his girlfriend, super slut," Ian says and even she responds by swatting his arm. He rubs it, grinning.

When Kyle comes out, a shorter girl follows. She has long black hair and super short shorts despite the cooler weather. She smacks her lips while chewing on a piece of gum and waddles when she walks. I am very grateful for being the one with the spotlight for once only because I don't feel like being stuck sitting next to her.

"Where are we going?" she asks with her voice pitched high and unexpectedly snooty.

"Just some place to watch some crazy shit, alright? We leavin' the house for a second, why don' you grab a coat?" Kyle tells her while holding her waist.

"Nuh uh, I just got these, I'm gonna show them off." When she says that, I don't believe she is talking about her outfit. I'm not sure what exactly about her has given me such a violent reaction to her presence. But I said the more the merrier and can't be rude to anyone willing to venture into the woods with no idea what they're going into the woods for.

Everyone follows her lead and gets into the car. I strap myself into the front and beg that they do not ask to play certain music or whatever. To avoid that situation, I plug in my phone before they even have a chance. I play my simplest playlist, one with punk rock bands and alternative rock. It seems to keep them quiet for the rest of the ride.

I feel like a parent trying to keep their kids' mouths shut even though I am the youngest in the group. I think to myself that they're probably all high or something and won't be very trustworthy when we ask if they saw what had happened. I know probably two out of the four we have with us seem capable of judging whatever's going to happen.

When Spencer pulls the car up to the side of the road next to the woods, Izzy starts up, "Oh, hell no. These are expensive heels. You didn't tell me we were going traipsing around the woods."

"Calm down, Iz," Kyle consoles her. "You wanna help me help a friend, right?"

"Yeah, whatever." She smacks her lips some more and walks awkwardly ahead of us like she did before.

Part of me wants to convince her to go in the water instead and make the monster eat her as a distraction, but then I look at Kyle as he apologizes for her attitude. She is lucky to have someone that cares about her because this would have been her death day. It would be easy to pretend she got caught while I tried to help her escape, an easy, non-guilty verdict.

These thoughts help me ignore her constant complaining as we step through the muddy path to the pond. Sticks break and Izzy trips more than me in those stupid heels she has on. What helps me more is that Spencer holds my hand as we dodge low hanging branches and poisonous plants.

I stop suddenly at first sight of the clear pond water.

"This is feeling like some sort of joke. Are you going to grab a fish and throw it at us or something?" Kyle starts and his voice quavers a bit. Are they nervous?

Well, a complete stranger did just lure them into the woods with no explanation. I say, "I'm going to step into the water and either disappear or look like an idiot who got their ankles wet for no reason."

"Are you Houdini?" Izzy asks and it's one of those genuine questions played off as a joke.

I ease up on her and respond calmly, "If it is someone's idea of a prank, I'm not the one pulling the strings."

"You're serious?" Ian bites at the piercing in his lip again, but nervously instead of out of habit. His leg bounces uncertainly and I wonder again just how reliable these witnesses will be. Something tells me he's seen things that aren't real before and seeing someone vanish into thin air won't be all that surprising to him.

"Am I the type of guy to bring you out here for a joke?" Spencer poses to the group and everyone stops their questioning.

Andrew makes a gesture like he's giving us the floor and I turn to Spencer, slow my breathing, and whisper to him, "Wish me luck."

"Good luck," he tells me back and hugs me really tight. He thinks this can be the last time we see each other, but I know I'm coming back.

"Give me ten minutes at the most, okay?" I grab my watch and set a timer for ten minutes. "If I'm not out by then, well, I will be so that's not even something you should worry about."

"Be careful." He gives me another hug and a kiss on top of my head before I step into the icy water.

I give a weak smile and take my steps slowly. I feel dumb, reaching down to touch the surface with my finger. Thankfully, the same thing happens as last time and it is just as magnificent as it was then, I just couldn't appreciate it at the time.

The water ripples from where my hands are going outwards and the water shines, I watch as their amazed faces disappear due to the bright light that I can't quite get used to myself. When that light fades, I'm back in the cold blue world that I had feared so much the first time I entered.

The air is filled with that same, slow-motion descent of glinting white ash. I know to stay near the water, for now, and look around for any sign of the monster that lurked here just yesterday. The only sounds are the others' voices freaking out back on the other side. Their voices echo like Spencer's did when he was calling my name.

"Woah! Where'd she go?"

"This can't be real, man."

"Ain't no way. Ain't no goddamn way!"

Somehow hearing them is a comfort, is confirmation, that this… is real.

Their voices give me the strength to move. I step out of the water onto crisp and dry leaves that crunch beneath my feet causing me to slow down even more in hopes of preventing drawing the attention of a creature.

As I walk, I see nothing but forest for miles ahead, it doesn't look like it leads back to a road. It would be very easy to get lost, so I do not venture far. I turn my head in every direction constantly looking behind my back to make sure I am not being followed by some other surprise.

I've done all I needed to. I made it here, proved that some part of this is real, but I want more than that. I have to find out more about the 'truth' Lanni said Lilith wanted me to see.

Circling around the pond in search of a sign of life, I see a figure run ahead of me. It is definitely a human, a teenage boy. He's not just running, he's running from something, and when I turn around, I see what it is.

"I knew you'd be back." Lilith is standing before me, her hair as shiny and black as ever. Her white dress billows, untouched by the dirt and her eyes have their color this time, a glimmering and silvery blue. "That boy is no good."

"The one that just ran by?" *No more fear of the unknown anymore, Elle,* I think before ridiculing myself for talking to her, *no more.*

"He wanted to get rid of me, he was trying to stop me."

"Stop you from what?"

"From playing with you." She giggles and skips towards the boy.

I follow her wanting to see what she is going to do to the boy who was supposedly trying to "stop her." When I get close enough, I recognize him. It's Alex. Only, it must be the fake Alex that I saw when we picked up Ian, Kyle, and Izzy. He's wearing what he wore to the dance, a light blue suit with a t-shirt underneath. His hair is coiffed in a way that makes a single loose curl dangle on his forehead.

Now, he's hanging his head low and holding rocks in his hand.

"I really tried to hold onto this one for you." He looks at me with mournful eyes and I'm taken aback. "It seemed like such a good one. I wanted you to be able to return to this moment, but it's just not strong enough. She caught me. Or maybe it's you who won't keep it—Unh!"

Blood splutters out of his mouth as his face opens with shock and I scream. "Alex!"

A pointed wooden pole forces its way into his back and out of his chest, dark red liquid coating the spear. Giant spikes shoot out of the ground and pierce through him one after the other as if the first shot was not enough.

The blood comes out of him trickling into the pond and turning clear. The slow dripping of the blood into the pond creates ripples, but these ones do not seem as beautiful as the ones back in the real world, although the sight is mesmerizing as the crimson streams turn into crystal clear water.

"He said too much, but you're a slow one, you won't figure it out," Lilith tells me while moving her hand towards the ground causing the spears to retract into the earth.

"What is going on? Explain to me something, anything," I beg her to give me some sort of information.

She paces and gives a thinking look, she puts her finger to her chin and says, "Alright. The enemy of Courage plants the seed of doubt that grows in darkness until it's out."

A riddle? She won't give me any direct facts. I take it and accept it. I try to figure it out when a roar comes from somewhere in the distance. "What was that? Was that the thing from before?"

"Don't worry about that. See, we don't want to kill you," she giggles more showing just how much she's enjoying my confusion, "We only want to play."

"Umm." While I have her here, I might as well ask her more questions, "Why'd you kill Alex?"

Was that really him?

"Oh, that's easy." She sits down on a fallen tree trunk. "He was helping you lose your insanity, he was holding onto your 'normal' experiences."

"Why is that such a bad thing?" I think about the clear mind I had while skating and after and if there's another being holding onto that moment running around, trying not to get caught.

"Well, it counteracts my job, silly," she tells me as if the answer was obvious, "If I want to keep my position, I have to obey orders."

"What are those orders?" I look her up and down watching her carry herself with the authority of someone much older than she is.

"To keep you believing you've gone crazy. To stop you from stopping him."

"The enemy of Courage? What is that? Fear? Yeah," I scoff, "I don't think you'll have to worry about that."

"Because I'm doing my job correctly," she says and then gets up suddenly saying one last thing before skipping off into the shiny atmosphere, "You might want to keep an eye on the time."

I look down at my watch and see it has been way longer than it felt, I am two minutes late from getting back to them. I walk into the water which I cannot stop myself from seeing as innocent blood. Taking my steps and closing my eyes, I reappear back in the woods in which I came from.

"What happened?" Spencer comes up to me hugging me even tighter than he did before I left, "You said you'd be back in ten minutes."

"I was learning something, I got information." I become quiet and wonder why until the images come back to me from both visits and my mind starts thinking about how this will not end well. I am putting everyone in danger, even Alex, or that apparition of Alex that only existed because I had a normal moment. I'm shivering.

"Hey, I thought you said you were prepared." This is his way of asking if I'm okay without saying the words.

"Yeah, just trying to figure some stuff out," I tell him and look around. The others are all staring at me, wide-eyed and in awe.

"And?" he sighs and rubs his hands together.

"Oh, I'm sorry I'm so cold," I step away to let him remain warm, but he pulls me back into his arms.

"No, it's okay."

"Okay." I say, trying to believe it.

My heart beats fast and I hope he doesn't notice too much, I don't want this to feel uncomfortable. I enjoy feeling his head lay down on mine. My arms take on the same position as Spencer's so that I can hold his hands as they hold onto each other, trapping me between them and Spencer. I let his warmth cover me, ridding me of any cold left inside.

As we stand here, I feel the nice autumn air blow in my face and hear leaves being blown off of the trees. This prolonged silence is sweet until I start to think over the conversation I had with Lilith and the… Alex. How he said that he was holding onto something for me, that that was why Lilith had to kill him; because she has to keep the good things out of my life.

I'm afraid again, afraid to close my eyes this time. I don't want to even blink for whenever I do, I see the spears that impaled Alex. I see his sad and depressed face. I see him kicking rocks beneath his feet and stuttering for words, whatever words he'd been trying to say to me when I ran after Lanni instead.

I feel sorry for something that I created, something that isn't real.

I start to cry without realizing it and once Spencer notices, he turns me around. Without letting him speak, I move my head onto Spencer, crying into his chest grabbing his shirt. He puts his arms around me again and rubs up and down my back, resting his head back down and making soft shushing sounds to calm me down.

"Is she…?" Izzy starts.

"What just happened?" Kyle adds.

Ian is the loudest in his panic. "This is some fucking devil shit going on here."

"Do I need my kit?" Andrew's voice is steady, serious.

I almost completely forget that they are here until they all speak up as a mix of an astounded peanut gallery. I feel embarrassed as I wipe the tears off of my face and let go of Spencer to face them. They have all turned pale and Izzy seems to have forgotten about the fact that she is in the woods as she sits upon a fallen tree trunk in exasperation.

Kyle opens his mouth to say something else, but quickly shuts it, sucking in his lip and going over the piercing again like a bad habit he has when anxiety kicks in. He finally puts together words, "You disappeared through the pond, like gone, completely gone."

"You weren't hiding under or nothing, either. You were just, *poof*, gone," Izzy waves her plastic manicured nails around dramatically expressing the event that even she can't find a way to downplay.

I just watch them all freak out silently, their heads to the ground or the sky, never at me or at the pond as if just looking at it will make something supernatural happen again. Spencer grabs a hold of me again, turning me to face him. His face is not at all in shock, somehow used to strange occurrences already.

"Do you believe me?" He asks as my tears slow down.

"No, I don't know," I tell him and it's true, none of that proved to me that it's not inside my head.

Sure I heard them and they're all saying I disappeared, but there's also nothing convincing me that Spencer didn't tell them to react that way just to make me feel better. Lilith said that I created Alex, but could I have manifested an entire place? What would that mean? How much darkness am I responsible for?

"Then show me how to get there," Spencer interrupts my confused thoughts.

"You're crazy," Izzy provides her insight.

"If it's in my head, you won't go anywhere," I tell him and get up on my toes so that I could put my hand through his hair, "But if you're right, I can't let you go to that place."

"You shouldn't have to face this alone." He hugs me and then turns towards the pond.

I grab his arm, using every muscle in my body to hold him in place, and say, "You're not going in."

"You can't stop me," he pushes me aside, "I'm sorry." Tossing the keys towards Kyle, Kyle fumbling to keep them in his hands still processing what is going on, Spencer faces the pond, hesitant to enter as he should be.

"You're not going in by yourself if you're going." I feel the need to protect him as if I'm the older one here.

"Fine." We walk into the water together, holding hands so that we don't lose each other.

"What do we do?" Andrew asks. "I can call the others."

Others?

Spencer responds, "Just give us ten minutes, then storm in here and grab until your hands find flesh."

CHAPTER FIFTEEN

In Deep

Spencer copies me, placing one finger on the water's surface, and I remember exactly why I don't like being the leader. I don't want to be responsible for what happens to him.

My hand squeezes his tightly, desperate not to lose him in transport. I don't know what I will do if Spencer isn't there when I arrive, but I'm equally unsure of what to do if he is. I can't even decide which one would be more comforting.

Sure, if he appears there with me and can testify to all the things I see, then I have to believe that what I see is real and I'm not crazy, but then Spencer is in danger of the creature.

On the other hand, if he doesn't appear there with me, then… well, I don't even know.

And that's just as terrifying.

My hand brushes against something on Spencer when he flinches from the brightness of the rings that encase us. I can't keep my eyes open to keep an eye on him. The cold sweeps over first and I know I'm back before I can see it.

Spencer has let go of my hand but before I can panic, my vision is restored and I can see him spinning in circles staring at the strange world around him, "Elle? Where are you? Why is everything so dull?"

"Dull? What do you mean? Everything's glowing blue. It's almost magical if I let myself admit it."

He shakes his head, "No, it's all white and blank. There's nothing but white as far as I can see."

"If we're not in the same place, why can I see you?"

"I have no clue, but… I can't see you." His lips move and his eyes search for something, probably me.

"None of this makes any sense," I talk to myself, but I don't doubt he hears me.

Then a familiar laughter arises from somewhere behind a tree and Spencer turns in different directions more frantic than he was before, "What's that?"

"Lilith?" I shout, but she doesn't show herself.

"Who's Lilith? Elle? What's going on?" He barely moves an inch from where he stands. He's terrified and this is worse, so much worse than if he was here with me, worse than if he didn't go anywhere at all. His voice shakes, "There's no one here."

"No one where you are, maybe, but I've been seeing a little girl. She's dangerous, I think."

"Oh, that's not weird." He laughs nervously and forgets that I can see him rolling his eyes.

The wind begins to pick up, blowing the leaves off of the ground in a rush of swirls, wrapping around me and distracting me from Spencer. Leaves rise in a sort of cyclone above the ground, rustling intensely as they approach me. Through their whirling haze, I see Lilith standing before me again. This is her doing.

I raise my arms and shut my eyes to the whipping wind until it all stops. Everything is still again. Everything is different again.

I am no longer in the glowing woods but at a country house with an open plain around it. A hot summer breeze blows by me and I almost begin to instantly sweat in my wintry clothing. I take the sweatshirt off and tie it around my waist.

"Spencer!" I cry out his name. He's gone. I don't see him any more. What is this place?

The door to a house opens and slams shut just as the old door at my grandparents house did so many times when I would go in and out. By some unseen force, I am compelled toward the house and can't stop myself from going to investigate. Suddenly, nothing else matters. Something has a hold on me and I relinquish control.

It is as if I have stepped into a memory, like Lilith is trying to show me something, remind me of something I have forgotten from ten years ago. As I climb up the pale blue steps that lead to the porch, the paint crumbles into soft curls beneath my feet. I move my hands along the small beams that hold up the awning. The plain old glider sits on its lonesome, beaten down and overused.

When my hand reaches towards the door, my foot falls through the floor. I reach desperately for the sides so that I don't fall all the way down. But like rotting wood does, the rest of the porch falls out from beneath me, sending me falling down, down, down.

There is utter and complete darkness where I finally land. Something howls at my side and I shrink, backing myself into a corner.

A whimper sounds from my mouth, or at least I think it does, but I make myself stop moving altogether, stop breathing, and stop making sound. A collapsing sound cracks from above me and I look up to see a small circle of light shining a spotlight into the darkness. The small cries continue and I follow the sound to right beside me.

Sitting there with tears beginning to fall down her face, each one collecting into a little puddle in front of me, is a small girl.

An old couple comes out from the house, I recognize them as my grandparents as their faces peer down into the space to find the girl and I realize that that little girl trapped under the porch is me.

I continue to watch, wanting to remember what was happening. This little girl, the younger version of myself, is scared to death trapped in the small dark area that she has seen many raccoons and other pests roam in and out of.

"Just think of a made-up place inside your head, go on," her grandfather comforts her with words to help her calm down, "Now tell me what you see, sweety."

"It's a-a forest, in the night," she says while slowing down her sobs.

"Yes, yes, that's good," he says to her as he watches his wife go into the house in search of something that will help them lift her out, "Now I want you to hide all of your fears here, shove them away and when you do, leave that place and don't ever go back."

"Okay, okay," the girl stops crying and her grandmother returns with a cord, like the kind used to tie down large items on top of a car. The girl takes a hold of one end while the old couple work together to lift her up, the grandmother nearest to the hole to receive her once she is high enough.

Upon rescue, the image seems to disappear before my eyes and I find myself back in the gloomy forest somewhat wishing to go back to the scene, to replay it, to be a part of it again so that I can see my grandfather up close again.

Where I am, there is no one that I want to see. Spencer is still nowhere to be seen and Lilith is standing proudly before me.

"What was that? Where is Spencer?" I almost yell at her. I am over being confused, I just want some answers already.

"No more riddles or games, tell me what is going on. What is this place, what was that? Straight answers, no more giggling and acting psychotic like you're some messed up little bitch from an asylum."

"Ooh, harsh words," she says sarcastically, "Such a one track mind for a girl with impeccable storage. How did that not answer at least one of your questions?"

My grandfather said in that memory, *hide all of your fears here.* A small piece of the puzzle clicks into place. I created this place, this is my forest of fears, so to speak.

Somehow, everything I've ever seen or feared has lodged itself into one place, creating an entire world inside my head where all of my hallucinations reside. A shiver runs down my back wondering what else might be hidden behind the trees.

Spencer said he was in a plain white place, a blank canvas. He hasn't created a place in his head, however surprising that sounds. It all seems to make the sort of sense that only makes sense to me, not so much in words. In words, it's incomprehensible. It's nonsense. Everyone has a mindspace.

"There you go," Lilith takes my hand.

"Hey, what are you doing?" I try tugging my arm back, but she holds on, unaffected by my attempt to get free.

"I'm going to show you Spencer," and all resistance stops. I follow her, desperate to get him out of here, or at least near me because his presence is the only thing that can calm my nerves.

She better not have done anything to him. Since this little girl seems to know everything that I don't, she can't possibly be a part of me, some mindless being forced here by my thoughts.

For some reason, she has placed a target on my back, which means she is the villain. Everyone knows what villains do to their targets. They find the ones they care for, and make them suffer. It was foolish to let Spencer come here, but he wasn't giving me a choice. The only thing I can feel secure about is my choice to come with him rather than wait outside for his return.

With my hand in hers, trusting her to take me somewhere that will give me more clues, we walk. Something tells me that she isn't trying to trick me into my own demise. We stray far from the pond and that makes me nervous. I start trying to memorize specific landmarks around us, but we seem to be walking along the same trees, never passing anything that separates it from the rest.

Everything looks exactly the same. There's nothing different about where we are walking now than where we were walking two minutes ago. I begin to slow down until the sound of rushing water sounds softly, getting louder and louder as we continue to walk towards it.

There's a smell in the air from the waterfall that makes me feel lighter and a bit more relaxed until I remember why the waterfall is here. Everything is here for a reason. I almost drowned myself once and it had reminded me of a waterfall the way I had left the water running and my face underneath it. I get goosebumps from this forgotten attempt at suicide, I was only nine years old.

My parents took me to the pool once, standing on the edge watching their daughter float around with arm floaties. My mom insisted on taking me, but would never even consider putting on a bathing suit, and my father hated water. So they read as I played, trying to get the water on my face. The other kids were all diving underneath, sprouting out of the water in laughter and anticipation to dive again.

While my parents weren't looking, I removed the floaties, telling myself that it didn't matter what happened. I knew better than to think that I could swim, this was my first time in a pool. I also decided to omit the fact that my parents were too isolated to sit with the other parents near the three-foot section, so I'd been floating around somewhere in the five-foot area. The second I removed the floaties, my feet felt like weights that were pulling me down an abyss.

My head went under, the water wetting my dry face, making my entire body feel like one entity again. The coolness beckoned me deeper and deeper, the water trying to get everywhere that it could. It tickled my nostrils, and I wondered if I could breathe the water, if I was special.

The second the water came rushing in, something inside me began to burn, an uncomfortable, chemical sting in my nose. I wanted to breathe it in more, let it fill up my insides. I swallowed it too, feeling it travel down my throat and to my stomach. I wanted to become the water and would have too, if it weren't for the lifeguard on duty. It was only when I got out of the water that I knew what was happening was bad, and I became scared of both the water and myself.

My heartbeat quickens as Lilith and I walk straight towards the waterfall. I remember what it feels like to not be able to choke out the water, not being able to breathe. I clutch my throat with my free hand out of instinct. As we get closer, small splashes of water bounce off of the rocks and hit my skin, bringing my attention back to the cold, but I don't pull the sweatshirt back on.

Lilith points to a cave that lies behind the wall of falling water. I take it that she wants me to go inside the cave, and I don't think I have a choice. I don't want to walk away either. She says she's going to show me Spencer, and I believe her because she probably did something terrible to him. Tied him up and tortured him for however long I was stuck inside my memory. She wants to see me break down.

The cave's entrance is above ground, so I begin to climb, slipping on the wetted stone as I struggle to find any footholds. I try to avoid getting hit by the few larger splashes that come towards me, but I fail in this attempt and end up losing my grip on the rocks with my left hand.

I slam myself against the wall to try and balance myself enough to find another place to put my hand. A sharp edge cuts into the bare skin on my right arm. The blood drips down my arm, and just like the blood of the speared young boy, it turns clear after coming in contact with the water.

Biting my lip to keep my mouth shut, I find a place to put my hand. I glance over at Lilith who is standing on the edge where I had started. She's smiling and I believe laughing. I take a deep breath and reach the cave entrance. Whether this is a trap or not—it most definitely is—I have to believe this is the way to Spencer. I have to find him.

When I reach the mouth of the cave, I lie down on the ground and breathe. I feel my heart slow so that it's not as easy to detect unless I put my fingers to a vein or focus on the now pulsing cut on my arm. It feels good to have a small thing like this to happen, to prove that this is not in my head, that this is very real.

When I catch my breath, I get up off the ground and look down the narrow path that I had tried so hard to get to. Deeper into the cave, there's a flickering light like a pale fire. And I hesitate to go to it. Lilith knows I want to find Spencer, so she told me she took him, and that he is here, but in reality, Spencer could already be back in the real world and what's actually waiting for me is a monster, or something worse.

I stumble along the cave, very slowly, putting my hands along the walls that seem to be getting narrower with each step I take. I find it difficult to breathe the farther back I go. The light is brighter and I can see where I am going. I was wrong about the light coming from a fire. It's one of those light strips you see in hospitals, long and fluorescent, buzzing incessantly.

The cave has morphed into a proper hallway leading to a research center. I know this when I step in because I used to have dreams about being sent away to one by my parents. I never thought they'd put me in an asylum, I thought they'd make me some sort of freak with supernatural abilities and scientists would want to poke and prod me like aliens would in horror films.

The room I enter is circular and very clean. A dark grey and grated metal makes up the floor that I'm now standing on. Above my head, metal steps lead down to the large room where cubicles and computer spaces are lined up facing a large clear wall like the glass between spectator and zoo animal. Behind the glass is a metal slab with straps. I always dreamt of myself being tied down to it, with all those eyes watching the other scientists hook up weird machines to me.

But the table is empty and vacant except for a single slip of paper taped to the viewing window. I make my way over to it, cringing away from everything in fear that something will shoot out at me, like some sort of trip wire or hidden laser protection throughout the lab will trigger some defense-mechanism to fire at me. To my surprise, nothing happens and when I grab the paper off of the wall, I read what is neatly written:

Subject 2:
   Shows signs of mental instability. May portray the ability to enter different dimensions. Further studies will be necessary. Move to room 502.

This has to be Spencer, no one else from this world would be placed here. My footsteps echo down the corridor as I run to find the room in which the note had stated. The lab looks more and more deserted and damaged the farther down the halls I go. My eyes glide from crooked sign to crooked sign and blinking light to broken ones. I follow the numbers etched into the walls and reach 502.

I try pulling on the handle of the large pale green door, but it does not budge. I look through the window and see a girl sitting up on the edge of the hospital bed that lays inside. She's staring out a window without a view, but perhaps I am wrong and she can see the outside of the cave that now seems like a mountain.

A clipboard hangs from beside the door reading almost exactly what had been written about her in the note I found in the main research room. But I don't engage, no matter what answers I may be able to get from her. I need to find Spencer. Everything else is just a distraction.

I get to the end of the hall and find nothing. I venture back to room 502 and look inside again. There has to be a reason that the paper implied for me to go here. I turn away, but then there's a banging sound that makes a loud thump echo down the hallway. I turn back towards the window on the door and see her face.

It was as if I was staring into a mirror, only the image doesn't quite match. Her hair is matted and tangled, and her face is ghost-pale with dark, purple circles under her eyes. My heart races in her wake. Is she meant to resemble me? Is she some version of myself I once believed I was and ended up trapped in here with the other things I've forgotten?

With this question in mind, I walk the hall again and take a closer look at the people inside. Every patient is now standing by the door just far away enough for me to see their faces. There's a little girl like the one I saw that was myself in the memory shown to me earlier, six-year-old Leighanna trapped under the porch. Her skirt is dirtied with mud and dust, and her legs are scratched up by the prickly weeds that grew under there.

Each room holds a different age of myself at different dramatic points in my life.

The very last room on the side of the hall has one of me from just yesterday. It's hard to believe that I had been at a dance, that everything that has happened between then and now has taken place in less than a day. I stare at her in disbelief, seeing what I must have looked like running through the woods after someone I thought was real.

The dress is ripped, her legs scratched by the thorns that tore her dress. Her hair has teased, sticking out in different directions and I imagine all the bobby pins that must have fallen out and are now riddled on the forest floor. Her face is a mixture of everything I hadn't realized I was feeling: embarrassment, fear, worry, curiosity, and bewilderment. She shakes her head at me disapprovingly, and I know exactly what she means.

I never should have come here, and even if I couldn't help it the first time, I never should have come back. I know because I agree. None of this would be happening. I wouldn't be seeing any of this if it weren't for my stubborn brain pulling me to it in search of answers to questions about myself. Questions that every teenager asks but none ever gets the answers to.

Looking away from her in guilt more than anything else, I hesitate before the window of the room on the very end of the hall. This room is marginally different than all the others. There's a large steel door with a window the size of every other. When I look inside, I find a glittering atmosphere just as if I was back outside.

Way back in the darkest corner of the room, I see what is being held inside. It is the creature that I had encountered on my first visit to the forest.

I back away slowly and trip over my own feet. When I get up and turn around, I see Lilith standing by a lever. She's smiling, giddy as she pulls the lever. Red lights flash and spin, a loud siren rings, and the doors to each and every room slowly open.

The sirens cease suddenly and the lights go out except for one single light shining on a young boy. By young, I mean he must be five, maybe younger. I walk towards him although his back is facing me.

When I reach him, I sit down on my knees and ask him to turn around for me. Expecting to see a mangled face of some tortured subject, I see the face of a young child. His cheeks are chubby like mine still are as if the baby skin won't go away, as it shouldn't on a kid his age. His hair is the same color as mine and falls down in waves around his ears.

Written on the name tag on his chest is the name, "Toby?"

"Yes," Toby's speech is that of a child and my mind spins.

Like when the wind picked up before, everything spins. The buzzing from the lights intensifies as they grow brighter and brighter.

CHAPTER SIXTEEN

Truth in Memory

The scene before me has changed again. I'm being shown another memory. The back-and-forth is a nauseating sort of whiplash, but I hold myself together. I have to endure. I have to get to the end of all of this to find Spencer, to find our way out.

The version of myself I'm watching now is laying on the ground, beaten in an alleyway and holding a tattered gift box. I remember this clearly to be the day I met Spencer. Only, I do not stay here for long before the memory is lifted away and replaced.

What I am next led to watch is the day my mom lost her baby. The me I'm faced with now is sitting in the lobby, knees bouncing, hands wringing. I had driven my mom down to her doctor after she began crying from pain.

My father thought nothing of it, having been the one to shove her down a flight of stairs in utter impatience for her to get down. He hadn't intended to knock her over, but she was so weak from having been hit just moments before that she fell down.

The worst thing is that my mom didn't just have a miscarriage. She was six months into the pregnancy and the doctors decided that the only thing they could do to attempt to keep the baby alive was to perform an emergency c-section. They didn't know that it would have been better to let the infant die. They didn't know why she was having complications. They were going to deliver the baby at six months because it was their job to protect life.

As young as I was, I sat in that lobby and didn't think once about calling my dad, thinking that the hospital would have done that anyway. Instead, I researched similar cases. There were few reports of babies who survived that kind of procedure, so it was no shock to me when the doctors came around to tell me that the baby was lost.

I'm watching them in their white coats approach me— the memory me—now and it is all over my face. The relief that there wouldn't be another child brought up by my father, but also a feeling of loss. I knew that we'd be there for one another and it might have made things easier, but in the long run, I also knew that it was for the best that this child didn't survive.

"Leighanna?" Toby's voice is so soft and sweet as he appears beside me, watching the memory with me. The child looks up at me with big blue, pleading eyes.

I swallow and clean my voice. I'm talking to my brother, even if it is just the one I made up in my head. "Yes?"

"Is everything going to be okay?"

The lie gets caught in my throat. I want to tell him that everything will be alright, that there is nothing to be afraid of, but I can't find the right way to say it.

I take one more look at his face, so young and innocent, so real. The words come out of me, "You're safe. There's nothing to be afraid of."

He wraps his arms around my waist and hugs me. The urgency in the hug, like he has been waiting for it for a long time does not send its apprehension through me like these things tend to do.

Instead of his pain transferring to me, a sort of tranquility comes from the center of my body, expanding outwards, expelling the bad and replacing it with something good. His cold, fragile body turns warm before the weight that I am holding onto disappears.

He is gone.

The lights sear again and fade back into those fluorescent light tubes.

The memory is over, Toby is gone, and I'm back in the eerie hallway. Only, as I look around me, the different versions of myself take a single unified step out of their rooms. Behind me, the creature has not moved from its corner despite the open door.

The other me's continue to stand still unsure what to do. I approach my six-year-old self and she speaks to me, "Hi, how did you end up here?"

"I walked into the ripples, did you make that possible?"

"I once believed in a portal through water, but never did I imagine it was really real."

I smile at myself. She's small, cute, and innocent. She doesn't deserve to be here. "Did you create all of this?"

"Yes, it's exactly how I imagined it, and more." As if I had suddenly reminded her of something terrible, she takes a few steps back into the room.

"No, no, it's okay. You don't have to fear this place."

"But the dark is scary. It can swallow me whole."

"Something really bad must have happened once. Do you want to tell me about it?"

She tilts her head. "But you already know."

I kneel down so that we are almost eye to eye, "How would I know?"

"The memory that Lilith showed you, we all saw it."

I feel a sudden ache and sadness for her as I realize she is referring to the one before Toby, the one when I had fallen at my grandparents' house. "You had to watch that? It must have felt like you were reliving it."

"Well, that's kind of what happens here." She points to a sign above my head labeling the residents of this hallway as BUILDING BLOCKS.

"What does that mean?"

"There are many of us here, ones that look like me and you. In this part of the lab, we each relive our moments when we experienced the greatest fear or pain. The things that make us who we are. Who *you* are. Keeping us here is also a way they can keep us from getting out."

"By trapping the fear inside of you, you're stuck?"

"Yes, and since we are here holding these moments in us," one of the teenage versions of me speaks up, her tone irritated, "you get to forget all about them and go on living like it never happened."

"You say that like it's my fault," I turn towards her getting up off the ground.

"It is, you just don't remember."

"So what's your story? What memory are you?"

"Oh, that's a long one." She crosses her arms and gets real close to me trying to look like some badass. "Wouldn't you like to know?"

"Umm, yeah, that's why I asked," I give her the same tough-girl tone that she's giving me. When was I ever like this?

"Quite a smart mouth for someone so oblivious." She cocks her head and a few others laugh at this. "Fine. Do you remember when you went camping about a year ago?"

"No, I mean faintly." That was the trip we hit the deer on the way to. "It was just a two-day trip that I obviously forgot about."

"Of course you forgot, because you decided to shove it away. Hide it in your now called 'forest of fear' so that you wouldn't have to remember. Shoving it away created me, fifteen- year-old Leighanna trying to forget the only memory she has." She keeps her attitude, but it's slower and softer, "You were camping with your parents, forced to go camping, wondering what on earth he was going to do."

I remember the feeling of my dad's hand grabbing onto mine as I refrained from getting into the car with them.

"You get to camp and sit above the rushing water in the middle of the night," she pauses, trying not to shake, "right after your own father puts his hands on you, and you attempt to jump down into the rocky river."

"No," and that's all I can manage as my throat dries, as the memory comes flooding in.

It all comes back to me like a slap in the face and my fifteen-year-old self fades in and out of focus, parts of her seeming to go away as I remember bits and pieces of that event. It's as if I'm back, watching it just as I had watched the other memory.

The intensity of the memory forcing its way to the front of my thoughts sends me back to the incident. It was the strangest thing. Details come to me that I never noticed before, never noticed because I was too busy forcing the memory away. The laboratory hallway disappears, replaced by a campsite.

I am watching this scene from some distance away like I had when I was beneath the surface at my grandparents house. Only, now, I seem to be an onlooker lurking behind the trees. The memory character of my father has just finished setting up the tent, an orange tarp lays lazily over the whole thing and cords are tethered to stakes that are desperately gripping into the ground.

It is stranger than anything else I have experienced to see my father from this angle, to look at him when he can't see me and watch him in a way I never got to before because I am not me in this scenario, but rather a stranger happening to view the coming disgraceful event.

This memory version of my mom is sitting idly by the fire, tossing in twigs and moss to feed the flames. Her face never lifts to a level height, I've never seen it look out into the horizon. It is like she is stuck trying to get back to something instead of watching for the future because what is happening now is too painful to accept and what lies ahead is too painful to anticipate. She flinches at the sound of something crashing. Something metal has clattered with other metal, twinkling sounds of small individual bits colliding with one another as they fall.

Both of them have turned their heads to see what had happened and my eyes follow their gaze. A little ways off in the distance, appearing as a shadow in the glowing, orange sunset, is me, the me from last year. She's not a child, but she is cowering behind a tree like one because she just knocked over a tackle box near my father's fishing set-up.

Just when I think the memory will speed up at my recollection of how my father came after me, drove my mom away, and did things to me, it freezes for a moment as if to tell me that that is not the case. Something prompts me to walk closer, to get a better look and be able to listen more closely.

I see my father start towards her, the memory me, and my mother shouts at him to let her be, that it had only been an accident. He seems to allow himself to be convinced and relaxes the fists he had formed with his hands. Once he returns to the tent to unknot a cord, he turns to my mother and asks her why she won't move about and take in the scenery like I had been.

"The whole point of coming out here was to loosen up a bit, you know, get out of our heads." This is the calmest and most thoughtful way that I have ever heard my father speak. Something about it turns a sensor on in my head, like something making me itch all over to plug it into some puzzle I've been working on to piece together everything.

"Of course, John… I just… I don't know what to say…," she's trying to choose her words wisely. "I'm just not used to everyone being together like this."

"Well, it's nice, isn't it? Like you've always wanted?" There's something childlike in his voice the way he seems so desperate to please my mother.

Something's not right. It's not right. He has never been so caring.

We went on the trip as advice from their boss who gave us permission to use his campgrounds.

That's how the story has always gone.

We went, my parents fought, my mom left, my dad crept close to me in the middle of the night, and that was that.

"Of course it is, John…"

"But…?"

"But I don't know what's going on. I'm exhausted, Leighanna is exhausted, and I'm sure you are too. Don't you think it would be better to just… to just…," she is at a loss for words once more, but when they come to her, I wish they hadn't, "be like this at home and give our daughter a safe place at home?"

"You think our home isn't safe for our daughter?" Everything about the way he speaks is double-sided, impossible to tell if he's daring her to confirm or if he's genuinely wondering if that's what she thinks.

Only, for some reason, this feels different. It is almost as if there is something inside of him debating his next actions, like he's fighting an urge as his fists clench and unclench at a rapid pace.

"Of course I don't think that, John." She has stood up now, her arms up in front of her in a sort of surrender as she backs away from him, staring at the ground in fear of his next move, wishing to go back to before all of this. She could never get her head up.

"If you think our daughter doesn't trust me, then leave." His words come out the way I have always heard words come out of his mouth, but there's something wrong with his face. His eyes won't look up either, almost as if he doesn't want to say the things he is saying. "We will come home to you tomorrow and she can tell you all about how much fun we had together while you sat in the home that you think is so unsafe."

My mother opens her mouth in protest, but shuts it in defeat. She is aware that everything she has said so far has only gotten her into trouble. I look for myself, finding her hiding behind a tree like she had been before and as I am doing now.

She looks frightened, but only for a moment as she walks towards her father, pretending she hadn't heard. "Where'd Mom go?"

"Can't handle the outdoors." His laugh is dry as he tries to reclaim the casual tone he had earlier. "It upsets her allergies. She had to go home."

"Okay." I watch myself nod and wonder why on earth I didn't suggest we go home with her. This was only a year ago. I would have said something. Right?

They awkwardly sit by the fire together, tossing kindling into it the way my mother had been. He tries some small talk and she indulges with short responses that seem to satisfy him. He's aware of her hesitation to do or say anything upon request, but he isn't annoyed by it. He actually looks like he was expecting these shy comments. There is a sort of guilt on his face, something he'd never say out loud because he did not want to ruin whatever progress he was making by bringing up the horrors of the past.

And I fell for it, this false calm.

They sit by each other as the sun finally sinks to oblivion and there is even some nervous laughter from the two of them from time to time.

But this isn't how it went. Things are supposed to be going very poorly.

Why am I not remembering this?

Then, it happens, that turning point, that flip of the switch. In all of the light-hearted air between the two of them, this younger apparition of myself knocks over one of the logs that had been positioned upright in the fire.

Sparks fly into the air, shimmering light fading as they fall to the ground. A few remain hot as they land on the overlying flap of the inadequate tent. The material catches fire and the girl has begun to cower in fear of what is going on, not sure what to do or what to expect.

This is it.

But my father only removes the burning tarp from the tent and tosses it to the side, stomping out the burning plastic with his boot. He's even laughing until he looks at the girl who has become so overcome with fear and shame that she has hid her head between her chest and her knees, rocking back and forth to comfort herself.

My father has also become so overcome with shame that he kneels beside her and tells her that it's alright, that it was only an accident. To show her that it was fine, he gets her to lift her head up and see that the poorly put together tent was still standing and nothing was terribly damaged.

How is he doing that? *Why* is he doing that?

"Perhaps your mother was right. We've had a long day. Gosh, you remind me so much of her." His brows pinch together as he turns his head to the ground and shakes it as if dismissing a thought. "Come, let's get inside, shall we?"

The girl looks at him, more concerned than ever, but too naive to question it. She only wants to believe that things are really changing. The feelings course through me, answering a question I didn't even know I had. This is why I have grown to fear him less. This very night is the reason why I stopped fearing the worst and began expecting it.

He let me into the tent, extinguishing the fire before following me inside. He told me that I could get dressed into my pajamas, swearing he wouldn't look over as long as I didn't look at him. It was supposed to be something like a joke. But when she lifted her shirt, he turned over his shoulder to see.

You remind me so much of her, his words ring in my head. I should have known from that very statement what was coming. Only, he immediately begins shaking his head as if fighting with a voice inside of him again, trying to resist any temptations that flashed across his mind.

They say goodnight to each other, turning off the flashlight that was hanging overhead. Then, my father turns over to look at her, his hand reaches out and pets her head, but his fingers don't stop at the end of the strands.

He continues to travel her outline with his fingers, following the curves of her maturing body. She squirms, but not awoken by his touch. His hand darts back to him all the same, reaching out and coming back to him in rapid movements like he can't make up his mind.

My cheeks hurt from clenching my jaw, knowing there is nothing I can do to stop this because it already happened.

Then, he does it. He grabs her shoulder to lay her on her back. Then, he traces her figure again as if trying to convince himself that she is nothing but a beautiful woman. A woman so much like his wife that she might as well be her. And with her away, what else was he to do? He has to be thinking. She must be expecting something awful, she's always expecting the worst from him, so what was stopping him from doing exactly what he was being accused of?

"Stop. Stop!" I try to shout as he climbs over top of her. But he can't hear me. "Make it stop! Please!"

Her eyes open, but his hand covers her mouth before she can make a sound. Her questions are muffled by the hand over her mouth and they only turn into louder muffled nonsense as he passes his other hand beneath her shirt.

She tries to squirm, and I try to turn away from it all but the scene stays in front of me, making me watch, making me remember. He has her, me, trapped beneath him. His head is turned away as if unable to look at me. His hands continue to feel my skin, trailing down to cup my thighs and I can feel it, I can feel it all.

He whispers into her ear, but I can feel his hot breath on mine and hear him as if he were right beside me. "It's okay. It's okay. It's okay."

Hot tears start streaming down my face as my body is flooded with the memory of his touch.

I shut my eyes, begging for it to stop. My hands swat at the ghost of his.

I don't want to see it, I don't want to *feel* it anymore.

The air around me becomes colder, the way it does when I return to the forest. I fall to my knees in sobs, clutching my aching stomach, sick with disgust. The memory is over, but the truth of it lingers inside of me no matter how much I try to shove it back away, to forget.

God, I want to forget.

The ground beneath me turns cold and rock-hard. I know I've returned to the laboratory's cursed hallway even before I open my eyes. Expecting to find myself eye to eye with a horrific sight, I only see my own face staring back at me, the one I just saw get violated.

She has her gaze fixated on me, trying to be as threatening as possible, turned stone-cold by the event and hatred at me for her pain. But her eyes have watered as I suppose they do every time she is forced to relive that moment. I want to feel sad for her, but feeling sad for her is really only feeling sad for myself.

Yet there is something external about her, about every single version of myself staring at me with a pleading or menacing look in their eye. They hold these vivid flashbacks in ways that I couldn't possibly remember on my own.

Everything is more unreal than fiction with every second that passes. I'm dumbstruck with how much I've been able to set aside, with how much I've gone through and how I'm still alive.

How haven't I been swallowed by all of the darkness in my life?

The lights flicker.

Every head turns towards the end of the hallway. Slick, black fingers grip the sides of the doorway. With slow, careful steps, the creature emerges. It saunters down the hall more human than monster, merciful in its approach to its new prey.

I don't move.

I let it creep nearer. I meet its vacant white stare.

Its arms made of shadows and impossible depths wrap around me, and I let them take hold.

CHAPTER SEVENTEEN

Happy Things

When I come to, I'm surrounded by white.

Where's the darkness? The shadows?

Then I remember.

I'm in their home now.

I evaluate myself first just to find I'm still in a t-shirt, the sweatshirt is still wrapped around my waist, and my arm is still wounded, though the bleeding has stopped. My arm is soaked in dry blood.

Then, I turn my attention to the room. The walls are white. The bed is short and small, decorated in white sheets, and the world outside my window is not a gathering of trees.

There is nothing but water running over it preventing me from seeing anything else on the outside.

There's no way out. I'm trapped. The door won't open for me. The window doesn't open at all. I've nothing to break it with and no way of knowing what would be waiting for me at the bottom of the waterfall even if there was.

All there is to do is sit here and wait. Wait and remember. I remember what had happened, how the different forms of myself talked to me, how they reminded me of a past I have forgotten. I know I am still in the lab.

The door opens quietly. At first, I only stare, waiting. Always waiting for something to happen, something for me to react to. I never make the first move.

I start towards the open door, slowly stepping out into the hallway.

I am officially lost. The numbers outside my door read in the three hundreds. The sign above my head says HAPPY THINGS, but the words have been crossed out by something sharp and just beneath the words instead is a single word scratched into the metal: BRIGHTS.

There is not a single reason for me to hesitate, but I do. Most of my instincts are telling me to run, but I never quite learned to run from danger. I only learned to leave *after* the danger had passed, *after* getting hurt, *after* knowing the answer to *what if I don't walk away?*

Instead of running, I peruse this new hallway. Each door I pass sends a fresh wave of chills down my back. Shivering, I look into the rooms as I go, finding different versions of myself like I did last time. They don't react, so I just keep walking.

What is new, however, is the end of the wing. There is no demonic creature crouching in the dark corner. Instead, there are linoleum floors and fluorescent lights filling the room with utter white A lone boy sits on a bed identical to the one I woke up in. His face is turned towards the opposite wall.

Dressed in all white, slacks provided by the lab no doubt, he looks tall. As he sits, he slouches with his feet beneath him. His head is tilted downward, the light reflecting off of his shiny brown hair. *Too light to be Spencer's.* I let the thought pass but quicken my pace. For a moment, I can swear that I can hear him muttering something under his breath and take note that his hands are pressed together in front of him in some sort of prayer.

To get his attention, I tap on the door. Almost as if he is a fish in a tank, he jolts upward, turns his head towards me, and backs away. I take a few steps back myself, disbelief consuming me.

While I stupidly believed that only bad things are here, here is Lanni, trembling at the sight of me. He is shaking so badly, sweat beading on his forehead and his head keeps turning back and forth between me and the corner as if he needs to continually check that I am really here while also wishing not to see me. It's the same way I used to look at Lilith. He doesn't believe I'm real.

I put my hand on the glass. "Lanni? What happened to you? What is going on?"

He shakes his head and turns around to face the wall. I pull on the handle, begging it to budge but it won't. My eyes drift everywhere searching for someone, a key, a padlock, anything that might have the password etched inside of it. I find nothing.

A lever sitting casually at the other end of the hall glints as if calling to me. It's been waiting for someone to warm its cool steel with their touch, begging someone to bring movement back to it and adjust its stiff position. Lilith had pulled the last lever to unleash my own darkness against me. She's not pulling this one, so maybe when I do, it will release the "happy things," unleash something *bright*.

I tug on the rusty piece of metal wondering why it looks so old in this clean place. The rusting machinery scrapes against itself. Its screech bounces off of the walls. The lever shifts with a clang and when each door opens, Lanni runs at me, screaming.

I throw my arms in front of my face as he tackles me to the ground. The wind is knocked out of me and fresh drops of blood splatter on the both of us as my arm splits back open. Lanni's face grows red as he pins my arms to the floor and straddles my waist, holding me in place. Freeing a hand by holding both of mine above my head, he begins throwing punches.

I turn my head so that each hit is in the same spot. This must not be Lanni. That must have been a trick. This is some monster version of my father, the one that never stops.

He'll never stop.

When my face gets hot, I finally start screaming.

I can do that.

This *isn't* my father.

This is Lanni. It has to be.

"Stop! What—why? Lanni, it's me. Stop!"

It seems as though his mind has been erased, like he doesn't even know who I am. His face is full of hate and tears. With his fingers around my throat, my voice is choked off. I feel myself stop struggling to fight back and as if seeing my body go limp triggered something inside of him, Lanni stops. I gasp trying to breathe without choking on the air.

When I gain control of myself, I look over at him. He has pulled his knees up to his chest and put his hands on his head, rocking back and forth.

"Lanni?"

"You should go," his voice is raspy and weak.

"I won't leave you."

"You still don't understand!" He takes his hands off his head and hugs his knees, "I'm stuck here, I'm not real, that's what Lilith—she told me..."

"What did she tell you?" I think I know what he's going to say, but I so wish that I am wrong.

"That I wasn't real… That I'm not real." He starts to get tears in his eyes and I want to join him. My chest hurts in the unbelievable surrealism of this image, him and me, because, well, he is me.

"I—I didn't know either," saying this leaves a strange taste on my tongue as I think I am only repeating myself, that this is a whole new level of talking to myself. "I'm sorry, but I have to ask. Do you know the way out of here?"

"Why? So you can be free from it and I have to remain here when I thought I had a normal life?" He gets angry with me now.

"No, a way to stop everyone's suffering."

"You don't want to hear the answer to that one." He laughs and relaxes a little bit.

"What is it?" I beg him, now having confirmation that it is possible to stop everything. To stop myself from breaking myself down.

"You are going to have to die." He laughs even more now as if this is some joke. He's playing with me. At first he attacks me physically and now he taunts me with words.

"What the hell happened to you? Why are you doing this?" I plead and go up to him, but he only pushes me away.

"You got yourself into this mess, you created me and didn't even know it. What the hell happened to *you*?"

His words cut deep and I try so hard to actually process this situation instead of letting the fact that it is all made up slip by me. I am stuck inside my own mind, everything in here is fake and made up, but yet I know I'm awake and I know this isn't a dream.

Spencer had walked into his own world, it's not only me that has a place like this, a place for their own thoughts to hide away. But I believe I am the first person to enter their forgotten past.

All the things held inside of oneself are put into a place that is capable of being visited somehow. I just have to accept it because there is no denying that it is happening.

Spencer's world is blank, empty because he never shoved away any of his fears. He's always been fearless.

I have to get him out.

Determination takes over and I turn my emotions off so that I can focus. There's one thing that confuses me the most on this, and that is that Lilith says she has Spencer. But that doesn't mean anything. Lilith has developed into a powerful thing of mind whose goal is to become a real person outside of my head. That means she has been lying to me—not exactly unbelievable—and used Spencer as a way to keep me inside longer.

The hallway gets darker and I see two glowing red eyes in the distance. "You weren't supposed to find him, he's not supposed to be here."

"I'm sorry, I'm sorry, but I just can't!" Lanni shouts over to the spot where the voice came from. "I can't do what you ask, I won't!"

The entire hall takes on a red glow and I can see Lilith in her little white dress staring Lanni down. "You know what happens when you disobey me."

"Yes, yes, oh, please, don't! I'll do anything, please don't make me do that again! Please!"

"Then why don't you do what I ask? Embody my will."

Everything gets eerily quiet and I look at Lilith as she watches Lanni who turns his head towards me. His voice turns flat, empty, "Follow me."

Run, I tell myself again. And again, I don't listen.

Lanni grabs my arm and it's no longer my choice. I am forced to go along with him wherever he is going. My heartbeat races at the touch of his hands hoping he will stop holding on so tightly. We pass by more signs and more rooms down a seemingly endless hallway.

One turn is all it takes for the entire atmosphere to completely change. This hall is metallic with silver steel covering each wall. The ceiling and the doors are thick and strong, undoubtedly meant to keep whatever's inside from coming out.

Before I am even able to begin thinking about what's inside, the door opens and Lanni drags me in. I try making my way out of his arms and out the door, but Lilith is right behind us and slams it shut. The heavy metal reverberates, sealing us in. My heart is pounding in my ears and out of my chest with the fear that I have been trying to force away.

The room is dark, no light glows in any part of the room and I feel as if I'm being walked through a haunted house where at any moment there will be flashing lights and people in my face. I hate haunted houses.

My entire body caves in on itself, slowly trudging along to Lanni's tugging. He won't look at me and he is not at all comfortable with whatever he is doing. His last exchange of words sounded like he was being ordered around. I've never seen fear on Lanni's face, but that look had definitely come over him at the thought of punishment. On the other hand, I have no reason to trust him after leading me here and attacking me, his fault or not.

What we end up coming to is another room, this one just like every other, but so out of place. Alone in its own corridor, the steely grey cell is illuminated by a single strip of light that winks in and out of power.

Lanni pushes me towards the door, his voice even thinner, "Look inside."

I have no choice but to do as he says as he forces my face against the small square window on the door. One look inside makes my blood turn cold.

Crouched like an animal in a cage is Spencer. His hair and clothes are ragged like he'd been thrown around. He's facing the far wall, working at something in the corner. and black paint stains the white garments he's been changed into. The paint coats his now shaking hands. The once white walls of his room are covered in markings, one repeated over and over: the letter **D**.

Lanni pulls me away like a guard forcing people down a line. Tears sting the corners of my eyes, but I hold them back. I rip my arm from Lanni's grasp and turn to face him, fuming, "Why? What did you do to him? Leave him alone!"

"I didn't do it, I only had to show you, I promise." He tries to show me innocence, but I don't find it. He still can't look at me.

My voice turns to a whisper. "If you were meant to be good, why are you so evil?"

"I didn't do this, I didn't want to." His apologetic eyes shift into resolve. "I'll show you what I mean."

He shuts his eyes and the room changes, but only for a second. In this second, like a blink, everything is dark. Words of profanity scream at me and waves of electricity course beneath my skin continuously, making every fiber of my body feel as if it is being ripped apart slowly and then sewn back together just to be torn again.

We return to where we were before, but the feeling lingers on my skin. I try to catch my breath with an entirely different reason to cry. "Did Lilith do this?"

"Yes… and no. She's shown me things, Elle. Things about myself that I'm honestly terrified of."

"Why did you follow her?"

"She was calling to me, begging for help. You have to remember, I thought I was a normal teenage guy and that the world was normal. She was a little girl wandering around at a high school dance. I wanted to help her."

He pauses but I have nothing to say. It's too unreal.

"When she started to run, I couldn't let her go off on her own. When I came here, a man was waiting and they took me and made me into this. There is so much that I finally understand now, which has made me a target."

"What man?"

As if in reply, a crashing clatter erupts from the dark room that led us here.

We both rush to it, seeing sparks fly and sunlight coming in from the giant hole in the roof. I wave my hand through the plume of dusty debris. A large pile of rubble now covers what had been a completely empty room all along.

One figure is crouched on the top of the pile.

CHAPTER EIGHTEEN

King of Shadow

His figure is shrouded in a blueish spotlight, glittering flakes visible in the ray of the night glow. Massive shoulders rear back, the muscles stretching with the movement. Golden hair falls in ringlets around the sharp angles of his face. Two yellow eyes glow above the glint of a pearly smirk. His skin is like slate, a chalky grey, inhuman. Shadows swarm around him.

Lilith comes in from the hallway, her lips just as deviously curled as the man who just came crashing in. Lanni quivers and takes steps back towards the wall with a face full of shock and fear.

But I stay where I am, staring at the man as if he is nothing more than a statue. I'm intrigued when I should be frightened. I can't help but wonder what exactly it is that has come from the sky, shedding light on this dark and dreary lab.

"Why do you stare?" His voice echoes and rings deep throughout the place, making more dirt and debris fall from what's left of the ceiling. With the hole, the sound of the waterfall sounds almost as loud as it was when I was making my way into the cave.

"You—I—" I find myself speechless in front of this bare-chested man.

"Don't fret," he says casually as he buttons the cuffs of a jacket Lilith brings to him. "Most people tremble at the sight of me."

"Who are you?"

"Why, I'm you." His smile somehow widens. "Well, I'm in you."

"You mean the others here in the lab?"

"Ah, yes, 'the others here in the lab,'" he laughs as he mocks me.

I feel too intensely for a moment that I have to remind myself to turn my emotions off, but all that does is make me start talking a bit too confidently, "Listen, somehow, those other people are storing my memories. Somehow, they developed and are here in a world inside my own mind. I don't see why it is so hilarious that I am confused."

"Oh, but it is simple, really." He steps down from his throne of debris, shaking his head like he's genuinely amused. "You've been given so many hints. How could you not notice that all of this, *all* of it, is from your head?"

"So you mean I'm asleep?"

"No, no, that is not what I mean at all." He creates more corrupt laughter as he moves past me and towards Spencer's door. "How could he be here?"

"It's not a dream, but it's in my head?"

"No, you're still getting it wrong. It's *from* your head." He comes up behind me and almost whispers to me, "You are merely our temporary host. We came to you. You didn't create me or the happy soldiers. You just gave us enough power to start entering reality."

"How?"

"Simple. You were always destined to be broken. But the natural course didn't quite please us enough." He moves his hands when he talks, excited to explain. "I sent Lilith into your head and your fear suddenly had no bounds. The greater your fear, the more power it gives me. For now, I'm stuck in your headspace. In time, I'll be free."

"So where did you come from then?" I cross my arms to try and hide the wild thumping inside my chest. "What makes you any different than the flesh-eating monster down the hallway?"

"I am not one, but all of your fears. Damus I believe you called me."

"My imaginary friend from the fifth grade?" Counselors said it was normal for a child to develop imaginary friends after a tragedy.

"Ah, so you do remember me." A satisfied sort of smile curled his full lips.

"You were nothing." Even as I say it, I know it's a lie. "Just someone who showed up one day and never really made anything better."

"You only say that now, but I was so much more to you until you came across someone more life-like, someone who you knew was actually going to be there in real life." He looks over at Lanni who stands rigid in the presence of Damus. "It was your stronger feelings about happiness that caused me to need to act."

"But why? Why do I need to suffer?"

"Because I don't want to!" His voice is enraged, no longer feeling in control under my every question. The heat of his anger radiates off of his skin and the power of his fury shakes the mountain to make dust fall from above. He takes a breath to gather himself. "The only way for evil to thrive is to get rid of the good. But then, you didn't just have a happy memory that I could destroy, you had a real person.

"Imagine that! You met someone you didn't make up. With him around, how was I supposed to become real? With him bringing happiness and joy," he says this with a snarl and hits Spencer's door. The metal rattles its echo throughout the empty room. I jump and he laughs.

He takes slow steps into the room and I'm about to beg him to leave Spencer alone when I see the dagger he holds behind his back. He doesn't need to explain to me the rest.

I look around on the ground for something to use to attack Damus with, but the only eligible candidate is a large rock. In my fear and adrenaline, the rock is easy to lift. I raise it above my head as I approach Damus. For someone who's been living in my mind, he doesn't seem to be much of a predictor of my actions.

With one quick motion, I slam the rock down onto his upper back while it is turned to me. The action hardly phases him as he turns around, hovering over me with his body of slate, blocking my vision with his darkness.

He walks into me, forcing me to take backward steps, but I can only go so far in fear of meeting an edge. My feet don't move well enough and I trip over myself, barely throwing my arms back in time to brace my fall.

It seems that all he can do is laugh, the cackle echoing off the walls in this large empty room. Damus holds the dagger above my chest and my heartbeat quickens. He can hear it. He knows exactly where to find it, where to aim, where to press the blade.

My hands cover Damus's slate-grey ones as we fight for leverage over the dagger trembling above my heart. Sweat glosses my skin and my eyes dart around the room for something to get me out of the situation.

I can't give in. It would be like running away.

Realizing I'm trapped, Damus enters another monologue, "Leighanna, poor, young, naive Leighanna. You have no idea how long I've been waiting for—"

I let him talk, using the time to watch Lanni and Lilith in the corner. They're in a fight of their own, the little girl's strength proving to be inhuman. They take turns grabbing onto one another, rolling over and over, pinning each other to the ground.

"Of course, your grandfather was truly demented, but it was the perfect starting point to get to you. You are profound, powerful beyond comprehension, and—"

Lanni takes a fistful of Lilith's hair in his hand to pull her off of him. He rams her head onto the ground and runs my way. I want to reach out to him, but I cannot let go of the dagger.

"The entire world will fall on their knees at the mere thought of me," Damus continues, unaware of Lanni's approach. He just pushes harder against me, our breaths heavy with effort, but still, he goes on, "You can't possibly know what it is like to exist on this plane, jumping from subconscious to subconscious to survive. To be my own entity, to be whole, will allow me to bring the world what it deserves—"

Lanni's lips are moving, trying to talk to me, something like "link" or "thing." He points to his head, then at me, then makes some sort of sharp forward motion with his arm, his hand enclosed, as he mouths the only word I catch, "weapon."

"Once your little buddy was discovered"—Damus throws one hand out and Lanni is launched back against the wall—"I was furious. See, I thought I was the only one."

Lanni was saying "think," and now he's being crushed by an invisible force.

I have to think to give him a weapon. I have to imagine he has one so he can get us out of this mess, like this is a dream I can control but can't wake myself up from.

Concentrating every ounce of energy I have on creating something effective enough to take down Damus, I stare at him, but I don't see him. Even with one hand, Damus is too strong. I can't push the dagger away. I can't *physically* push the dagger away. All I can think is, *no, not today.*

Damus's hand goes limp and the dagger is in my control. But I don't need to use it.

He reaches behind himself as he turns around, his back now towards me so that I can see the knife in his shoulder, liquid darker than blood excreting from the wound.

Lanni's standing behind him with just as much surprise on his face as there is on mine. Damus growls and pulls the knife from his shoulder, throwing it to the ground in tinkling disregard.

With him focusing his anger at Lanni, I take my own opportunity to run. I go over to Spencer's cell, knowing that he will not return to the real world if he is not with me. My head turns back and forth from the lever I am trying desperately to pull and the fight between Lanni and Damus.

Lanni keeps Damus distracted for me, taking the blows that were meant for me. I shake the thought. This is different, this is insanity. As long as the real people get out, the rest will sort itself out. I have to believe it.

The lever finally shifts and I scream from the pain in my arm, feeling the blood start to flow again.

I hastily squeeze myself inside as the door opens at a snail's pace. I rush to Spencer's side to help him up off the ground. "Come on, no time for explanation, we have to go."

The door is still opening slowly, but not enough for me to support Spencer through so I continue to look back at the fight but I don't see much. They circle each other, move as if hit, but neither one actually touches the other. Just as the door is open wide enough, Damus collapses to the ground and I stop to stare, anticipating movement.

We have to go. I know he isn't dead, but at least he is stopped for a while, enough time for us to get out. Of course, it would be enough time if Lilith wasn't standing in front of the door. I hadn't noticed her rise from where Lanni had knocked her down. With her childish grin and curious tilt of her bloodied head, she thinks she can stop me from leaving.

I begin leading Spencer up the pile of rubble that leads outside, assuming it would be faster than crawling back out the way I came, and start heading in the direction we need to go. It seems almost too easy to reach the outside.

As we climb down the rocky slope and onto the forest ground, somewhat fresh air filling our lungs better than before, we begin heading to the original pond. I have no choice but to trust the tugging in my stomach like a needle pointing me in the right direction.

About a minute into the walk, our heads snap up to noise coming from the trees. We don't see anything above us, but I know something is up there. My eyes search the treetops and I walk Spencer along a little faster. He hasn't said a word, but that's probably just because he's in shock.

This is all new to him, none of this will click in his mind the way it does with me. This is all my fault. I should've fought him harder.

Once my fast walk turns into a run, I hear a zip-like sound pass my ear and feel a small pinch. I put my fingers up to it and when I pull it away, there is blood. Something shot at me and will probably shoot again. I pull Spencer closer to me in hopes I can somehow shield him.

Every part of me screams as my legs grow tired of running and I can barely breathe. Another arrow comes by and I can't judge where it will go until it hits Spencer's leg. He cries out in pain and falls to the ground. In my rush and fear, I tear the sweatshirt off from around my waist and tie it above Spencer's wound.

This has only slowed him down and I groan in an attempt to get him on his feet, supporting his weight. I somehow manage to get him up, but now we have to jog instead of run. The cut on my arm is throbbing under the pressure, but I fight through it in my desperate attempt to get us out before Damus or even Lilith finds us. I feel like I'm getting slower and slower.

The pond isn't far, I can smell the water. I don't stop until we're standing in the pond, its water remaining still despite our rough actions.

"You have to do as I do, okay?" My voice is trembling, but I am staring at Spencer to make sure he's listening, to make sure he's following. My hand is in his, but I can't hold him up anymore.

He nods his head and slowly follows. I see when his hand dips into the water when only a finger should have grazed it.

He did it wrong.

Shit.

A large gust of wind rushes by, and rings of light ripple outwards up from the pond's surface.

Rally

I sigh in relief when the light embraces us both.

Spencer falls back onto the ground, obviously in agony. I'm too angry to give attention to any pain and kick the water in my frustration. It's cold and I know my feet will freeze any time soon, but I would soak the pond up completely if it would destroy everything on the other side. I settle for picking up nearby rocks and throwing them into the water. Once my energy finally gives out, I fall to the ground beside Spencer.

He stops writhing in pain long enough to ask me a question, "Are you hurt?"

"Me? You got shot by a fucking arrow!" He puts me into hysterics with his concern.

A scream breaks whatever conversation is about to commence and Spencer and I both turn our heads to find the source. His reaction relieves me, confirming that the scream was not in my head.

We raise our heads to see Izzy turned pale by the sight of our wounds. Kyle has grabbed onto her, but it seems to be more of a way to comfort himself rather than her. His eyes are wide, staring at the stick coming out of Spencer's calf. I don't realize how strange it is until I allow myself to look at it as well.

Blood has streamed from the puncture, streaks of red falling down his leg and staining his socks. But the area around the entry isn't puffed up and different colors like I would expect it to be. That must mean it isn't as bad as I thought, but bad nonetheless. That world can physically hurt us.

Upon seeing that he isn't harmed as badly as I thought, the fear and adrenaline fades away, my body becoming less tense and more relaxed. But this isn't good. The more the energy flushes from my body, the more I can feel the cut on my arm. For the first time, I look at it.

The cut is down the inside, blood coating my forearm, the red-hot stickiness finally coming to my attention. It has begun matting onto my skin, not quite dried, not quite finished bleeding. How much blood can there be left to pour out?

My head gets dizzy, fading out of focus, like my entire being is falling away into nothing. Just as my upper body begins to descend, two sets of arms rush in to grab me. Someone shouts my name, but I shut my eyes too soon to see who it is. Everyone around me sounds the same, a blur of voices making noises of nonsense as my mind strays from consciousness.

My eyes flutter but won't open. I'm still aware of touch, slightly. I can feel something lift me up, my head getting dizzier with each rushed step that the person holding me makes. They're all talking to each other, their voices frantic, yet certain in action as if they've dealt with this sort of thing before.

I'm surrounded by people, people who care… about me.

I awake somewhat again at the rumbled startup of machinery—the car—and the sound of suction releasing—a door. Whoever was holding onto me lays me down onto someone else and then there's a slam—the door closing. This new person has one hand on my head and the other holding mine, but I cannot hold it back. I cannot do anything but lie here, consciously unconscious.

The thoughts become less and less intelligible in my own mind. I wish the darkness would sweep me away, release me from this hazy sense to the certainty of unconsciousness. In this state, everything is unpredictable, unknown, unsure.

Would Damus follow me into death? Would everyone else be safe?

The suction sound—the car door again—breaks through the muffled field surrounding me and hands are on me once again. The desperate shouting of people is indiscernible, but eventually the hands of someone more steady, sure, and strong take hold of me and I finally fade into the black.

○◉○

This time, my eyes open. I actually feel awake.

Spencer's face is in front of mine, eyes shut and pale. Weak. I've never seen him look so weak.

"He's okay." I turn my head to a third person in the room. Andrew's leaning on the wall of what I now realize is his trailer. It's musty with the air of years of cigarette smoke, and the air conditioner fixated in the window is rattling something fierce.

"H-he woke up?" It's difficult to speak. My throat is like sand.

"Yeah, and he refused to go back to sleep for a while." Andrew steps away from the wall and sits on the floor at the foot of the air mattress Spencer's been laid on. His leg is being propped up by an unstable looking pile of pillows and blankets. "He wanted to be awake when you came around."

I turn to face him where he stands, leaning against that whimsy partition. "How long has he been asleep?"

"Only a few hours."

As if he heard us talking, Spencer stirs and opens his eyes, shifting his gaze between the two of us. He smacks his lips, thirsty, he must be so thirsty. "'Morning."

"Spencer, are you alright?" I mean, I know he's not, but what else can I ask?

"I'm fine, Andrew's the best," he sounds just as groggy as me, but he remains able to make a joke and make me smile.

"That's all Ian, man. You can't imagine what he swipes from the ward." Andrew lifts himself off the floor and throws the flimsy wood panel door aside to make his leave, "I'll let you two discuss… whatever it is you might need to discuss, but don't keep us waiting?"

"We'll explain." Spencer offers to him and then he's out the door.

I don't get hung up on the fact that he said "us," though I could. They stayed. They're here. But I'm not getting hung up on that.

Instead, Spencer and I find each others' gaze, smiling. I move myself into a sitting position, cradling a bandaged arm, and look back at Spencer, "How bad is it?"

"It's a lot better than it looks."

"And we were asleep because?"

"You can't seriously wonder why you passed out." He's bemused by my confusion and everything is so much better when he's laughing. "You were kind of bleeding, like, a lot."

"Fine." I roll my eyes and get the rest of the answer out of him, "But what about you?"

"Painkillers. I wasn't kidding. Andrew has some pretty intense stuff stashed here. I was out like a light for him to patch us up. Couldn't sit still otherwise." In a flash, his light fades and I know that look. I've lived my whole life wearing that look.

"Spencer, what happened to you?"

"It's a long story."

"I want to hear it," I beg him like a little child as I find his sweatshirt crumpled by his feet and put it back on. It may be stained by the forest floor and bloodied from holding his leg, but it's his and it's cold and I want it.

"Alright, fine," he sighs, his inability to withhold information from me working to my advantage, and settles himself for a really long story. "It was just moments after you stopped responding to me. To pass the time, I began spraying the wall with the paints. Just a picture. I thought we would go back when you were ready. But when I finished painting, there was this rip in the wallpaper. I pulled it back and stepped through it hoping there'd be something more, hoping I'd find you. What I found was just another, smaller, blank room.

"I had forgotten the paints behind me and as if by magic"—he rolls his eyes and licks his dry lips—"the wall sealed itself shut and I couldn't go back to get them. There was no more paint besides a single can of black. I looked around for another way out and tried talking to you again, but my words just echoed back to me.

"A little girl appeared behind me wearing a little white dress and she was tilting her head like she didn't know what was going on, but she talked as if she knew I was there, like she was how I got there." His voice grows rough, "She said something about focusing hard enough on something can make it come true. She was cheering me on to think about finding you. But it was just demands shouting over and over, echoing and overlapping, driving me insane."

He takes a long pause and I reach out to him having no idea what to say. Neither of us could have imagined what was going to happen. I knew I didn't want him going there and I curse myself again for not trying harder to stop him.

The thin wooden door slides over again. Andrew steps in, "Sorry to intrude, but I was kind of hoping sooner rather than later?"

"Yeah, of course," I say and stop staring at Spencer. Having a crew of people waiting to hear from me and it's not so that they can berate me is different, but I have to hear the rest of Spencer's story. We need a goddamn minute. Spencer deserves a goddamn minute. "We just need a couple more minutes."

"If you're worried about moving, I'll let you both know you're good to go, relatively speaking."

"Thanks," I respond, lifting my bandaged arm to show him I know I can move.

"The whole leg raised thing just felt like the right move, Spence. You're fine, though, physically. Might limp a bit, but right as rain otherwise." Andrew's prattling, rambling, nervous. He's nervous. I suppose they all are, standing outside, waiting. Spencer's family.

"Just a minute," Spencer assures him, but his voice is quiet. Something tells me he won't be sharing the details of the story with the others.

Andrew slinks back out and we are left alone again. When my attention focuses back on Spencer, his look is vacant. He looks as if he's looking back into it and reliving the whole thing and for a moment I consider telling him he doesn't have to explain.

But then he starts again, suddenly figuring out how to say what he needs to. "I didn't understand what was going on. She told me she was going to bring you to me, but it seemed too long after she left me. I thought I was going to be left alone forever with that voice yelling at me. I tried finding another rip somewhere or something that I could use to break free, but my brain was scattered.

"I started thinking about you the more I listened. I wondered what was happening with you and I felt like I needed to *do* something to the walls to get rid of at least one annoyingly insanity-inducing feature. That was what you saw." He sighs and doesn't look over to me once, but if he did, he'd see nothing but compassion. Is this what it feels like when he listens to me talk about my father?

"I know you're going to tell me not to say it, but I'm sorry," I say, and he sighs as if trying to brush it off. I don't let him. "Not in a this-is-all-my-fault kind of way, but in the no-one-should-have-to-go-through-that kind of way. You're not crazy."

"If that's true, then neither are you." He finally looks up at me and his look says everything. His hair is wild, his jaw is tense, and those liquid caramel eyes of his are shining with all of the restraint that comes with having too many emotions to know which one to show.

"The jury is still out on that one, but not about this. Lilith…" I trail off and swallow. I have to say it. "Lilith is real. That's who you saw, the girl I told you I sometimes saw in the garden."

"She's terrifying, Elle." He could have said any number of things, but every single one of them would be a different way of simultaneously apologizing, confiding, and stating solidarity. Seeing her is like a shared experience now, like when Spencer had witnessed my father's abuse.

We know without speaking what the other is thinking. It's a combination of reliving the events and vowing to do something about it.

To make him feel safe, to provide him with the same comfort he gives me, I slip myself off of the couch and beside him on the air mattress. My fingers play with his hair. We each take deep breaths and stay this way until I remember the group of people that got us here, that got us safe. "We should go out there."

"Yeah, I suppose we should."

I squeeze the hand that is lying down flat beside him. "Thank you."

He knows exactly what I mean by it. He knows that it is thanks for not letting me believe I'm crazy, for letting me involve his crew, for coming with me, for insisting on protecting me, for always being there for me, and for showing me the care that I had no idea existed.

Spencer's the first to move and we help each other off the mattress with little grace. I'm grateful for it as it makes us laugh and we wear these cheeky expressions out of the trailer to where the others are huddled by a small fire.

Night has officially taken over and there's a chill in the wind much cooler than the usual autumn breeze. I can't believe they all stayed here.

"About time," Izzy greets us in her fashion. She's now wearing Kyle's grey jacket.

The others simply look at us expectantly and I hear every question they have without anyone actually asking. One second, we were there. The next, nothing. Then we were gone far longer than ten minutes. At which point, I can't imagine what was going through their heads.

"Thank you all, truly. I thought I was making it up."

"We're not looking for thanks," Kyle offers, though smiling. Everyone likes to hear it.

"Yeah." Ian adds, "We just want to know what's going on."

"Well," I start and look at Spencer. He's just as lost for an answer as I am.

I wonder how much, if anything, he heard from Damus, or how much of it he understands. I bite my lip for a moment so they know I'm thinking, but I have to say *something*.

When I open my mouth to speak, no words come out, so I breathe. I breathe and remove a filter. "Have you ever pushed things down? Like bad memories or thoughts, creating a world for them to disappear into so you could forget about them?"

My question is met by nods of various speeds, and I continue, "The pond is a portal to that place. It takes you to the parts of your mind that you ignore. Except, mine is… there are things there. Things that want out, that want to be real.… Monsters."

Everyone's eyes are on me and it's all I can do not to shrink away from it. But they aren't shadowed. I can see their faces. They are real and not just watching. They're also listening. They're hearing me, actually hearing me. And they are anything but amused.

"There's nothing for you to worry about, though." At that, they release a collective breath like that was what they were waiting to hear.

Everyone except Ian relaxes. After mulling on his lip piercing for a solid minute, he comes up with something to say, "Demons."

My eyebrows shoot up. "Um, yeah, I guess that's another word for them."

"So, when's the fight?" Kyle asks.

"The what?" Spencer says, and I'm grateful I'm not the only one thinking it.

"The fight." Kyle repeats himself.

"Yeah," Andrew agrees. "Monsters, demons, their bad guys either way. And they hurt you. We've got to hurt 'em back."

The others nod in agreement, standing upright and fixing their posture like a proper ragtag group of individuals bucking up for a fight.

It's not just the fire that's warming me now. Here are four people who had nothing better to do on a Saturday than wander into the woods at the request of a friend's friend. They watched, bore witness, and *believed*. For once, standing in a group of people, I'm not only a part of the group, but it's real, they're real, and they're not calling me crazy and running away. They want to run right into the crazy, guns blazing.

"Thanks, guys," Spencer speaks for me as I lack words to say, "but we're not going back."

The energy shifts and it shifts the right way. We'd all been teetering off a cliff when there's safe land to walk on if we just go the other way. Spencer's right, but I can't say it doesn't deluminate the night, like the fire died a little bit at the cancellation of battle.

"He's right," I urge as the others look ready to argue. It's like they all have a death wish of their own and this sort of thing is the perfect excuse to run haphazardly into danger. "We've all experienced something… bizarre today. I think we should take the night to think about what to do, if we do anything at all."

I add that last bit as Spencer gives me a look and I know that that look means he wants to put this behind us. He'll be there if I go, but if he has things his way, he'll never be within a mile of that pond again. And I can't blame him. But I also can't stand the thought of this becoming the one thing he shoves away, that I'm the reason he has something he wants to shove away.

Everyone's feet kick at the pebbles around the fire, mumbling a chorus of agreements as yawns split through the group.

Andrew interrupts his own yawn to say, "There isn't room for all of you here."

"Yeah, yeah," Kyle waves him off.

"Like we'd want to stay here anyway," Izzy confirms their plans to leave as Kyle drapes an arm around her shoulders and they start walking towards the street, Ian in tow. "You keep us in the loop, alright?"

"You got it," Spencer calls back in response. Then to Andrew, he asks, "Do you mind if we crash? I'm not exactly up for driving."

He makes a motion with his wounded leg and Andrew nods, "Of course. I didn't put anything away, so you've got where you were before."

"Thanks," we both say as the three of us head back inside the trailer.

CHAPTER TWENTY

Home

Spencer and I shared the air mattress. I awake with his arms still around me.

His voice is rough with sleep when brushes the hair from my face and gently whispers, "'Morning, beautiful."

I allow a sarcastic giggle to escape me, "Your eyes are closed. Otherwise, you'd see me with this untamed hair and your ruined sweatshirt."

"It's not ruined." He licks his lips as he opens his eyes, "You look as good as me."

We each laugh, but the loud sound of it makes me pause. "You know, we've probably overstayed our welcome."

"Yeah." He takes a deep breath in and out, "But you're coming with me."

"How could I refuse?"

Yet, for a moment, neither of us move. We both look out the small part of the sun-beaten windows that we can actually see through. It's wordless, and Spencer keeps his hand on top of mine stroking it with his thumb.

There's a slightly violet tint beyond the window—or because of the window—making the outside world look fuzzy, as if we are looking at a picture taken with a bad camera. It is still better than the forest we had been in before.

Then, we break the stillness. Still not speaking, because the silence is too clean, too nice, too pure to break with what we will have to discuss at some point.

I lean against the trailer as he talks to Andrew. I'd join him, but my throat is still raw and I don't have anything more to say than I did last night. What can you say to someone you randomly met when you needed a wound glued shut and then again when you randomly decided to roller skate in an empty warehouse which was followed shortly by a trip to the woods where he watched his friend and some girl disappear into a pond just to emerge beaten and bloody?

Thank you isn't enough. Nothing is enough. But he strikes me as the kind of guy who understands that.

However, I listen in on their conversation as if I do wish to be a part of it. It's a struggle to make sense of things until I catch a clear word from Spencer, then the collapsible wood is what it is, a paperthin partition. Spencer says, "No."

"You knew what it meant bringing her here the first time. She's one of us now." Andrew is serious, more serious than Kyle when he bared to take arms. "And we don't back away when someone threatens one of our own."

Spencer takes a while to respond and I can picture the look on his face, the one that means he's about to give in even though his muscles are tense in protest. "Okay, but this isn't someone, it's something that might not be as easy to outrun or beat down as you're used to."

"I know you're scared, and you're only scared when you care. But don't you see? *That's* when fighting matters the most; when you have something worth fighting for." There's a moment when it seems that's the end of the conversation, but after a breath, Andrew speaks even softer, "I've seen you fight for less."

"Take this," is all Spencer has to say in response and I wish I could see what *this* is, but their conversation is over.

I make myself look busy, probably doing the exact opposite of making myself inconspicuous, but Spencer doesn't address it when he returns to this side of the makeshift door. When he sees me, he smiles, and it's like all the questions their quiet conversation gave me never crossed my mind in the first place.

"Come on, Little Fawn. It's time to get out of here." Spencer reaches for the keys in his pocket. I listen, almost dazed by the sound of them jingling.

I don't want to leave this haze where everything feels perfect. I have an *us*, I'm with Spencer, and I no longer want to torture myself by investigating the psychosis that lies within the water. I don't even have to think about it.

I do anyway. My mind wanders, thinking that something wrong is bound to happen, that I am not okay just because we aren't there. Being out could make it worse. At least inside the forest, I knew exactly what he was doing, but as I am outside in the natural world, I have no idea what horrible new reality the demon has in store for me.

Should I believe what Damus said? About becoming real? It can't be possible that someone in my head materializes out of thin air, but what about everything that happened with Spencer?

If I can get there just by walking into the pond and Spencer can be pulled inside, then it has to be possible. If I can go in, why should I believe they can't come out?

I sit in the car with my head against the window wondering what I can do to stop what may be happening. My entire life seems out of my control. Everything that has ever happened has had its negative side enhanced tenfold by this Damus character. It's not like I can make him go away just by thinking about it. That's what got us into this mess.

There almost seems to be no point in living other than to keep Damus inside me and nowhere else. He called me a host, so that has to mean he can jump from person to person if he needs to. As long as he is convinced that I can fulfill his wishes, he is going to remain inside of me.

The idea of living the rest of my life with this demon in my head sickens me because I can't bear to consider burdening anyone with the complications. If I stay with Spencer, I will be forcing him to live with it as well.

A nauseous pit forms in my stomach, an ache I can't ignore. I can feel its discomfort taking over my body, the hints of something gnawing at me evident on the outside in signs that I don't notice, but I know are there. This has got to be the single most frustrating thing that I have yet to wrap my mind around because it makes complete sense without making sense.

"Hey, are you okay?" Spencer puts his hand on my shoulder and his warm touch seems to go through me. I almost jump from surprise.

"Yeah, I'm fine," I sort of whisper unconvincingly.

"Well, we're here." He parks the car and opens the door walking over to my side to open my door. I don't know if I want to go though. Can I risk everyone? Spencer? Can I hurt a whole town, cities, states, maybe even countries, if it means I get to forget about it?

"I can't."

"Can't what? What's wrong?" He looks me up and down, scared for me.

"Damus, he—" I try to find a way to explain myself, to explain what's going through my head, "My ignorance feeds him, makes him more real, able to leave the forest."

He wipes his face with his hand and leans on the door while I stay sitting, "So what? You think you have to leave me? I thought you said you'd stay?"

"Spencer, I can't. I can't hurt you."

"This guy might have been lying to you, Elle! You seriously think isolating yourself is a good idea?"

"But the evidence is so strong. You were pulled there, we can go there. It's a place. If we can get there, don't you think they can come here?" I pause to take a breath and stop myself from getting too worked up. I don't want to argue, I want him to listen. "I can't let any of this insanity hurt you. You already can't walk now."

"I can walk." He stands back up straight but winces almost immediately and leans back against the door. "I can't believe this."

"What? That you fell for a young, damaged girl? That she's more insane than you thought? That you're part of all of this?"

"That you don't want me around for this," he is quiet. I wish he had yelled. He's looking at me like he had when I stopped by before the dance, before all of this, like I'm disappointing him all over again, hurting him more than any time he's seen me in pain. "That the girl who has come to me for everything ever since I first found her in the alley no longer wants me. That she doesn't think I can protect her anymore."

His words make me cry and I get up to hug him big and deep, "I—I can't think of anything other to say than 'I'm sorry.'"

He wraps an arm around me, but this time, I think it's for him. "But you don't have to do this."

"This is all my fault, all of it, and I should've stopped you from going, should've known Lanni was screwing with me, should've stayed with you without going there again."

"Then Damus would get out without you even knowing who he is or what he is doing."

"I thought you didn't believe it." I keep talking into his chest, tears not seeming to stop.

"I don't, but," I can tell the words hurt to get out, "I have to believe *you*. I always have. And that is why you shouldn't do this."

I pull away and wipe my eyes with my sleeves, "I have to go."

The second I turn away from him, the anger that was boiling inside of Spencer comes to the surface. He slams the car door that I just walked out of so hard that I stop in my tracks mere inches from the car.

Instinct makes me turn back to him, but I don't have time to process anything as he grabs my shoulders in his hands and pushes me against the door that he just slammed. One arm is across my chest while the other's hand is flat against the car above the side of my head, his body trapping me in place.

I let out a whimper of pain from my head and shoulders colliding with the door. "Spencer, you're hurting me."

My arms and legs squirm looking for an angle to get myself out of his confinement, but he only pushes back harder. Has he done this before? He speaks, barely moving his mouth, "I can't let you go, Elle. I won't."

"Spencer, get off of me."

"See, you're fighting things right now." As strong as his hold is on me, pressing into every bruise, there's anguish in his eyes, a plea. "Why can't you fight him? I can't let you go back there."

"What is this about?"

"Home, Elle! I can't let you go." This time, it's less of a request and more of a demand. Is this the side of Spencer that owns a gun? The side that vandalizes buildings and talks in hushed tones with people scraping by on the wrong side of the tracks?

He's never been more of a stranger, or maybe I never knew him to begin with. It's all so clear. "Did you really think we would be able to do this? There was no way I'd be able to live with you, Spencer. There is absolutely no circumstance where we would get away with it, that we would be able to make it work."

His arm relaxes and the anger that screwed up the lines of his face disappears as he looks at me, begging, "Do you love me?"

When I started this entire conversation, I knew it would be hard, but I thought it would hurt more like ripping off a band-aid, one and done. This is more like a band-aid that has been placed on incorrectly so that the sticky sides are adhered to the wound and tearing it off is like peeling off skin, especially with how long he is dragging it out. It is one long, excruciating rip trying to tear the band-aid that is Spencer off of me.

But with this question, it is like the band-aid has been completely removed. There is a brief second of breath that is the time he has given me to gather myself, but then the question lingers in my head making that open wound burn in the wind, not ceasing to bring me pain. My throat is dry and I try to swallow my own spit, but there seems to be nothing inside of me, so it is like a gulp of nothing that doesn't make me feel any better.

I am torn between the truth and what I need to say to get him to let me go. What is happening right now is exactly what I want to avoid. This is the only time I will hurt him. I don't know what will happen if Damus becomes too powerful. He could take control of my body for all I know and the first thing he would do if I am anywhere near Spencer if it happens is cause him harm. But I just can't lie.

"Of course I do."

This answer seems to be the opposite of what he wanted. He lets out a long sigh, hanging his head down towards the ground. Then, he turns around to put his back against the car next to me and lets himself fall to the ground, pulling his good leg towards him and putting his head in his hands. His entire body is shaking with sobs and I can't even try to imagine what is going through his head.

As I start to come down beside him, he motions for me not to. He reaches for the door handle to pull himself back onto his feet.

The thought never occurred to me about actually going home until Spencer begins to walk away from me. He travels towards the grey, going inside without another word, just a solemn face.

I slam my fists against the car door and wish to externalize this agony through screams, but I don't want him to hear me.

I walk home. It's long and quiet besides the cars passing.

The one large duffel bag that has all my things in it that I was going to keep at Spencer's hangs over my shoulder and I'm pretty sure the stitches in my arm have come undone. The wind created by the rush of speeding vehicles ripples my clothing against the bandages and I can feel it cling to the wet bandage.

The sun has begun to fall down, darkening the sky to match the mood that won't blow off of me and into the wind for somebody else to catch. I've been walking for what feels like forever. I know I have to go home, but it can wait for just a little while longer. I'm not ready to be there again, not yet, not with every memory flashing before my eyes every time I think about turning in that direction.

My feet feel blistered and bruised from everything that I can't even begin to summarize. My brain is pounding against my skull in no sort of rhythm, just a random thumping of pain that I allow to infuriate me to mask the other feelings.

I try to stop the tears that the cold wind has helped me cry, and develop myself into an emotionless being so that I won't break down when encountering my parents. It's late enough and it's been long enough to the point that I have no idea what they could be thinking. The last time they saw me was Thursday night, before school the next day and the dance and everything that has happened.

It's been over two whole days since then. I can't begin to predict what will happen as I walk in the door, noting the fact that there is only one car in the crooked driveway.

It frightens me when I reach it. My hand hovers over the worn down, metal doorknob and I take a deep breath before walking in.

What I find is not what I expected, not by a mile. My dad is home but not my mom. He's sitting in his usual chair in the living room and I catch my breath.

I cry briefly, a little hiccup. But I don't cry of fear, I cry for Spencer, but I'm unsure why.

"Where the hell have you been?" His deep, tired voice is thick, passing the air between us.

"Why do you care?"

"I'm your father. You had me worried."

"Yeah, right." I don't know who I am right now, but I do not stop these careless words from coming out of my mouth. If I can make him angry enough to beat me to death today, I will take that chance. "I'm sure you were missing me as you sat here finishing your case instead of calling. As far as I'm concerned, I can go anywhere I want at any time I want and you won't give a rat's ass as long as you've got someone to beat. Sorry your wife and child weren't home so that you had to think about your day at work with your head instead of your fists."

My words, although oddly empowering, enrage my father. He pulls himself out of the recliner. Something that used to be a man walks towards me. He does what he always does and mutters insults just before shoving me hard in the chest. I fall on the ground from habit.

He stops himself from striking again and I begin to get up to fight back this time, but he uses his foot to keep me on the ground. He drinks what is left in his bottle, he tosses it to the side, the glass shatters.

"You're filthy," he sneers and hits me again. I don't resist, and he strikes me over the top of my head.

Everything gets a little fuzzy. Everything that happens afterward is a blur. This time must be different, there's a reason. He is pissed at me for being gone, like he still is concerned about me. Or maybe there's just too much pent up inside of him for him to be able to stop himself. That face I saw in my memory, the one that wanted to be stopped, is absent.

I'm tired of guessing every time, I'm tired of my life and how everything is crumbling even more than it had been before.

I'm tired. And frustrated. And heartbroken.

I get hot all over and not only from the burning marks of his belt, but from my anger.

Without thinking, with only the desire to get rid of some of the bad in my life as I hear Spencer's voice telling me to fight, I grab the bottle he had dropped on the ground.

I attempt standing, but he kicks me back down with his foot again.

I stab the piece of bottle into his leg and am given a window to stand and get away, but…

I don't leave.

My entire body is shaking as I stand over my father, a full sense of power coursing through me. With my dad now kneeling and clutching his bleeding leg, I finally feel bigger, stronger. In this moment, I'm not the small and fragile toy anymore.

There's nothing in this room except for the man who has made my life what it is.

Every word he has ever used to insult me, every excuse he has ever made for hurting us, every swing of his arm and look of guilt that crossed his face before doing something he knew was wrong crosses my mind. The confusion I felt before about his debating nature during attacks turns into rage as I realize that that is an excuse he has made without realizing it.

My father curses as he tries to stop the bleeding.

The glimpses of a sorry man were meant to show me something, to spark something. They showed me that he was well aware of the evil he was doing, the evil that he continues to do despite whatever remorse floods him at the thought of doing something again.

He forgets his wound and overtakes me. Our roles are reversed before I can finish taking a breath. His blood-soaked hands leave wet prints on my body as he grasps for the control I'd taken. And he gets it back.

It is like I can feel him all over me, everything he has ever done from wrapping his hands around my throat to touching me under covers. I can feel the hard collision of his rough knuckles against my cheek as well as the gentle stroking of fingertips around my waist.

"Why?" His question is more of a plea. A desperate, sorry, and a threat all at once. It's my question, one I'm done asking.

Instead, I wonder if he has ever been hurt the way he has hurt me, breaking my skin and my spirit. I wonder if he has ever been touched the way he has touched me, forcefully and without consent. I wonder if he has thought about the day I retaliated during one of those regretful thought-sessions. I want to give him that pain, to make him hurt like I have hurt my entire life.

Gasping for breath, I stick my arm out, reaching for the glass, or any of the glass to use to free myself. The moment I feel something smooth move under my fingers, I fidget to get my grip around it—

A thunderous crack explodes through the house, drawing the creeping shadows towards the source. A sound that I will never be able to put into words escapes me. It's like a scream, but it is not. It's like a loud cry, but it's not.

My ears are ringing as I first feel the full weight of my father collapse on top of me. I just have to breathe. Once I can breathe, I'll know what's happening. Pushing him off of me feels as impossible as it always has.

Someone helps lift his body enough for me to crawl out from under it. *His body.* Is that all he is now?

"Mom?" The word comes out as a sob as I take in the sight of her.

Her thin hair, white from the years, is still tied back in the tight ponytail she does up for work. Her entire body is trembling and tense. On the floor, dropped or thrown aside, I can't tell, is a gun. I'd never seen it. I only knew it had been there, tucked in their closet beneath the gift box that held my mother's old dress. A dress I'd worn and destroyed. Had it been her gun all along? Set up there for this very moment?

I see it all but it doesn't look right. I don't feel like I am here. This has got to be some kind of lucid dream.

I stare down at it, seeing my shoes become surrounded by the pooling of his blood. He is completely still, not a sliver of life seeming to remain, but it can't be true. He's warm, the blood is warm. The red is bright, everything is normal in color. Death is supposed to be cold and dull, so he can't be… it's just not possible.

A lump gathers in my throat and there is nothing I can do to make it go away as I bend down to check his wrist for the determining factor. My two fingers can't find anything. I hear myself repeating the word "no" over and over as I climb around him, checking for any sign of breath or a pulse. My ear lies against his chest, listening for a heartbeat, but I can't hear anything.

"What did you do?" I don't hate that she did it, I just can't believe that she did it. And I can't believe she's just standing there, gaping at me with her stare transfixed on my father's unflinching body. "What do *we* do? Mom? Mom!"

"Listen to me, Leighanna, and listen close." Something's snapped in her, it's in her eyes and the way they don't blink as she locks into focus. I listen.

My stomach flips, sickness taking over me. But I swallow whatever comes up as I follow her instructions. I remove my shoes, stepping outside of the blood so that I do not leave a trail. The second I step foot in the bathroom, it comes out of me, unable to remain an internal disgust.

Once the wretching stops, I sit on the floor with my head back against the wall and eyes shut just trying to think of what happens next, but there doesn't seem to be anything outside of this moment as my mind tries not to remember what just happened while also avoiding facing the truth.

I feel numb.

My body moves in a way that is unfamiliar as I get up and into the shower. I am moving without thinking and I don't think, I don't do anything but scrub. I clean the blood that was both mine and my father's from every inch of my body even though it's not everywhere.

As I watch the blood mix with the water and go down the drain, I can't help but feel like it's still on me, covering my neck and my shoulders and all over my hands. I rub until my skin turns raw, burning under the pressure of the warm water.

When I can't think of what to do and the cuts on my hands finally start to hurt, I stop what I'm doing and leave the shower running. I sit down on the tub floor. I just sit. I don't cry, I don't sleep, I don't even blink. It hasn't set in, I can't let it sink in.

I don't want to move. I don't want to do anything.
But my mother said to get clean and get out.

CHAPTER TWENTY-ONE

Aftermath

For some reason, I think about the day that I was alone in the hollow beneath my grandparent's porch. I was crying and I could've sworn that there was a creature hiding in there ready to pounce on me. I begged my grandfather not to leave me alone and he responded with, "You're so special. Whatever it is down there, you need to forget about it. It can become strong but only if you let it control who you are."

After that was when the police arrived to help lift me up and out of the hole. I was grateful and happy to be out. I didn't think anything of my grandfather's words other than that he was comforting me and helping me stay calm.

Another memory shines bright through my moment of thinking. I'm eleven now and I am hiding behind a wall to listen in on my father and grandfather's conversation.

"You need to stop what you are doing, my son," my grandfather tried reasoning with him.

"I don't know what a dad is supposed to do. If you don't recall, you were barely ever there when I needed you."

"Shouldn't that make you want to be better than me? Please, son, take care of your family."

"I'm not taking advice from you. I will be how I am, I will parent my own child."

"You don't know what you're doing to her," he continues to beg the younger man before him. My dad had been long since trapped in the rhythm of his ways, he wasn't going to listen, obviously.

The image falls away and I find myself sitting in the bathtub with the water still streaming onto me. I slowly get up and get dressed, finally putting on a different outfit than the one that ties me back to the blue forest, the one now covered in my father's blood.

The bandages on my arm are wet, pointless. I remove it to reveal the tattered remains of what was so neatly repaired. Everything needs to be re-taken care of. We have gauze from an old, dumpy bag of first-aid stuff like antiseptic and medical tape. So I mummify myself, my hands and arm wrapped somewhat securely.

I reach for Spencer's sweatshirt, but it's covered in blood. So much blood. Bile rises in my throat again, but I push it down. Everything I own is in that duffel bag back in the living room. So I put the sweatshirt back on.

Hesitantly, I step out of the bathroom towards the scene, my stomach turning in knots just thinking of seeing it all again even though the image is burned into my memory.

The now darkened blood is falling into the cracks of the tile by the door and soaking in the fibers of the carpet. No one has moved, not even my mother who's still standing beside him, staring at him, as if afraid to take her eyes off of him or else he'll rise and take his revenge.

"Go." Her voice is a whisper. "Take your things."

I creep around the mess and pick up my duffel. She doesn't want there to be any reason for someone to think I was home when this happened, doctoring the crime scene... he's dead.

Without a look back—I wouldn't be able to stomach it—I walk out the door.

My hands have stopped shaking and I get Spencer's sweatshirt off of me to replace it with one from the bag. It seems crazy to me the amount of calm I am after what had just happened because as much as I can't believe it, this is calm. Nothing about what has happened in the span of the last 48 hours is sane, yet it all makes a sort of sense that just has to be accepted or else I would lose my mind.

I have to do something. I tried to escape the world inside of me, but now I'm stuck inside my head anyway; and the things my thoughts are leading me to do are too much for me to really process. Before I get sick from revisiting the event, I bring my walk to a run, begging for motion to clear my head of any thought.

I'm outside in the fresh air that is more clear than it has been for a while. My throat is dry and the wind on my face as I run causes my eyes to water, the tears being drawn out and towards the sides of my face in cooling streams. I wipe them with my bandaged arm and keep running. I don't think I'll be able to stop.

I run straight down the main road that leads down to the center of town. I run across the street even as I am instructed to stop. I would run in the woods and open plains, but if I broke down, no one would come to get me and I would never get up.

I can barely hold myself together and when I reach the canopy that stands in the middle of the large yard in the city's center, no one else is walking across. People on the sidewalks are having calm and quiet conversations with their loved ones either on the phone or whoever they're walking with. I just want to stand in the middle of it all, noticing everything else while nobody notices me. No one passes through the center of a roller rink.

It's almost funny to think that everyone else around has real lives apart from what you see. That no one around me knows what just happened. That at any moment something could happen to one of them and turn their lives upside down on a day when someone else's day is just like any other.

That at one of your best moments, someone else could be at their worst.

In the middle of town square, upon the wooden gazebo, I kneel down and just scream. Loud and confused with the obvious distress ringing out long and almost painful. My head falls to my knees and I hug myself, crying.

How is it my life could change in the blink of an eye? Forcing myself to be without Spencer, nearly killing my own father, running away from my problems and my mother who *did*, in hopes of what? Saving the world?

I must be insane.

Someone comes up behind me and I try to take deep breaths to slow my sobbing. He speaks to me in a soft tone, "Are you alright?"

"Funny, I used to hate that question." It's not funny, but I have to act normal now that I've got my screaming in public out of the way. I finally stop crying and get up to face the young man. I almost laugh when I see who it is. I stumble for words at first due to the surprise of seeing Alex here, but then it just comes out, "I'm going through a lot."

"And screaming in Norwood's Community Gazebo at the center of town seemed like a good idea?"

I give a slight laugh and he smiles. "My dad is… not well."

"Oh, I'm so sorry." He moves closer and I feel compelled to hug him, this person who has just shown up every now and then recently. This guy who suddenly decided to notice me. The one person completely unaware of everything that's been going on. Completely unaware that an other-worldly being murdered an apparition of him that I'd conjured up to hold onto a pleasant memory.

"It…"—I stand up and wipe my nose on my sleeve. There aren't any other words—"sucks."

"What is wrong with him?"

"He…" sobs threaten to rack my body once more, but I try to choke them down. "I… and my mom…."

"It's okay. You don't have to." Although completely appropriate, his words remind me of what I just said. Somehow, it is easier to say the truth now that it might be over. He furthers his condolences, "I don't think I'd be able to go out if I were you."

"But here I am." The wind blows under the gazebo, brushing back the hair from my face and I welcome its attempt to clear up everything.

Alex inches closer. "Do you have other family?"

I hesitate to answer. It could be Alex's supposed infatuation with me compelling him to get information, but it could also be something else, something darker, as everything in my life has come to be. But I respond honestly on the off chance that he is normal and this is a normal conversation, "My mom."

"And how is she taking this?"

"Why are you being so nice to me? You don't even know me."

"What are you talking about? We see each other every day." And he's right. We see each other every day, at school, in one class, and no one else gets involved. For all I know, he isn't real. Saundler could have been another character created to try and convince me that Alex is real.

The entire scene in the cafeteria could have been completely nonexistent. How am I supposed to know what is real and what isn't? He could be just another apparition.

My breath quickens and Alex keeps stepping closer to me with every step away I take. Only dark things want to be near me. I swallow, trying to act normal because, *God,* I need normal. "Exposure isn't the same as having a connection."

"I like to think we're connected."

No.

I can't let him get close to me. I won't. "I have to go."

He grabs my arm to pull me back, "Let me get you something to eat, huh?"

"No, thanks," I need to detach myself from this person.

"I insist."

"And I reject," I get stern, "Listen, I know what you are and I don't want to see you die. I am done with these stupid games. Tell any others who plan on showing themselves to stay the hell away."

He gives me back my arm and stands still, terrified, as I walk away. As long as he stays away, I know I will be fine. But my mom won't be.

CHAPTER TWENTY-TWO

Loss

Before I even get around the corner towards my house, I hear sirens.

My heart skips a beat and when I finally turn, there's an ambulance parked by our house. Why is there an ambulance parked by our house? They don't send blaring vehicles for dead people.

As tired as my legs are, I force them to sprint again, dashing for the spinning lights. I nearly trip over three different cracks on my way down the hill. Between pants, I try to fix my expression to not give anything away. I'm not supposed to know what happened. I wish I didn't know what happened.

I almost run into the truck when I make the turn into the driveway. I use my arm to shield my eyes from the lights that are shining and spinning. I shouldn't notice it, but I do notice it. I can't help but notice it. But my hair falls out, tumbling down into my face like it's trying to keep me from seeing what's going on.

But I know what's going on. Don't I?

A mat lies under my mom and she looks as if she's asleep. "Mom? Mom!"

One of the taller male paramedics steps between me and my mom. His voice is brisk, detached, strictly business. "Are you the daughter of Jenise Groeman?"

"I am. What happened to my mother?!"

"Your parents were often sent home early for aggressive behavior, does that sound right?" He looks at his clipboard as if he were some doctor.

"You aren't answering my question. What happened?"

"Listen, I need to make sure I have the right notes, I am only trying to do my job."

"Fine, you want the truth?" I say it in complete annoyance and enunciate every single word like a student giving an oral report. The paramedic takes scribbles on his paper as I go, breath ragged in hysterics, "Yes, they were sent home early sometimes. Yes, they're not great people. My father is abusive."

My words seem to have no effect on him, but he finally tells me what I've asked to hear. Only, it is not at all what I want to hear. "It seems your mother has had a heart attack, and your father has been shot."

"A heart attack? She's too young for that. And—And why—H-How?" This isn't real. This can't be real.

"We can only assume your mother was the shooter and the stress of it was too much on her heart." Shouldn't he slow down? Shouldn't he be asking me what I think before telling me their theories? He needs to slow down.

"Slow down." My voice drops so low I can feel it shaking in my stomach. "Is my mother dead?"

Before I let the paramedic answer, I shove past him and fall down to the ground beside my mother. She's lying right next to where my father was, the blood still sticky on the surfaces.

I take her hand and it is already getting cold. Something tells me she won't come out of this. I talk to her even though I doubt she can hear me, "Mom? Please, please don't leave me. You're all I have left. Everything was supposed to be okay. This shouldn't be happening."

Tears roll down my cheeks and I lay my head down on my mother's chest. A female paramedic puts her hand on my shoulder and speaks to me, but I don't understand a word she says. Everything is falling apart in front of me, my entire world is ripping at the seams.

Aren't terrible events supposed to come to you periodically? Everything that's been happening hits me. Lilith, the ripples, Lanni, Damus, my father. Everything's been going downhill. All but one thing and I can't even have it because I pushed it away.

I'd be foolish to believe that the world balances out the good and the bad for each person. I'd be even more foolish to believe that this is just my luck because I know, I *know* something else has a hand in all of this.

I'm torn away from my mother, I hadn't realized I was holding onto her so tight. A strong man is pulling me back as I kick and scream, begging to be put down. They pull me into a separate room and close the door. I am set down, but the person that was carrying me keeps me in his arms. He holds onto me tightly.

I just stay here, rocking and shaking, listening to the sound of the front door slamming and the slow fading of the sirens. The house sounds hollow with wind blowing in through the window that is always open in the kitchen. I take a moment to look back at who stayed with me, who is now holding me tighter than before.

It's Lanni.

Without thinking, I sink deeper into his hold and cry more into his shoulder. He rubs my back and pets my head. "It's okay."

"But—But how did you get here?" I calm myself again, something I will undoubtedly be a master of by the end of the week.

"That doesn't matter," he dismisses. "I'm here so that you don't get out of hand."

"Out of hand?" I don't think I was ever *in* hand.

"I have to make sure you're safe."

I pull away from him and wipe my eyes with my already tear soaked sleeve. "Is this all a part of their plan? Are you still helping them?"

"What? No, that's not what I meant." He pinching his features and twisting his fingers as if what he means to say can somehow be wiggled free. "I mean, I don't want you to be alone."

"You don't understand, I have to be like this." I turn away from him and hug my knees facing the corner like a kid in time out.

"You're right." He puts his hand on my shoulder. "I don't understand, but I don't think you do either."

"What is that supposed to mean?"

"That you have it all wrong."

"But if you don't understand, how can you think I'm wrong?"

"I have a guess." He turns me towards him and we look at each other for a while until he speaks again, "You think that by removing hope, you won't get hurt enough to give Damus power."

"You would know."

"I do, and you're wrong."

I shake my head implying that I have no clue what he means, "So you get insight about the man behind everything and become what, a double agent?"

"Hey! Do you want my help or not? Because it wasn't that easy to get on his good side, especially when I'm on the Brights' side."

"The what?"

"The Brights, the happy things inside of you." He points to my head.

That hall that Lilith didn't want me in.

Happy Things. Brights.

I can only picture Alex or not-Alex in the woods getting pierced. I remember the way I had thought he was a part of the group of junkies that Spencer had brought with us to the second visit. He was the memory of the dance before it went so wrong.

In my head, I'm watching his red blood turn clear in that damned pond.

I'm not aware of my daydream-like daze, staring at the wall, until Lanni grabs me again and pulls me out of it. "Stop, please, stop doing that to yourself."

"Doing what?"

"Seeing those things in your head over and over."

"How'd you—?"

He cuts me off, takes his hands off of me, and sighs as if realizing he has a lot to explain to me still. "Ever since I found out what I am, how I am connected to your mind, I've been able to know what you think about."

"I guess that would make sense" *in the same way that everything else has.* I turn to face him again. He's looking at the ground. "Hey. It's okay."

"No, no it's not." Here comes the pity train. Or sympathy. I don't know anymore. "This kind of thing doesn't happen to everyone. Why does it have to be you?"

"You know that's what I'm asking myself right now."

He pulls me into another hug and I breathe in deep, though all I can smell is the cold autumn air that blows through the open window. I should leave. This place is going to turn into an official crime scene eventually now that the emergency squad has found the blood. I can't be here for questioning. It would only get worse from there, wouldn't it?

"It would, you're right," Lanni answers me. I'm so used to someone answering my questions like that that I don't really notice that he does.

"Lanni?"

"Yeah, Elle?"

"What can I do to stop it?"

"I already told you."

"You lied to me the first time, tell me the truth. How can I stop it?"

He rubs his eyebrows apart and back together a few times, "You know the obvious, be happy. But even that isn't guaranteed. There's no such thing as pure happiness, especially now with everything that has happened."

"Yeah, I guess people can't just jump to a good life after all of that. Any other ideas? I can't have this on my conscience anymore. There's too much going on."

"You know the other option."

I put my head down because I do know, I just don't want to accept it. There has to be another way, there just has to be. As I think this, Lanni shakes his head. There has got to be something, anything I can do to make this problem go away, anything but that.

"I'm sorry," Lanni gets up and walks out of the room.

"Where do you think you're going?"

"Where you are thinking of going. Duty calls." It only takes a single blink for him to disappear from three feet in front of me.

I run around the house even though I know I will not find him. Even though I know I have to leave again, I'm just as unsure about where to go. It's déjà vu. I'm blindly running down the street. This time I avoid the crowds and run to the nearest area of unowned woodland.

I use my arm to push aside any branches that might try to get in my way, ripping and tearing holes in my clothes all the while. When I finish pushing my way through, there's an open field before me. I fall down and lie there with my face towards the sky that is so dense with clouds that I can't even find the moon that should be high up in the sky by now.

The sky turns dark quickly and the dense air foreshadows a rainstorm. I play with the grass beneath my fingers and close my eyes, breathing in the weather. The smell is relaxing and I can almost forget about everything. I want so desperately to forget everything. Which is exactly why I can't.

To fill the void I've put in my head, the memory of a time when my grandfather took my dad on some sort of trip and I was left with my mom enters my forethought. I was so little, and my mom was so happy.

I didn't know it then, but that was the happiest I was ever going to see my mother. Her hair was still alive with the colors of autumn and she smelled like cinnamon. She took me to the park and pushed me on the swing. We were there until the sky was dark and then we stopped for milkshakes. That night she held onto me so tightly, I couldn't move.

Before I fall asleep daydreaming about when my mom was the angel I still think she could be, I get up off the ground and start walking to the hospital. I guess it would be easier to deal with it now instead of later. My shoes are grassy and I try wiping whatever I can off of my clothes as my pace slows down.

I don't want to face the result of any of this. If my dad survives, but my mother doesn't, then I am stuck with a father who has every excuse to harm me now without anyone there to keep him under check. If they both die, I'll be an orphan, forced to live in a home with other children. Teenagers, especially ones like me, never find homes or at least face the hardest time getting there.

What will become of me when I have to live alone? Who will I be once left to my own devices? Yet again, my mother might not be dead, so if she comes out and my father doesn't, then everything will be okay. Suddenly, I can feel the cold touch of her skin and think that it is impossible for her to still be alive.

The ground is muddy and my tennis shoes are filthy. I leave wet footprints on the sidewalk once I reach it. The wind coming from passing cars makes it that much colder. I pull the sleeves up past my hands and hug myself taking really slow steps to the hospital. I couldn't drive away from the house in my mother's car. It just wouldn't be right.

A car pulls over and drives slowly in pace with me. Whoever is driving rolls down their window and starts talking to me, "You need a ride?"

Her voice is sweet and seemingly full of good intentions, so I respond. "I'm just walking to the hospital."

"Are you injured?"

"No." I keep my head down and forward as I talk, "My mom is there."

"Are you sure I can't give you a lift, it looks very cold out there."

I look over at her finally and see that she has a cross hanging on her mirror. Her eyes are full of pity and she has a baby boy in the backseat. Suddenly, the idea of sitting down, of not moving, sounds so relieving. I don't care if she isn't real, if she's actually a man with tools in his back seat instead of a child. "On second thought, if you have nowhere to be, that would be great."

She smiles and stops the car, unlocking the passenger door, "I'm always willing to help. In fact, we just came from mother and son story-time at the library."

We both look back at the baby sleeping soundlessly without a care in the world, spit dribbling down his shirt. If only that childhood innocence stayed longer than it does. Babies are smarter than those older than them. If I could steal their perfect peace for a moment, I'd be so thankful. This ride is as good as I'm going to get.

"What happened to your mom?" She breaks me out of my train of thought.

"What? Oh, she had a heart attack earlier today and they wheeled her in for immediate medical attention."

"I'm so sorry." She puts her hand over her heart and then back on the steering wheel. "I'm Olivia by the way."

"Elle," I answer her while pulling on the seatbelt.

"Is that short for anything?"

"Yeah." For the first time, I don't grimace when I say it, "Leighanna."

"That's a lovely name. Do you have any other family?"

"Just my parents, and my dad has been hospitalized for a while now. Cancer."

There's a long moment of silence and it stays this way with her christian music playing gently in the background. My eyes look at the buildings and signs saying 'Now Hiring" or "OPEN." Just normal places where normal people go, doing their normal day-to-day things.

We turn into the hospital parking lot and Olivia says, "You and your family will be in my prayers."

Feeling slightly uncomfortable, I thank her for the ride before entering the pure and out of place building. The sterile white atmosphere of the hospital is less than comforting. I only know loss within these walls. My grandparents and my would-be brother. The antiseptic and linoleum are an omen.

The lady at the desk waves her hand to get my attention and dons a serene smile. "Are you looking for something?"

"Some*one,* actually." I hesitate to go on. The hospital can't know that they're my parents. CPS would be here in a heartbeat. "I've come to see my friend's parents."

"Names of the patients?" She's looking down at her computer screen now.

"John and Jenise Groeman."

"I'm not at liberty to give you the details without informing the family first."

"You don't even know if they have family." Why would she ask if she knew she couldn't tell me anything? "Please, I'm supposed to be the-the messenger, the contact."

"I'm sorry," and she truly looks apologetic, a look I'm sure she's mastered from practice. "But policy is policy."

"You are basically telling me that they're dead. Both of them. It is not that hard to just tell me, I need to know."

With a frustrated sigh, she turns back to her computer, hitting keys on the keyboard in that seemingly unnecessarily exaggerated way that hospital workers do. Finally landing on the information, she reads off of the screen without looking at me, "Mr. Groeman has left the hospital and Mrs. Groeman is in the operating room at the moment."

My heart skips a beat, "What for?"

She types more, keeping her eyes glued to the screen, but all she says is, "I really can't tell you."

Another member of the hospital staff, the label on his coat embroidered with the letters "DR," walks behind the desk, fumbling comfortably around the nurse until he gets her to pull to the side with him.

They speak in hushed tones, but not hushed enough. I've been listening through walls my entire life, a few feet is nothing.

"When family arrives…tell them…best we can."

Best we can is not hospital lingo you want to hear. Best we can means they are not confident. Best we can means my mom is dying.

"Are you okay, miss?" The nurse addresses me, but it comes in all muffled.

My father *left*, and my mother is…

"Miss?"

I should have been better to her, I should have told her that I noticed her attempts, that I love her and I need her. I shouldn't have fought my dad.

"Doctor!" the nurse shouts down the hall as I crash to the floor.

CHAPTER TWENTY-THREE

All There Is is This

My eyes open and I'm grateful to not find myself lying in a hospital bed. That would be just the thing I need, to look like one of my doubles, one of my memories…

I'm still in the hospital, but seated in the lobby with my head on someone's shoulder. When I feel a hand on mine, I'm less unnerved and turn to see who has come to me this time, hoping while also not hoping that Lanni has come back to me.

"Hey, Little Fawn." It's Spencer, and I am so thankful that it is. I don't want a doctor or a nurse standing beside me. I want him. I *always* want him and I was stupid to push him away.

"My mom?"

His smile goes away and he shakes his head. "She didn't make it."

How would he know? He's not related?

But I believe him.

A short, high-pitched gasp escapes me. "What am I going to do?"

"Try to forget it?" He shrugs. "Or get through it."

"You look like hell." He's pale with dark circles under his eyes just like me. His clothes are filthy and we're both just dirty people sitting in a hospital lobby with no one in the rooms to be here for. "What happened?"

"Just some street art and running from the police." He's lying to me. I can read it on his face and by the fact that there's no spray on his clothes.

"Why do you lie to me?"

"You see right through me." He smiles and leans back in his chair.

"Spencer?" I won't let him get without answering.

"I can't tell you."

"And why not?"

"They called me from your phone. Elle, you were so stressed that you passed out not even knowing about your mom and I just told you she's—" *Dead, just say it.* He doesn't. "I can't risk overwhelming you like that again."

"Spencer, do you think I care? No secrets, please."

He licks his lips and takes a deep breath. Everything has changed so much since that one day. He is barely the bright and happy soul that I've always known him to be. There's not one thing left the same as it was only two days ago. I want to be back at the roller rink being completely crazy and stupid.

"Fine," he sighs. I finally broke him, whether it was my pleading or his own choice. "I went through the ripples."

"Spencer…." He bows his head ashamed. "Why would you do that?"

"I thought I could fight Damus, but I got stopped halfway, I didn't make it to him." I grab his hand before he can cover his face. "I thought I could protect you."

"Spencer, you don't need to protect me, you can't. Take care of yourself, please. I wouldn't know what to do if I lost you too." I begin to cry although not wanting to. A single tear rolls down my cheek and I feel it fall off of my chin. I wipe away the line it had created and stop myself from going on any longer.

Spencer wraps both arms around me. "I'm so sorry. I didn't want any of this for you, I just wanted to help, I didn't know all of this was happening. I'm so sorry."

I can hear the absolute sympathy in his voice and can't help but shake with him as he begins to cry. A gust of cold air blows in as the entrance doors flap open and shut with the passing of people. I just can't seem to escape it, the cold.

Yet I don't want to leave this moment. Finally, I feel like someone needs me and not the other way around. I'm so tired of playing the damsel in distress. I rub his back as he puts his face down into my chest.

With inopportune timing, a nurse walks over, talking and staring at her clipboard, "No need to keep you here, just had to keep you nearby after you knocked yourself unconscious. I take it you and your friend's mom were close?"

"Yeah," I say as Spencer gets up off of me wiping away all the sadness for a moment, "We got along really well."

"I'm so sorry for your loss."

"Thank you."

The nurse leaves the room and I watch until her shadow is no longer visible. I turn towards Spencer and his expression is almost lifeless. I reach out to him, but he doesn't move towards me. My heart sinks and I want to help him feel better just as he has done for me so many times.

In reality, he probably would have been better off without me, if I was never thoughtful about my mom so many years ago. I would have never seen him tagging the building. There would probably be a mural where his name is now. My appearance, so limp like a deer that was hit and left at the side of the road, seems to not have changed. I am still that broken girl.

"You never told me what the present was for." He must have been thinking the same thing as me, what his life would be like without me in it.

"It was my mom's favorite book." I remember this because it is also mine. I gave it to her and started reading it almost immediately. I was curious and eager to find out what my mom had thought was so interesting.

"Any special occasion?"

"Yeah." I get lost in memory like I do so often and speak to him as it plays out in my head, "We had just found out that my mom lost the baby. She was five months in. She didn't want to know the gender, but I secretly hoped it was a boy."

"I'm sorry." He leans back and stretches as a pause. "My God."

"What is it?"

"There never seems to be a good thing for you. Hell, you were also robbed that day." He shakes his head.

"Well, I know you didn't have a perfect childhood."

"Oh yeah, like being a runaway street artist is anything compared to that."

"It is. Your family tossed you out because you didn't take after them. You did your passion and had run-ins with the police at age twelve. You suffered all alone besides you're here-and-there friends."

"But I was never beaten or forced to go back to my family." As I look at him, that concern mixed with some sort of guilt weighs down on me, but I acknowledge it as his feelings.

In this moment, I finally understand the reason behind everyone's actions. The reason is that they are human. Everyone has their own share of shit, a voice that is their own speaking to them inside their head. Everyone hears themselves reminding them of the past or enforcing feelings as a result of those experiences.

Suddenly, the voice in my head is yelling at me for pushing him away and being scared of him for even a fraction of a second because his intentions were nothing like my father's. His thoughts made him scared of being let go the way his family let him go. I can only imagine how many things that he has cared about have gotten lost or taken away, or how many times he has been given up on.

I don't blame him for trying to make me stay. And I can't blame him for caring about me, no matter how incomprehensible it is to me, because to be human means to not be in control of who you love.

"Spencer," I look into his eyes as he stares deep into mine and a spark is shared between us. "You are all the family I am ever going to need."

Without warning, but with full expectancy, Spencer gets up out of his chair and kisses me. A deep, breath-taking kiss that makes me wonder why we haven't been doing this the whole time. It's all I ever want to do.

"I am never letting you go," he whispers to me before sweeping me up out of the chair and into his arms. He carries me all the way out to his car, sets me in the passenger seat, and walks around to the other side.

I watch his movements, slow and graceful even with   his slight limp. He gets inside and I smile. Once he puts the car in drive and we are on the road, I take one of his hands off of the steering wheel and hold it. He squeezes and I return it.

I take a deep breath like I always do when I am about to go into a deep thought. I can be happy, it is very much possible. As long as I have Spencer, I have family, and with family, I can really do it. Even with the images of each horror

I have endured crossing my mind. It all seems to be passing in front of my eyes as a look back at how I got where I am.

"Stop thinking," a panicked voice sounds and I know it's Lanni but I don't see him, "Stop." His voice fades in and out like a camera going out of focus and then returning over and over again.

The strain he's putting into talking to me shows by the headache that follows his warning. I have to take my hand back from Spencer's warm touch and reach into the glove compartment for ibuprofen. Only, instead of pain relief, I see the glinting handle of the pistol I once saw within his coffee table and quickly shut the compartment.

"Are you okay?" Spencer doesn't look, doesn't realize what I did, what I saw. "Sorry to ask."

"No, you're fine. I just got a headache, that's all," I say leaning back and rolling the window down, maybe the rush of the brisk air will help. It worked when my grandpa took me on fishing trips.

We would hop in his truck and drive down to the creek they had not too far from their house. It was full of those tiny fish but every once in a while you could find a big blue gale. The very first time we went, we didn't catch anything.

One day, my grandpa had caught a single fish and the hook had gone through its eye. I kept thinking the fish was dead, but I watched terrified for the fish and for my grandfather if it were to bite him or scale him. It made me feel sick and I'd get headaches.

He made me rest my head on the little part in the door and close my eyes as the wind blew by. It had made my face really cold, but it helped my headache so I continued to keep my head down as my grandpa drove silently down the dirt road.

When Spencer hits the brakes and the smell of smoke from a nearby bus blows in my face, I pull my head back in and put up the window. I realize just how quiet it is between the two of us, but I enjoy it, like this time is full of sweet innocence. Nothing can go wrong now and we both need a time where we neither talk about the past events nor regret. Something to look at later as a sort of reminder that there is always something good to look back on.

It stays this way until we reach his apartment and I am so grateful not to see my house that is now filled with even more darkness than I thought possible. We slowly make our way up the stairs with his arm around my shoulders and mine his waist. It feels strange to go to his home alone even though I've done it so many times before.

I have no one to punish me for anything that happens afterwards. I can literally do whatever I want and no one will care as long as it's within the law or kept very secret. My heart races as we make it in and close the door behind us.

CHAPTER TWENTY-FOUR

Not Out of the Woods

A gunshot wakes me.

I bolt upright, alone in Spencer's bed, and race out of the bedroom where…

Nothing is happening, nothing but Spencer standing over the stove, pouring batter onto a pan.

"'Morning," he says when he notices my entrance.

"Good morning." I come up behind him and hug him. It must have been a dream. "What are we having today?"

"Just some french toast."

"Delicious," I get up on my tip toes and kiss his cheek before setting the table.

We eat and it's quick because neither of us want to be sitting apart for so long. His feet play with my feet under the table and we giggle as we focus more on kicking each other than eating. It's a little foot war between us and we have to hold onto the table to keep from falling off the chairs.

We laugh as we swing and miss each other or knock a fork to the floor. Although this is fun, we both know we'd much rather get on the couch and cuddle to a good movie proving to the world that our lives are just as normal as everyone else's. I spent so long believing this could never happen to me which makes it so much better now. He takes me into his arms and we lie down on the couch, my body fitting into his like two pieces of a puzzle.

This right here, this is what I want to—*need* to—be doing for the rest of my life. Here, with Spencer laughing and us enjoying ourselves without a care in the world. If I close my eyes, I can breathe him in, the smell of fresh herbs strong after the shower he must have taken before I woke up. This is easy, simply living in the moment. I don't have to think about where Spencer's gun is now, if he brought it in, or why he got it out in the first place.

A ringing fills my ears like radio static and Lanni's voice warns me once again, "Stop that," a muffle like a radio going in and out of range breaks up his words, "I told you before… thinking… helping him."

The more strain he put into contacting me causes my entire body to clench in a strange discomfort. Spencer starts to rub my arm to loosen me up, "Hey, what happened?"

"Just another headache," I tell him. It's not a lie, but it's not necessarily the whole truth. I have to shut him out and make it seem like he is not a problem. He told me happiness will stop Damus, so why does he bring up things like this? What is the point in reaching me?

That is hardly the big question. I want to know what he is trying to say. Maybe if it happens again, I'll be able to try and let him talk. I wasn't pushing him out before, but if I put an effort into listening to him, maybe I will get a clearer message. I don't understand why it is so hard for him to talk to me in my own head.

I hadn't even noticed that Spencer got up until he returns with more ibuprofen in his hand. "I saw you take one in the truck and it seemed to help then."

"Thanks."

"Are you sure it's just a headache? Something else seems to be bothering you." We read each other so well, too well. Thinking of how close we are, I smile, but it fades as I realize I have to give him some sort of explanation.

I lie to him no matter how much I don't want to. According to him, we are fine. "I was just thinking about having to get a job and pay rent."

"Living independently isn't so bad, especially living independently together."

I wasn't actually anticipating a whole conversation, but since it is off topic, I don't argue. "How exactly *do* you pay rent?"

"Well, that's not what's important." *Would others stop deciding what is and isn't important?* "Besides, you don't have too much to worry about. Seventeen-year-olds get assisted living or something like that."

"You mean seventeen-year-old orphans…" He looks upset, so I quickly say, "Don't make that face. He won't find me, and I doubt he's even looking."

He seems to want to ask questions, but I know he knows my "don't ask" face.

I sit up, grab Spencer's hand, and make him return to the couch. He lies back down and I lie right next to him. An old film is playing on t.v., some black and white romance.

There are always those moments in time where you wish you could stop thinking. Just stay where you are without a single thought going through your head. I guess I got my time in the car and all those silent but perfect moments earlier.

"I can stay here forever," he tells me and then squeezes me tight.

I can't help but smile and move myself closer to him, hiding my face in his chest and feeling his warmth. I know he is real. I am incapable of making up someone as complicatedly perfect as him. He is alive, human, flawed but beautiful. Taking in his presence, feeling this moment, I feel a part of something outside myself. There is absolutely nowhere else I'd rather be.

As the movie finishes, Spencer starts to move so I get up to let him do so. He stands up and grabs my sweatshirt off the place on the floor where I had left it last night. The sleeves are stained with dirt and a few holes have managed to grow larger and more noticeable. "You need a new wardrobe."

Except, all of my things are already packed in a duffle bag—shit. I have no idea where I left that. It could be sitting suspiciously in town square, in the well of the passenger seat of a stranger's car, or still on the living room floor… by the bloodstains and silenced shadows. What will they watch now?

I can see my parents' bodies lying on the ground, stiff, on the brink of death. I sit myself down to avoid falling.

"I know you don't want to go back there, but I will run in for you." He gets close to me and crouches down so his face is even with mine. "It's okay."

I breathe and nod like a child who just got persuaded to talk to someone they never met. All that goes through my mind is seeing people in there photographing the damage, preserving the crime scene, insisting that we go in and out as quickly as possible to avoid contaminating evidence or disturbing the investigation.

By the time I go back to school, everybody will undoubtedly have heard about the attack on Clamer Street. I will receive stares and the halls will get quiet when I walk through them as everyone suddenly has a new idea about me, a cautious attitude around me. People will start rumors about how I probably murdered my parents or some other awful shit that they think of, even though they wouldn't know how close they were to the truth.

Teachers will be awkward around me, unsure how to deal with someone in my situation. People will say they understand what I am going through even though they can't possibly have any idea. Since I won't see a certified counselor, the ones at school will constantly call me down whether it is because what someone else said or something I did that seemed off.

Things will never be the same there. They'll give me a pass for missing school today, maybe even if I skip the entire week, but I'll only have their sympathy for so long before they start talking about making me repeat the school year or whatever it is they do with students whose parents leave them.

The best for me would be to stop going to school over all. I don't need a real career. I can join Spencer, maybe we can start a legal way of raising money, like a street permit to sell something or other for money. We could work at a warehouse or start a touring business where we take people around to the city's best graffiti, explaining the meaning and inspiration while taking a final stop at the pond, showing a captive audience the "fabled portal to another dimension."

We could tell them the legend of creatures that lie beyond the surface and warn them against entry, only we would never tell them how to get through in case they try. Or I can simply take up a minimum wage job while Spencer keeps up with whatever it is he does that keeps him here. His grandfather's account must be dry by now. Whatever ends up happening, we could make it work.

As my thinking drags itself out, we pull into the driveway with its gravel path. I see my mom's car still sitting here as if she's home. I curl myself up and lean against the window.

Spencer seems to want to say something, but only pets my head.

But when he reaches for the doorhandle, I stop him. "You have no idea what to look for."

You don't need to see what's behind that door.

"We already cleared out my bedroom," I explain when he just stares at me, confused.

"Oh, so you're…" He doesn't want to say it, so I do.

"I have to go through my mom's things."

"Do you want me to come in with you?"

"No. And I'm not saying so out of fear this time. It's just… better. It's… goodbye." I shrug and look out at the front food, chipped paint and all. "Let me say goodbye."

"Okay."

I take a deep breath before letting myself out of the car. The wind has stopped. It's quiet and still, nothing I'm not used to. Which is exactly why it's wrong. There's been violence behind this door. There's been blood. But never like this.

Crossing the threshold feels like crossing through the ripples. It's cold and dark and I'm still being watched. Quietly now, like this time, the shadows are the ones shying away, peeking through their flickering fingers like they want to look away but can't.

I'm not here to do anything, though. There's no one left to do anything for.

The floor creaks as I go down the hall to grab my bookbag from my bedroom and head to my parents'. Their closet is the same as it's always been, except for the empty space in the corner of the high shelf. The box that had the dress in it is still on my bedroom floor, the dress torn to ribbons and sitting somewhere at Spencer's, if he hasn't already thrown it out.

The small box that had been under it is down. I have no idea where it has gone, but I know it's empty wherever it is. The pistol is somewhere in police custody, dusted for fingerprints. The only ones on it being my mother's so that they'll be pinning the crime on a dead woman. Battered wife shoots abusive husband and dies from shock. Case closed.

Casket closed.

Will my mom get a funeral? Who would set it up? It can't possibly be on me.

My mom wore nothing but jeans or corduroy pants with t-shirts or sweaters. You don't need much when you only ever leave the house for work. As I remove clothing from their hangers, I reveal her old bowling shirt. Her name, Jenise, is stitched on the breast pocket in bright pink thread.

Why do I care so much?

I fold the shirt and neatly tuck it into my bookbag.

My chest tightens like it always does when the front door opens.

It can't be him. It can't be him.

Then, something crashes and like I always do when there's commotion within these walls, I go towards it.

"Sorry." Spencer's eyes catch mine as I peek over into the living room from the hallway to find him bent over the broken pieces of a picture frame. "I didn't think that anyone else should have this stuff."

"Thanks," I say, coming out to join him. "But I probably don't need all of this."

"You might not *need* it, but it's still you, Elle. Your things, your life, like trophies."

"How much of your stuff did you take with you when you left your family?"

"I wish I could have taken more," he lets those words set in for a minute. "The whole point of you doing this with me is so that you aren't alone and don't make the same mistakes that I did."

To avoid giving him any sort of look, I look to the ground, but I catch sight of his bandaged leg and the feeling of guilt consumes me. Everything he has gone through for me cannot possibly be worth it. "I'm not just another struggling kid, I'm seriously fucked up. Have you not thought for even a second that I might be the biggest mistake you've made?"

"Never."

This is one of those long-lasting words that resonate in the space between us. The doubt is faded, set aside in favor of desire for a better future. I smile and help him gather all of the things he deemed important not to leave behind.

He fumbles with the keys to unlock the car door and pops the trunk. We place the things inside and get back in the car just as we have so many times before. I already feel a pattern forming for the next few years ahead of us.

Everything that's happening all seems too perfect. Problems seem to have disappeared—or at the very least been de-escalated—and all is calm. I don't want to complain, but it is just a little boring after looking at how peaceful it is.

Is this really how I want to spend my time? In a sort of dream-like state where nothing but good things happen? We could end up going through the days without anything to really make them worth something.

I don't want to. I need something to happen. Not necessarily something bad, just something to make this all seem real. In my mind, I can imagine tearing through the sky as if it were only a paper background. All of this is a movie set where I am living one big lie.

"Right."

"Right what?" I turn towards Spencer admitting I was caught completely off guard.

"I didn't say anything." He looks back and forth between me and the road confused.

"Focus!" I know Spencer doesn't say this so it must be Lanni. I didn't notice, his voice has changed as if he is hurt, "Crack the code…not perfect…need…stop…Damus…he is still…do something…he's not…I can't… please… help… he's coming… help!"

I reel over almost sick. My head seems to be pulsing although to a different beat then my heart. It pounds against my skull making me wince and reflexively hold it with my hands. I open the glove compartment and find that the ibuprofen is missing. The gun is gone, too. I roll the window down, but it hurts more to move my head down beside it.

My moaning and facial expressions cause Spencer to pull over. He gets out of the car to get closer to me. I can't respond to any of his questions. "Elle? What's going on? What can I do?"

I want to say he's done more than he has needed to, but I mainly focus on trying to let the headache pass. It won't fade as I find myself thinking about what Lanni said. *Not perfect.* What is he trying to say?

It sounds as if my fairytale land of happiness isn't enough to stop whatever is going on in my own mind. Everything about the ripples is hidden from me, I have no idea what is going on there. But I guess that is the point of that place, somewhere to place things to forget about them. A perfect hiding place for Damus.

Just when I thought I could stop dwelling on the fact that Damus might destroy us, he shows up posing another threat. He's doing something to Lanni, something that makes it difficult for him to reach me. He's hurting him and I want it to stop. I want all of it to stop.

The thudding gets less and less noticeable and aggravating. I lean back letting myself breathe for a moment and calm myself. After it all seems to have dissipated, I turn towards Spencer who has remained standing beside me, quiet and patient.

"Something's wrong," the way he says it makes it true. "You lied when you said it was nothing."

"Because I didn't know what it was," I defend myself.

"So now you do?" After I don't respond, he insists, "Elle, I want to help you."

"And you have, my God, you have," I express my thankfulness to him, but go on to take on an almost angry tone, "I have to go back."

"Back? Back where?"

I look at him with apologetic eyes, "The ripples, Spencer. Our problem isn't solved."

The water hasn't stilled itself. Our disruption of the events that were taking place without me knowing are still in motion. This problem has not stopped, the pond is not steady.

He gapes without words to say, or with too many words to say. He just stands there slack-jawed at the idea of going there again. If I have to, I will leave him here alone. The absolute last thing I want is for him to go with me.

I need to keep my priorities together, I can't give Damus the advantage. If I am going to win this fight, I'm going to have to go in alone. This will be harder to explain to Spencer than the fact that I am going there at all. It will crush him to hear these words, but hopefully he will understand when it counts.

"Spencer?" I try to pull him back to Earth before saying anything else. If I hear how he actually feels, it might be easier to tell him.

"I just don't understand," he says, barely looking at me.

My body shivers. I don't want to leave him behind, but I have no other choice. I choke back tears, "I have to go. Me, not you."

"What are you trying to say?"

"That you will only make it worse." I breathe deeply trying to control my feelings. "That if I am going to win this battle, you can't come with me."

There are no more words. He just pulls me close and holds me tightly as if he's afraid to let go. I don't want him to, but I know he will have to eventually. I break away first. This can't last too much longer, it will only make it harder in the end.

I don't say goodbye because I plan on seeing him again. I don't want him to think this is over between us. I will be fine, but I can't tell him that. It will only make him think that I won't. No words is the easiest way to go. So I put one foot in front of the other, wiping away tears and trying to push aside all feelings but hate.

I must be full of rage to accomplish this. Damus will win if he is given any leverage, so I can't let my fear show. I have to shove it away this time in a new place, one where he can't find it. Fear makes you stronger, so I hide it with my good memories which is where I should have kept everything in the first place.

My grandfather was wrong to believe you had to create a place for all the bad things in life. In reality, we should consider everything to be good, that way you don't have anything bad to rediscover as you get older. No creating demons for yourself. I have to stop letting dark memories consume me and morph me into something I'm not.

This motivation helps me feel better and more confident about everything that is about to take place. I don't look back, but right when I need it, Spencer grabs my wrist and turns me back around.

He has nothing to say. I have nothing to say.

Instead, we pull each other in deep, our lips crushing each other with every word we have no idea how to say. It is warm. It is home. It is what will keep me going.

We need to breathe and that gives us the space we need to move forward.

He goes back to his car and I take a moment to stand up tall and pretend that it's power. Practicing now will make it more believable later.

CHAPTER TWENTY-FIVE

Obstacles

I have absolutely no idea what I am doing. Killing my demons? Yeah, that's not me. I hide them, throw them somewhere so that they are no longer my problem. I find it hard to believe I am the only person with this task at hand. There has got to be someone else with a made up monster trying to overcome their unrealistic world by materializing.

Leaves crunch beneath my feet as I turn into the forest. Trees are orange and yellow, showing more fall colors than I had noticed before. I recognize their beauty, their purity, and how they go about standing still, taking in chemicals to provide for the rest of us living beings. They change with the seasons and it seems perfect, like they are carefree.

Of course this is crazy, trees don't have a conscience, they aren't thinking creatures. Although it is nice to believe that these mute pieces of nature do have a known purpose to themselves and not just to humans. It is childish to believe the trees are really alive that way.

Everything about the forest, the real forest, seems alive. I let whatever warmth happens to break through the chill air come over me. It doesn't last long, but it lets me know there's something that sets this place apart, something about this reality to hold onto.

I feel like I have to savor every last second in this forest as I make my way to closing the gap between me and the other side. I try holding onto all the good things that have happened over the last few days, but they are cloudy memories just as they were when I was in them. Everything has a filter over them blocking me from getting any true emotion from them.

My steps are so loud, I can barely hear much else besides the leaves beneath my feet. If I were anywhere else, I'd feel as if I am giving myself away. I am most definitely not stealthy enough if I want any kind of surprise advantage.

Lucky for me, the leaves level out the ground making the roots of trees less of a problem for me and it is an effortless walk to the pond. As I get closer and the water becomes visible, my body stops itself. I stand still letting my fear take over.

The voices in my head are anything but encouraging. They tell me that I am crazy for thinking that I am capable of completing this task. My own thoughts taunt me for fighting this war inside my own head.

Only, there is an intruder. Something has tried claiming territory on land that already belongs to me. His army may be larger, but it can't possibly be stronger.

I have to take this risk. Otherwise, something larger and more terrible could happen. I'd rather do the irrational now then regret never trying later if it is true. It's like when you go to a new restaurant and decide whether or not to try something you've never had before. You are worried you'll waste your money on something you find out you don't like. Yet again you'll go on the rest of your time thinking, what if? Only, in this case, the results could be fatal.

The decision is made and I go into the pond, soaking yet another pair of pants. It feels like ice and I wonder what it will feel like on the other side. I try to prepare myself for the cold that awaits, but there really is no point. No matter the temperature, my nerves will keep me heated.

My hands are shaking as they hang over the water. With the slightest touch, the pond ripples outwards.

My body falls and I don't land on my feet, this time getting covered in the water from the inside pond. When I remove myself from the water, I notice that it is no longer water that covers me, but something red. It isn't as dark as one would think. It's almost pink the way it sinks into my clothes and shows up as little dots on my hands.

Seeing this on me, I remember being mesmerized by the way the young boy's blood had turned clear as it streamed from the holes in his body. But there's nothing here, no immediate danger. Damus had planned for this to happen, for this to be the first obstacle in my attempt to stop him.

He hoped the sight would frighten me. He knows I pose a threat and is trying to find anything to stop me. He believes creating fear will make him stronger, will make me weaker. I laugh at this. I shout into the lonely woods around me, "You're going to have to do better than that!"

I get hyped up on a moment of insanity. Everything seems to just hit me and I realize that at this point, it's a miracle my head is still on my shoulders. Enjoying being in this state, I use it to hide my true feelings about the situation. Both from him and from myself.

Indulging in the slight hysterics, I kick the leaves and continue to laugh like I have some hidden plan. Which means I should get to thinking. I have no weapon of any sort to protect me from the things that a physical weapon will work against. Many things are in store for me, so I need to gear up.

I walk over to the place where the blood had spilled before, hoping to find what I want. The spears that had risen from the ground are still protruding out slightly, the ends stained with the blood of the Bright version of Alex. I snap one from its place in the ground and touch the tip with my finger. Still sharp. I wipe the dry blood off with my wet shirt and it looks almost brand new.

With a tinge of self-congratulations, I continue to make the tool even better. With ropelike vines from the nearby rose bushes, I fashion a spiky edge to the shaft of the arrow that was once a spear. Those survival shows my grandfather always had on are paying off. All I have to do is retrieve each end of a spear to create multiple in case I need more. I know I will need more.

Now my only problem would be where to keep it so that I can use both my hands. The first idea that comes to mind is to gather leaves and somehow tie them together to make a quiver. Though as soon as I try, the thorns and arrowhead poke through the material. I have to try and find something stronger than fresh thick leaves.

I lean against a tree as I think about it and start picking at the holes in the trunk. That's when it hits me. I start searching for small twigs and less prickly, yet durable string-like plants. With these, I make a sort of quiver to place on my back.

There's nothing left to do but bring the fight to him, so I start towards the small mountain. Something tells me that this is where I need to go. And so I head out, tense and ready to fight whatever Damus tries to use to stop me.

This psychotic daze fades as my mind sharpens into action. The air has changed. Everything is grey and dull now, the exact opposite of everything outside. The only similarity is the way the leaves break beneath my feet, hardened from the cold and crumbling loudly. The overhead branches bend and sway with lively intent, but the effect is haunting in the absence of the shimmering blue that filled the air before.

Something tells me to ignore my grandfather's words from so long ago. Face my fears, don't hide them away. It's convincing enough to keep my head up while going through the forest in the direction that feels right. That compulsion like a compass in my stomach pulling me along.

I brace myself, moving so fast, I hardly recognize the wilting plants around me. The roaring of the water falling down onto the rocks grows the louder the closer I get. The sound of the trees above gives me chills as I remember what had happened to Spencer in our escape. I stop where I had began the first time, where everything started going extremely downhill. My arm burns remembering its injury.

Something glides past the trees that surround me. I stop and stand completely still after slowly retrieving my arrow. My fingers tingle to get the practice. I spin in circles as I pay close attention, following the movement of the shadows.

My fear of the dark. He's using my fears against me.

Evil things lurking around, no problem. I will just do what I have done for many years and push away all of the thoughts that fill my head of what the figures might be. Of course, the shapes form into images as they come to my mind because this is my mind and what I think goes.

The very first thing to cross my mind comes from the haunting appearance of a single tree among the plethora of other trees. Seemingly carved into the trunk is a face of tragic expression like the negative of a theater mask. The face rises into the air as the tree's roots lift slowly out of the ground, disentangling itself from the wildlife that has grown around it over the years.

As the legs rip out of the ground in a thunderous uprooting, the final leaves shake off to the ground leaving nothing but an ashen skeleton of something that was once beautiful. On its way, the ground beneath me rumbles and a shrieking roar sends black birds flying. I begin running down the path as fast as my legs will carry me. I don't have a weapon to use against a being created to be unbeatable.

The gears in my head turn as I dodge the branches that are thrown at me. The new monster screams as it rips itself apart for ammunition. What could I possibly do to get rid of or at least distract the tree until I reach the waterfall?

As I try to prepare for what comes next, a branch lands in front of me and I run right into it, flipping over and onto my back. I can feel the ache pulse outwards. It's going to hurt to run. The pain is like a paintball being shot point blank at my sides every time I take a step.

One measly attempt to send the tree monster staggering backwards with the shot of an arrow proves to be useless as the mildly pointed stick bounces off of the trunk with a pathetic and non-existent effect.

There has to be something I can do to get this tree to leave me alone. I need to do the trick I had thought up before, make this bad event into something good. The tree is another confidence boost. It has pushed me to get to where I need to be faster, it brought on a conflict that I might have faced later anyway. Being chased and the tree's inevitable unsuccessful attempt at stopping me proves to me that I can get through whatever my mind tries to use against me.

With this in mind, the loud stomps and shakes of the ground come to a sudden halt. I look behind me to see the tree root itself in the middle of the path. The bare tree glows and becomes more lively than the pale grey shade of the others around it.

The face brightens to match the trunk that has started to transform into a healthy maple brown color. In slow motion, leaves sprout from the previously decayed branches and small white flowers bloom on these bright green leaves. It looks beautiful and happy, accumulated with so much life.

I did it.

The waterfall's crashing flow is deafening as I approach. To make my way into the laboratory will undoubtedly be a challenge given my almost embarrassing failure to climb the slippery rocks the first time. And that was without manipulation of a man trying to slow me down.

My feet hesitate on the ground just before the rocks as if they have a mind of their own trying to tell me to turn back. With one quick motion, I force my foot to the first open place to rest it, following the movement with a grab onto a protruding rock with my hands.

Just as the path seems to look too easy, I spot movement underneath the surface of the water. Immediately, my mind races through a list of possibilities from a small version of the Loch Ness monster to evil mermaids from old lore. I shut my eyes to lock the images away before it can manifest, but I am too late.

Something wraps around my ankle, slithering up my leg. I open my eyes to see a live seaweed reaching up at me from deep under the water. Its slimy green leaves wrap around me, a piece per limb and another around my neck and waist.

The constriction forces the air out of my lungs and it begins pulling me down into the freezing water. It continues to force me under, dragging me below the surface, and all I can think about is trying to breathe.

I hate being in water like this, I haven't gone to a pool since the day I nearly drowned myself. I haven't even taken a bath since the last time I forced my head under water. Fear of so many things run across my mind as my body becomes surrounded by the fluid, trapping my clothes onto my skin and weighing me down even worse than if I had no clothes on at all. I feel like a child again falling under the surface wondering if anyone will notice me.

I care too much to let go this time.

My legs kick at a rapid force, I suppose due to survival instincts. My throat feels dry despite the situation and I grab at the plants that bind my waist. My hands can't grip on to the slimy material and continue to slip as I make restless attempts to escape.

I can see where the surface is above, but I can't reach it. The plant pulls me down further and I can feel the struggle as I try to work against it. No longer able to hold my breath, I make a desperate attempt at breathing in. Water rushes into my lungs and I choke while under the water. I'm not sure how much longer I can take this.

Black spots cover my vision. The plant pulls relentlessly despite my yanking and kicking, so I can tell that I am being forced further and further from the air. My lungs burn and I stop struggling, simply out of energy. I can't breathe anymore and I feel myself go limp just before passing out.

My eyes open to the shiny world around me. I know I didn't die because the world feels the same. Above me, I see Lanni and crawl away from him and his worried expression that he can't seem to shake.

If I could only go back to the day we met and treat him just as I treated everyone else. But he would have insisted because he is invisible to everyone else. He was put here for me. He's been by my side this entire time and I've taken him for granted.

"You have to get through this," he tells me, but is immediately made silent. He clutches his throat from his sudden inability to speak.

Damus appears behind him, "Shut it, puppet. She is supposed to get through alone."

There's an eerie silence, a moment, where all of us are motionless like statues. I would move, but what would be the point if my goal was to reach him anyway? My body tells me that I am not ready to fight him. I have no chance against him. The more the silence and stillness drags on, the more I negate myself and see that my fear controls me.

Damus makes a sudden movement and Lilith comes out from behind one of the nearby trees. She looks just as guilty and proud as Damus except she presents a more childish aspect to it. She makes a look at Damus expectantly, patiently awaiting his command.

Damus nods slowly and she jumps, clapping her hands. I stare and watch as she approaches Lanni. My heart races and I fear for the thing inside my head. She makes long wooden spears rise from the ground again, only this time, they surround him. He panics and I stay still fearing that any move I make will cause him to run into one.

Looking at me the whole time, Lilith snaps her fingers. Lanni is engulfed in flames. We both scream and it's like I can feel his pain, but I know there is no way I can know the true extent of it. The orange and yellow heat is a blinding sight in this midnight forest, yet I can't pull my eyes away and I wish for smoke to blow in my direction to force my attention off of his squirming struggle to escape.

My thoughts scream at me for my body to move, to do something to help him, but I remain restrained. My eyes refuse to shut, my mouth fails to speak, but I can't even find the words I'd say if I could say them.

There has to be a way to stop this, because for something like them, something unknown and unreal, this agony can last forever burning a pain in my head where his screams will never cease to paralyze me.

With that same brain I can stop this. I know there is something I can do to fight these intruders. A wave of water from the waterfall comes rushing towards us and Lanni is put out.

I am relieved by how Lanni is hardly scathed by the flames despite his howling. As if my brief moment of calm would tarnish everything they have worked for, Lilith jerks her head making the spears inch closer to Lanni. Their pointed tips remind me of my own, but when I go to reach for them, there is nothing there.

"Looking for these?" Damus says and holds up the arrows in their handmade quiver. "I managed to grab them while you were drowning. It was supposed to be while you died, but someone had to go and ruin things."

There's a tense feeling in the atmosphere as Lanni and Damus hold each other's gaze. Out of nowhere, vines rise from the ground and wrap around Lanni's throat. I reach out to him but am forced down to the ground. Damus pulls my head up to make me watch what he does to Lanni.

Lanni cannot move his hands to grab the ropes, but eventually he moves without intention. His movements make the spears poke him. A few pierce his skin and make him jump in the opposite direction, straight into another. I feel a tear escape my eye and can't believe I still have some to shed.

A part of me feels empty as Lanni goes limp.

The bad things set in again. I seem to have no good thing to look back at. There is only bad in everything and I feel cold and lonely. I see a montage before me, appearing all too real again here.

My father lies face down in his own blood.

My mom is stiff right beside him, both of them in line with Lanni's body.

The monsters previously seen in this forest and all of the negative versions of myself emerge from the trees, continuously feeding me bad memories:

"He smacked you and made you swallow your vomit."

"He pushed her into the wall, shattering picture frames and breaking his knuckles on her face while you had to stay and watch."

"They told you that you were imagining things."

"They never let you in."

"She turned the other way, never once looked at you."

"The creature spoke to you, telling you to do horrible things, and you listened."

"Darkness surrounded you, but you couldn't cry. You begged for the end."

"You didn't care if that car hit you."

"You didn't care if you were held under."

"You didn't care if he never stopped."

"You liked the pain."

I curl into a ball putting my hands over my ears as a screeching sound creates an ear-splitting shriek throughout the forest. I am driving myself mad. I feel the weight of it all pressing down on me. My entire body and mind can't take it.

The sky begins to crumble, small, dark blue pieces fall onto the ground revealing a pitch black nothing behind it. The people around me glitch and disappear as trees begin to fall.

It takes a branch to land beside me to get me standing on my feet. I need to find where they all disappeared to, but I have no willpower to do so. Everything seems dark and the only thing left after the world falls apart is the waterfall and its cave.

Fear

The one thing with the most evil and darkness, the only thing I have left to go to. I shake when I walk towards the cave.

There has to be something to do, something to draw back good, if there is any to draw back. I remember losing good things, but I have no idea what those things are. It all slipped away dramatically and I feel like I lost something important, but apparently not important enough.

I move slowly and carefully, but not with fear. Never again. There's no one that is going to save me anymore. I am alone in this battle. I've always been alone and I've survived this long. What's one more fight?

With my heart and mind full of condescending thoughts and events, I can either choose fear or hate. If I have any chance at changing what I am now, I have to embrace the hate and let it lead me.

I climb with a grace I've never had before. I move quickly enough that it seems I am moving in between the splashes. My hold in the rocky mountain side stays strong and I make my way to the cave entrance without a scratch. I continue to realize the irrational, yet devastating and seemingly real events. I feel myself shaking but don't consider the cause. I just keep moving forward.

My entire body shivers and the hairs raise on my arms and neck. I need to push away this fear, my anxiety. I must have hate, I can't hide in the shadows to avoid him. I cannot let him consume me and my thoughts. Although, that is all that I can think about.

No more thinking either. I take a single deep breath before I get down on all fours. The ground is like ice and my hands freeze at the touch. The cold water clinging to my skin makes the wind and stone that much more chilling. Continuing to shiver, I see a light flicker at the end just like I had the first time.

I do not sprint, I need to develop a plan and take my time. Shame on me for coming so soon. I should've thought of something before ever entering and I might have been able to go about things differently. But something tells me it wouldn't have made a difference.

He is me and I am him. He knows my every thought, plan, and scheme. My only option is to act without thinking so that he can't predict my next move. Now he knows I know to go without a plan, but that doesn't help him in the least. All he can do is guess what I will do instead. It will be almost as real as fighting a whole different person.

I take a single crawl forward and my hand sinks into the floor. I stop. Something hisses a release, like an airtight room was just opened, and I sit motionless as an arrow flies across my face. Booby traps, perfect. He knows he can't take me if I have full energy. The thing is, I didn't have that to begin with.

My body starts moving in very stiff and hurried motions so as to stay accurate in where I must move to next in order to avoid setting off another trap. My eyes search for any irregular shapes on the ground in the dim light that I am given. My hands feel for bumps and suspicious tiles.

I hold my breath so that I don't break focus. I need complete silence to do this, otherwise I might just fail. It's too late to bite back that thought. There are no physical objects that appear in the cave, but sounds echo off the cave walls as if there were.

Chirps of birds, whistling sounds, horse hooves, wings flapping, and other various animal noises bounce off of the cave walls. I close my eyes so as to try and shut it out, but it only gets louder and more annoying. I scream at the top of my lungs to let out some frustration.

There's another reason to rid myself from Damus. I am done suffering from his games. The only thing that can hurt me from now on is me.

I take a confident step forward and laughter erupts above the other noises as an axe swings down from one wall to the other, nearly slicing into my head. The momentum of each trap is slow. All I have to do is remain still or move back, and there is plenty of time to do so.

As I stand still again, the sounds get louder and more off beat of each other, like an elementary school band. As a ringing accompanies the noise, I bare my teeth and ready myself into a running stance. I am prepared to run through to the end of the cave.

There's a gunshot sound mimicking the sound-off for a race and I take off. Tiles fall out from beneath me and some don't even click all the way down. The ones that do, release smoke now to make it more difficult to see, but I continue crawling anyway.

I get to the end after metal falls and flies from every angle, but I have to feel with my hands to know where I'm going. There is no exit, the walls are closed around me and they begin to move. I press my hands against the walls trying to force them apart, but my strain is pointless. They continue to close in.

When my hand reaches above me, I feel a final tile move into place. My initial thought is that I need to move, but the walls are now so close that I am trapped in place. My heart beats fast and the noises start to get really loud again somehow breaking through the continuous buzzing already going on.

A red hot line breaks across my face, I can feel its heat as it forms. I reach my hand up to touch it, but the back of my hand is met by a fast sharpened piece of metal. Pulling the piece out of my skin, I decide to race forward once more and brace myself for more flying weapons made from scraps. The end of the temple-like tunnel relieves me enough for my body to think it can stop for a moment.

Everything starts feeling real. I'm out of a haze and realizing that what I am doing is dangerous yet again. I acted on a whim and now have no clue what I am doing. There's no unknown force pulling me in a certain direction. I am trapped. Helpless, cold, and alone. I don't know what I'm doing here, just that I want to get rid of Damus once and for all.

An all too familiar giggle comes from near me at the end of the cave entrance. My heart races and sweat beads on my forehead, but I do not stop. I'm trying to push away the feeling of being afraid and try to begin feeling brave. I was never the one that acted without thinking, never was outgoing and courageous. Having said that, I continue to move towards the noises, but something stops me.

My entire body is rigid and I can't move. Something turns me around and I see Damus, but he's different. His clothing is all black, his body itself seems to be a shadow, a wide smile spreads showing pure white teeth on a head-shaped figure, and his eyes glow a hazardous yellow.

"You, you cheater!" I spit at his ghastly form, "Face me yourself, you coward!"

My head turns in the direction of a cynical laughter. He says, "You still don't understand."

"Then explain."

"None of this is out of your control." He motions his arms outwards gesturing to this world. "You're injured now because you want to be."

"No, there's something about you that makes you different. There's something about everyone in here," I shout and point to my head trying to emphasize my point that this place is not all mine. "You may think you know me and that you have some sort of physical pull on me, but the only kind of manipulation you have is psychotic. You're a smooth talker, but that's all you have."

"Foolish girl, don't you know where this version of the truth has gotten you this far? Is it really that hard to believe that I am you and you are bringing me into the world because that's how broken you are? Doesn't this all seem too right?"

"You can't use your way of persuasion to make me back down." My theory only makes sense as my eyes find Spencer on the floor. He lies on the ground behind Damus, seemingly lifeless on the ground.

Damus notices me staring. "Oh, yeah, I found this one wandering around on his side."

His side. Spencer has a place of his own, the graffitied white rooms. There has to be more than just us. My mind is just over-imaginative, or I am a perfect target. Really, anyone could have entered their place, Damus could have chosen anyone, but I was so close to the entrance with an unstable teenage girl attitude and a life so pathetic that I couldn't possibly not fall into his lap. It really could have been anyone, but he chose to feed off of me.

"You know, your grandfather never believed me either."

"What did you say?" His statement catches me off guard and my teeth clench out of anger for what he could possibly mean by it.

"Louis Groeman was just as stubborn in his pre-adult ages as you. I finally laid off the hard stuff when he had a son, but trust me, I wanted your father, too. So, I used Louis, tried to force your father into becoming someone who would set me free, but your grandmother made that impossible. She taught John to hold his head high and have *faith* in his father." Damus spits the word like it left a bitter taste in his mouth.

I listen tentatively as he continues, "When John finally grew older, no matter how much his parents advised him against it and despite the life he had growing up, a daughter was on the way. Finally. An easily corrupted female. All I had to do was manipulate Jenise, a tortured soul of an orphan, to fall in love with your otherwise unlikeable father, and my new plan was in motion.

"Jenise was nothing but a bad influence. She polluted your father's mind with all of the bad things in life and thus the bad habits began."

Every word out of his mouth is a lie, but I keep listening because… I don't actually know that.

"John never saw a problem with her until well into their marriage. He tried persuading her to either raise the child on her own or give the baby to him; either way, he wanted her gone. That wasn't happening on my watch.

"So I messed with Jenise's head, got her to get him to have one more drink and eventually, he caved in to her and the fetal movements of the unborn child. Then, you were born. I leave Jenise alone to see the mess she made, the man who couldn't get through the day without making some depressing or aggressive comment.

"I'm sure you know the rest." Damus leans back, amused with himself.

"Enough." The tears start to blur my vision. I'm letting him get to me. The way he so coolly tells me my family's past, the reason we were the way that we were, angers me. He's proud to tear lives apart, taking away any possibility of my life being okay. "I don't know who you think you are, but you can't get away with this, you won't. I survived this long. I will not stop, especially knowing what you've done. I can't let you hurt anyone that comes after me. You're not psychological, you are physical, and I will hurt you."

He seems ready to mock me, but at my will, he winces from an invisible pain as I push his thoughts out of my mind and force them back at him. A bright light shines in my mind and the lights in the hall glow so strong they temporarily blind us all. The mountain shakes and begins to crumble beneath our feet. If the ground gave out, we'd fall forever.

I take this opportunity to quickly grab an arrow from beside him and plunge it into his heart from the back. The arrow and my arm pass right through him as if he were a ghost. I stumble but manage to hold my ground. How many more surprises can he hold? This is only getting less fair.

"You tried, I'll give you that." His hand is wrapped around my wrist, twisting it so that the arrow in my grip is less than an inch from my heart.

We writhe, pushing back on each other. The amateurly crafted, and therefore more harmful, piece of weaponry plunges into my side. I let out a shout of pain, excruciating agony like I've never felt before. I've been hurt, but never like this.

Damus pulls the arrow out aggressively and drops me on the floor. My body curls around the wound as I try to hold my blood inside with my hands, the liquid feeling warm as it escapes.

Somehow, I manage to stagger to my feet. Damus begins to enter into another speech, so I take this time to make my way to Spencer's side. My every thought now focuses on him as to distract me from everything else. Every possible emotion overcomes me to see Spencer back here. The black around us takes on its original blue shade.

As I begin to cry, the shiny things appear again. I realize now that it wasn't weather in the air, but slowly falling tears. There is no more mountain, but the tears from the sky land and cause small and leafy plants to sprout out from the ground.

"No! You can't, I destroyed the last Bright, there shouldn't be any more of this," Damus sounds mad as nature returns to the scene. "When will you finally let go! Give up! All I want is to come to the real world and give you a life that no one ever could. No longer will you be mocked or punished for frivolous things. You'll be free!"

His voice is rough and full of absolute anger just before nervously cowering at the return of vibrant color. All I do is stand beside Spencer, both of us supporting each other's weight. He turns me, holds my shoulders at arm's length, and nods at me like he has a plan. He steps forward towards Damus after taking the arrow from my hands. I focus my thoughts against Damus.

All it takes is to channel my anger at him. I remind myself of everything that has happened because of him. My grandfather's life, my father's, my mother's, and my own, all taken away. Lanni, someone who is probably like a good person of Damus's world, had to suffer through his games. Spencer fell in love with a girl whose family was controlled by this wicked creature, his life turning upside down.

Damus's whole plan altered the direction of so many lives, and I hope he burns in whatever hell his world offers.

I hate him for making my feelings go out of order. I hate that he is causing me pain, that he caused my family to be the way it was. I hate how he started with my grandfather, how he ruined the life I could've had, the life my father could have had. Generations of my family were forced to suffer.

As these thoughts continue, I see Damus cower before Spencer's broad stance. I force myself to believe this will destroy him for good. There is no reason it can't be this simple. I watch in anticipation as Spencer holds the arrow above the crouched form.

"Wait," I tell him and keep my eye on Damus. I wait for the Demon to turn solid again. "Now."

With a smirk, Spencer plunges the arrow into Damus's flesh. With a howl of pain, Damus's body leans backwards and he grabs the end of the arrow, pulling it out of him. The black blood oozing from the wound looks a lot more painful than it seems to be.

Damus uses his back hand to swipe Spencer off of his feet just before turning back towards me, his mouth deforming into a crooked smile, a nasty collection of teeth and blood red drool.

Running at me on all fours just like the creature had before, Damus is in for another attack. My mind loses focus, his ugly form getting closer and closer. I raise my arms in hopes that it will create some sort of shield to protect me from him. I can't go down, not like this. I've been through too much for this monster to beat me.

Right when I think he'll crash into me, a force sweeps the air across me and I look up to see one of the tar-black creatures wrestling with Damus, swinging its razor-clawed hands upon the demon's face in rapid succession.

"Let's get out of here." Spencer grabs my arm.

I wince.

"Shit," he utters and helps me up, my hands clutching my side. He repeats, "Shit."

CHAPTER TWENTY-SEVEN

One of Us

Climbing out of the mountain is easier than the hoops I had to jump through to get in, but it's made complicated by our injuries. We're moving too slowly.

The creatures won't be able to hold Damus back for long because with every passing second, every time one of our feet slips, my fear grows. I think of every horrible what-if about our failure to get away, to recover, to try again later. I think of how we're losing.

Even worse, I think about how this might be exactly what my father felt before my mother shot him. The last thing I need to be thinking about as my thoughts manifest around me.

But he survived it, all of it. I have to survive this, if for no other reason than to make sure Spencer survives this.

The blasted rock shifts beneath my feet and I think of the driveway to the house. I'm used to unsteady ground, even when there are icy wisps drifting through the air. That's all I picture, a snowy winter, as the two of us reach the outside of the mountain, stumbling our way back down to the forest floor.

At the bottom, everything in me stops. The cold reaches my skin and I can feel it inside of me, creeping in through the open wound until all there is is pain. "Spencer?"

He turns to see me as I fall.

When I come to, water is being poured on my face. I feel water all around me and wonder where it could have come from. This is until my eyes open and I see the blood around me and on Spencer. I am unable to speak, but I begin reaching towards him grabbing at his clothes.

His eyes are red and baggy from worry, and he tries to stop his crying. "Oh, Elle, I thought you were gone. I don't know what to do. I'm sorry."

I try swallowing to clear my throat and talk to him. It's hard for me to breathe. I want to tell him that this would have been worse if he wasn't here. That I could be dead instead of dying.

"You need to get up to leave," he begs me. "You need to get up. I already tried just taking you with me, but it doesn't work. You need to get up."

My eyes are half closed and his words come to me fuzzy. I understand, though. He brought us to the pond, to the ripples. And I have to get myself out, but it hurts when I try to move. He reaches his hand out to me and I grab it, both of them wet with blood. My blood.

He pulls me up and I lean against his body for support. The act of leaning over to put my finger above the surface of the water is such a simple task, but I find it difficult to perform as I fall on top of Spencer the second his grip loosens just slightly.

I feel like a stupid child. There's so much pain that tears start streaming. It's just tears, not an ugly cry, just wet streaks falling silently down my cheek. I know I have to try, I have to get out of here, get us out of here. This can't be the end, I won't let it be.

With more persistence, we try again. This time, he holds onto me tighter, moving just as slowly as me to make sure he doesn't leave without me. My finger grazes the top of the water as Spencer's did his first time out. It hurts to move at all and I feel the wound getting worse. I want to cry out and lie down, but I know I will be able to soon enough.

Glowing rings rise from the water, surrounding us in light as we're transported back to the real world, back to safety. From the direction of the mountain, a shriek pierces through the air, following us into the daylit forest…

Following us into the *real* forest.

"What was that?" Is that Ian?

"Grab them!" And… Andrew?

"Is she hurt?" Kyle?

"There's blood. Yes, she's hurt!" That's Izzy.

It feels like all of their hands are on me, pulling the clump that is me and Spencer out of the water and onto the mulch of the forest floor. We're a huddled mess as everyone fusses over the two of us, asking us what happened, what they can do, how to help.

They're scared, making me feel like I should be scared, and I am. I am terrified. More what-ifs than I have ever thought at once come rushing into my head and I am terrified of dying.

Everything hurts, no matter how carefully they try to handle me. But the pain isn't what makes me scream.

Another yell, a furious shout somewhere between rage and torment builds from within the still rippling water we just came out of. A bright flash momentarily blinds us until through the slowly receding light, I see it. I see him.

Damus's scream turns into laughter, airy at first, breathless, and then builds into something so wicked that it becomes even harder to shove my fears away. They only grow.

He's here.

He can hurt people.

And I have people I care about enough to not want to see them get hurt.

The eager crew around me all rise to face him.

"Demon," I hear Ian growl as he flicks out a switchblade he must've had tucked in his jacket sleeve.

I look at the others' hands and see nothing but balled fists and that does nothing to help the heavy pit of dread in my stomach. I am powerless to help them fight my fight.

"Yes. Yes!" Damus shouts as smaller flashes spark from the pond and more things appear. Creatures. Their black, tacky skin glistens with the water dripping off of them. Their white eyes are wide, adjusting to the yellow light or sizing up their prey. I prefer to believe the former.

"You're not getting her." Andrew steps towards Damus, his chest puffed up.

"I don't need her anymore."

"You got what you wanted." Spencer stands in front of them all as if he can keep Damus back if he just stands close enough. "Now what?"

"What I *wanted* was to bring everyone to their knees. Now I can." Damus's wicked smile falls. "I will."

The creatures sprint into attack, Kyle and Izzy facing after one, Ian and Andrew on the other as Spencer stands still, defiant, facing Damus. And all I can do is lay here, propped against a stump, hands pressed to my side without any strength to do anything else but watch.

Izzy full-on form tackles the creature in front of her as Kyle grabs for its arms so that when Izzy gathers herself again, it can't swipe at her as she throws her arm around its neck. Ian is thrown across them, flying through the air and slamming into a tree trunk before toppling down, but all he does is bare his teeth and growl as he rushes back at the creature who now has Andrew pinned to the ground.

Andrew's arm is reaching out for something just out of his reach when Ian knocks the creature off of him, but that only makes the creature pounce on Ian while Andrew collects himself enough to beat down on the creature. They are holding their own, but barely. They take turns having the advantage.

Izzy and Kyle's opponent has fought Kyle off and turned things over so it was the one with Izzy in its hold with Kyle using a stick he'd found to shove in its mouth and keep it from biting.

Their fight could go on forever this way, neither winning, neither losing. And then there's Spencer in a staring contest with Damus who has yet to make a move, waiting for… what can he possibly be waiting for?

I can't just watch.

These creatures, they come from me. They *were* me. Which means they're just scared. I have to remind them what they're scared of, channel their blind violence towards what they actually want to defeat.

Their fear.

Fear itself.

Damus.

I'm not afraid of my past. I'm afraid of how it might affect my future. But the past doesn't determine what's going to happen. *I* do. I will not be controlled by fear.

The fighting halts as the creatures abandon their foes and rise to stand, turning slowly to face the demon. When I think they're going to attack or run, they walk slowly back toward the water, somehow growing shorter with each step, the black tar of their skin sloughing off until they look almost human again… until they look like me again. The color of their eyes return, bringing life into their blank white stares.

As younger versions of me, they wade back into the pond, passing Damus without a second glance. They bend to touch the water's surface and rings of light reach up around them before they're gone, back on the other side, back in the forest of my mind.

Izzy, Kyle, Ian, and Andrew are heaving with lost breaths and undoubtedly screaming muscles, but they form a line standing side by side on either side of Spencer, forming a wall between me and Damus.

He's outside of my mind now. Would he still be affected by my mind? What would I be able to think of to get him to go away? All I can think of is how I can't feel my arms, can't feel the pressure of my hands on my side. I'm not even sure if I am still keeping pressure there. I've thought the creatures away for good and Damus still hasn't moved.

It could be that he doesn't know what to do. He dreamed and dreamed for this day but never thought of what he was going to do when it came. I hope he doesn't know what to do. He can't manipulate his surroundings, use our fears against us. The real world doesn't bend to anyone's will.

Damus starts towards the group. It's five to one and he's in our world now.

My friends.

They've got this.

I can let my eyes close.

They've got this.

A familiar voice speaks so clearly beside me, so gentle. "Not yet."

I open my eyes. Lanni's face is in front of mine, holding my hands against my wound. "But you—"

"He had me for a moment there, yeah." He pauses, remembering every stab of those wooden spears just as I am, before meeting my eyes again. "But you didn't need me then."

"Why are you here now?"

Grunts and battle cries give hints to the scene unfolding behind Lanni, but he's all I can see, all I can focus on. He says, "I didn't know until just now, when you needed me, when your friends called for me."

"I don't understand."

"I am… Will. Will to fight, to survive, to live."

"You're what can defeat Fear," my words come out slow, weak, soft. I am losing focus, but I know this much. I will not let go. I will see this battle won. I will see the other side of all of this pain.

Lanni only smiles before standing and turning to the fight. "Damus!"

The back of the demon's hand swipes across Ian's face, sending him hurtling to the ground again. Damus looks at

Lanni now. Can everyone see him? It doesn't matter. I connect with Lanni, gathering up all of my will and letting it fuel him the way fear fueled Damus.

I think of all of the same things, my life and all the moments that make it. But instead of hiding from it, I see my strength.

My father may have beaten me, and as much as I dwelled on his words, I know I never believed them. I certainly don't now. I didn't let his cruelty turn me cruel.

I still go to school, do well in it. I get out of bed every day. I change my clothes. I went to a school dance and actually danced. I sought help when I needed it instead of closing myself off completely.

I kept going back through the ripples, not because I wanted to be broken down by what's on the other side, but because it was a way to face myself, to make all of my pain make sense so that I could move on.

Lanni grabs Damus's wrists and pushes him back, their feet sloshing in the pond water. Spencer lets Lanni have the fight and comes rushing to my side. "I got you. I got you."

He's holding onto me, holding me together, but turns his head back to the group to shout, "Andrew, now!"

Then, a deafening sound like fireworks exploding in the room puts everything on pause.

My ears ring and my eyes shut, wincing from the rattling sensation of it all as Spencer holds me even tighter.

Something collapses into the water, splashing. I look past Spencer's shoulder to see Damus on his knee, clutching the other. Andrew is still holding the gun that fired the injuring bullet, ready to pull the trigger again.

Lanni drills a hole through the demon's head with a fiery glare as he says, "Do it."

And Damus obeys.

The demon grazes a fingertip upon the water's surface and we all watch as the rings rise and he vanishes.

CHAPTER TWENTY-EIGHT

What is Real

"Is that it?" Kyle asks.

"Did we win?" Izzy adds to it.

"But he's not dead, is he?" Ian adds. "Couldn't he come back?"

"I'd like to see him try," Andrew settles it.

Their voices come through all muddled. I'm fading.

Spencer picks me up in his arms in a cradle. "Whatever the case, we're done for now."

I lean my head back and close my eyes. I feel his steps and listen to his careful breathing. I notice all the moments when he tries his best to hold me gently and step around anything that might hurt me. The rest of the group's footsteps are a comforting cacophony of support.

They work together to situate me in the backseat of Spencer's car. I don't care where we go. I open my eyes for a moment and see nothing but a blur of colors because we're going so fast. I know where we're going. I need a hospital.

His voice sounds truthfully scared when the phone stops buzzing. "911, what's the emergency?"

My eyes flutter open and closed as if unable to decide whether to rest or stay awake. Bright white lights glow making it hard to keep them open. There's a mask over my face. Although my body is in a laying down position, I feel myself getting pushed forward and through a set of doors.

Around me, there are doctors with hands on the thing wheeling me around. I see Spencer running beside them until a pair of doctors grab him and tell him he can't go further. I reach a single arm towards him weakly. I don't want to go in with a bunch of strangers, but I also don't want him to see me die if they fail.

When a door closes and I can no longer see Spencer, the doctors disperse and nurses bring in the necessary equipment. A different air comes in through the mask that covers my face and I fall asleep.

But I reappear almost instantly in a park.

The sun shines bright and children run around playing tag. There is no hole in me and I am wearing a sort of nightgown. A little girl swings and laughs as someone that looks like her grandparent waits to catch her when she decides to jump off.

On the brick wall beside the park, there is a load of graffiti covering whatever the original color was. An older teenager is riding a skateboard as what looks like his girlfriend watches in awe. She is wearing roller skates waiting to take her turn on the halfpipe. Two people walk to the park with food in their hands and one is laughing at what the other said. A group of teenagers gather in a large circle on the grassy area moving their hands, rapidly engrossed in conversation. Everything here seems very happy and enjoyable.

I try to decide where to go and who to talk to when someone comes up behind me. A little girl about four years old tugs on the bottom of my dress, "Hello, Leighanna!"

"Hi." My face lights up immediately. She somehow knows my name and I am tempted to ask her why, but wait. "What are you doing here?"

"I'm playing hide and seek in the woods over there with my grandpa."

"Oh, fun. Am I in your way?"

"No, actually, you are out of my way. I just really wanted to see you."

"Why? How do you know me?"

She giggles a cute and innocent giggle and it's almost contagious. She has got to be the most adorable thing I have ever seen. "Doesn't it seem a little *bright* here?"

I give her a perplexed look, but then I get to thinking. When she sees that I understand what she said, she runs off in the other direction.

"Hello, Leighanna," a vaguely familiar voice comes from behind me and I turn towards him.

"Grandpa." Tears fill my eyes as we pull each other into our arms. "It's so good to see you. I'm so sorry."

"I am the one who should be sorry. I wasn't strong enough to put an end to his games. I couldn't guide you the way I wish I could. You turned out so strong."

"That's because of you. Before I knew what was going on, you were the only one I could hold onto, the only one I could trust. You may not have been able to send Damus running, but you kept him at bay. If you hadn't taught me how to push the thoughts he gave me away, he would have come sooner, and I would have given up."

As much as I had hated my grandfather for his advice, it is clear to me now why he had given it. How much that information helped me, how it made me grow and be able to resist the constant suicidal thoughts or depression that threatened to keep me from behaving. He taught me to be a girl and act like a girl should act. The face he gave me, gave me strength.

"I'm grateful to see you, but I will see you much much later, and not once until then. I love you." And with that, he playfully chases the little girl who had pulled on my gown earlier. My grandfather, a Bright.

"You didn't honestly believe they would go away forever did you?"

I turn around towards his voice and I see Lanni standing proud and ready to take in the hug that I am preparing for him. I jump onto him and he swings me around before letting go. "I thought—well, I don't know what I thought."

"I know," he chuckles.

"So what are you? What does it mean to *be* Will?"

"That's the part I still have to figure out." He smiles and shies away for a moment to shake it off as nothing even though I know it is something.

"Damus told me he destroyed all the Brights."

Lanni places a hand on my shoulder. "Nothing can destroy your memory besides time. Even then it is not completely gone, just in need of remembering."

"Is Damus still trying to hurt you?"

"We are all happy and safe here and glad to see you have finally come for a visit," he pauses to laugh for a second. I laugh too, realizing the reality of that statement. "The Bright who looked like Alex, the one you saw die before, was just sent back here. Your memories are safe."

"Then what was Damus?"

"Damus is the embodiment of Fear. He's pretty much everything that's bad in the world and just like Hades trying to be free of his dark dominion, Damus wants to escape the realm he is stuck in, the realm I belong to."

"So this means Damus must have survived as well. He's not defeated yet."

"Only if you let him be strong is when he may take over again. It's all up to you what happens. You have control here, more than anything inside because each one of us is only a fraction of you."

"Can't I just stay here and avoid it all?" I ask while sitting myself on an empty bench.

"Unfortunately"— he waves his hand to show me myself in the real world as the doctors are operating—"if you decide to let go, you move on to something different than this. I have no idea what that is, but we both know it's true, because all of this then moves on too."

"I must go back. I have to, right?"

"Fear of the unknown is known to be the greatest fear there is. It controls people and the decisions they make. Fear of what will happen to those you care about when you leave is a great part of that. That's why we need people, to find the ones we love and the ones that love us back."

The calm sunlight, like a perpetual Sunday afternoon on the cusp of summer, allows me to think the clearest thoughts I ever have and I let the debate roll over in my mind.

I can just as easily leave everything behind for the next adventure into the unknown as I can return to what I do know in hopes of the evil being subdued enough to attempt a normal life. I can forget it all: the possibility of returning to the forest, of my father finding me, of my mind continuing to play tricks on me as remnants of the events.

But I cannot leave Spencer behind. I could try to convince myself that we won't last forever, but I know that is not the case. Looking around this world, I see him as the other skater by the halfpipe and the person on the swingset and the person walking alongside one of me on the sidewalk.

He is everywhere, all the time, inside my head and out, literally and figuratively. If I have the choice to spend a lifetime with him, I have to take it, no matter the risk. Not everyone is granted the opportunity to make this decision. How many people might be waiting for me wherever the road beyond life leads? How many of them will wish I had chosen differently? How many of them are people I know?

There is no one beyond. There is no one but Spencer. And he is probably worried sick about me, waiting and watching for the slightest sign of consciousness. My heart burns at the thought of him hearing a flatline.

That feeling that would overcome him is a feeling I've felt before when my grandfather passed away. The feeling of losing the only one keeping you sane, keeping you feeling alive and that your life has meaning, is a feeling I won't be responsible for.

It is the contraction of all your muscles making it feel impossible for you to breathe, your heart bursting into flames until you feel like you could cough up smoke, your thoughts fading in and out as you wonder what happens now that the one you cling to is gone. I know he has felt it before as well when his family gave up on him, when his own grandfather passed away, and probably every time he waited for me to wake up just as he is doing now.

Taking just a moment to absorb the sun, a feeling I haven't been able to take in freely for the longest time. A feeling I took for granted in summers past. A breath in fills my senses with hope, if hope is a smell. It is like breathing in pure joy, a graceful and absolute assurance that everything is okay. The sense of it all, the slight breeze, the rays of muted light warming my skin, prompt me to action without a feeling of urgency or worry.

"I know what it feels like to be left behind, to feel like everything you've done was for nothing. I want to be able to say, 'we won.' I want to return to him for him and see the look on his face once he realizes that everything that ever threatened us is over. I want to give him that peace."

Lanni simply holds his hand out for mine and says with a smile, "Come on, this way."

Epilogue

I haven't seen the shadows in a month.

We cremated my mother. It was easiest that way. Her ashes are in the tin the funeral home gave me, sitting on Spencer's mantel like a non-specific knickknack that fits with the rest of the brick-a-brack his grandfather kept there. My mother sits between a plaster frog holding a fishing pole and a glass turtle.

As for my father... I have no idea. I haven't heard from him and the driveway has been empty every time we drive past it. I look out the window as we do so now, and part of me hopes to see something different. Not his presence. Just something different.

Spencer takes a hand off of the steering wheel and places it on my thigh so that I stop looking and return my gaze to the road. I reflexively brace myself for the unsteady motion of parking by Andrew's trailer. The pain is so dull now, it's like a phantom, but it's still there. It always will be in a way.

"Hey, Wonderland!" Kyle greets me with the nickname I've been given. I wear it with pride. There are about four, bright pink, scribbles of that name tagged across the city now.

Ian punches my arm as he comes up from behind. His hair is a new color and the stud of his lip piercing changed to match. His unclear style has fully committed to a demon-hunter look, complete with a black trench, half-fingered gloves with studs on the knuckles, and a simple cross pendant on a long silver chain around his neck.

"Careful, Ian," Andrew warns, wiping his hands on a grease-stained cloth as he comes out from behind his recently acquired motorbike.

"Yeah, I wouldn't knock Spence's girlfriend around if I were you," Izzy chimes in. "She's still recovering."

"She's tough. Try your worst."

"I know you mean well, Spencer, but let's maybe cool it on the violence, at least for a little while." To drive my point, I take a seat in a newly acquired lawn chair. The legs scrape against rock as the chair settles into the gravel in front of Andrew's trailer. I've made a few changes since making it a regular haunt.

"We've got a job for you, by the way. That is, if you're ready for it," Kyle says with a wink in his smile.

Spencer's jaw sets but he doesn't say anything. This might be what Spencer has been hiding from me, how he's managed to live on his own. But I've been tagging, I've been skating, and I've been doing it all without seeing demonic little girls, tarred creatures, hazy bodies, or even the slightest blue twinkle in the air.

She's one of us, Andrew's words come back to me from that first time he bore witness to the ripples.

In that one instant, everything erupted, one event after the next, wave after wave, and the water has only just begun to settle. But that was just the first skip of the rock. It's time for the second.

I can't stop the smile from forming. "I'm ready."

Acknowledgement

Ripples is my very first novel, which means it is very near and dear to my heart. That also means it has been through… a lot.

I wanted to take the time to write an acknowledgment despite not having a vast team backing me on this journey. My team is small but mighty.

In the beginning, all I had was my family (thank you Mom, Dad, Megan, Rachel, Matthew, and Nana) and very closest friends (thank you Evelyn, Jade, Morgan, Noah, and Sonya), but even they didn't get to see much of the story because, well, sharing creative work with your family and friends is like arriving to school naked.

Then, after an extensive education (thank you Larissa Szporluk, Amanda McGuire Rzicznek, and Abigail Cloud) and a decent bit of my own research into indie publishing, I found beta readers. My beta readers are my lifeline.

A special thanks goes to Courtney for the beautiful e-mail I was sent about how much my manuscript impacted her. I have the e-mail printed and taped to my wall as a reminder of why I started writing in the first place.

Another special thank you goes to Kevin, a quick friend made on social media who read a previous draft and immediately expressed such delighted anticipation for Ripples' release that I almost forgot to be nervous. It seriously made a difference in how I kept my head in regards to the self-marketing aspect of indie publishing.

Finally, thank you, readers. You are the reason people like me write, why we don't give up, and how we still manage to have hope.

Stay Tuned

To stay up to date and get an inside look at how I do this authoring thing, consider the following:

• Sign up for my monthly newsletter at aliciacharron.com
• Follow me on social media @aliciacharronauthor
• Like my Facebook Page Alicia Charron Author Page

ALICIACHARRON.COM

My website's highlights are the blog and the progress report pages. My blog is in typical old-school fashion where it serves as more of a journal where I offer book reviews, writing advice, and general views on various publishing topics from writing to editing to designing books to marketing them.

SOCIAL MEDIA

The top source for frequent content that is both (hopefully) entertaining and a good source to see what I'm working on is TikTok @aliciacharronauthor. I do Live writing sprints and post quirky, quick videos that often feature my cat.

Thank you for reading!